CAPTAIN FUTURE
WIZARD OF SCIENCE

Vol.1, No.1 Winter 1940

Captain Future and the
Space Emperor

By

EDMOND HAMILTON

D1733684

Photography and editing by A.F. Murphy

Reprint edition (c)Unspeakable Industries/Aundrea Murphy 2017

ISBN-13: 978-1978107694
ISBN-10: 1978107692

"I HAD TO BAIL OUT IN A PEA SOUP FOG!"

C. W. HARBERT
Aviation Cadet
Bristol, W. Va.

1 "I took off from Pensacola on a night training flight in my single-seater fighting plane," writes Cadet Harbert. "Later, as I started homeward, a heavy fog rolled in. The landing field was blotted out!

2 "It was too dangerous—for myself and those below—to attempt a landing. I had to bail out in that pea soup fog! Heading for open country, I circled at 5,000 feet until the gasoline gauge showed empty, then jammed the stick forward and catapulted into space!

3 "I landed waist-deep in the wide mouth of a river. Marooned by deep water on all sides, I grabbed my flashlight, and—despite the soaking—it worked! Guided by its beam, two fishermen eventually found and rescued me—thanks to 'Eveready' *fresh* DATED batteries—which you can depend on in emergencies! (Signed) *C. W. Harbert* "

EVEREADY
Nº 950
EXTRA LONG LIFE BATTERY
A NATIONAL CARBON COMPANY PRODUCT

FRESH BATTERIES LAST LONGER... *Look for the* **DATE-LINE**

CAPTAIN FUTURE
WIZARD OF SCIENCE

VOL. I, NO. I CONTENTS WINTER, 1940

A Complete Book-Length Scientifiction Novel

CAPTAIN FUTURE, published quarterly and copyright, 1939, by Better Publications, Inc., 22 West 48th Street, New York, N. Y. N. L. Pines, President. Single copies, 15 cents; yearly subscription, 60 cents. Application for entry as second-class matter pending. Manuscripts must be accompanied by self-addressed, stamped envelope, and are submitted at the author's risk. Names of all characters used in stories and semi-fiction articles are fictitious. If the name of any living person or existing institution is used it is a coincidence.

Read our companion magazines: The Phantom Detective, Thrilling Detective, Popular Detective, Thrilling Spy Stories, Thrilling Mystery, Thrilling Love, Thrilling Ranch Stories, Thrilling Western, Thrilling Sports, Thrilling Wonder Stories, The Lone Eagle, Sky Fighters, G-Men, West, Popular Sports Magazine, Popular Love, Popular Western, Everyday Astrology, Texas Rangers, Range Riders, Startling Stories, Strange Stories, Detective Novels Magazine, Masked Rider Western Magazine, Rio Kid Western, Thrilling Adventures, and Black Book Detective Magazine.

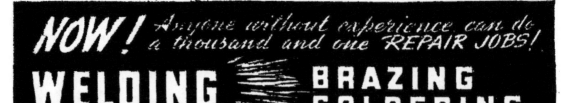

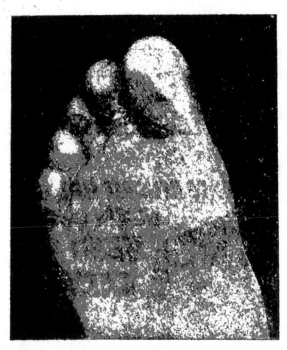

FOOT ITCH

ATHLETE'S FOOT

Send Coupon
Don't Pay Until Relieved

According to the Government Health Bulletin No. E-28, at least 50% of the adult population of the United States are being attacked by the disease known as Athlete's Foot.

Usually the disease starts between the toes. Little watery blisters form, and the skin cracks and peels. After a while, the itching becomes intense, and you feel as though you would like to scratch off all the skin.

BEWARE OF IT SPREADING

Often the disease travels all over the bottom of the feet. The soles of your feet become red and swollen. The skin also cracks and peels, and the itching becomes worse and worse.

Get relief from this disease as quickly as possible, because it is very contagious, and it may go to your hands or even to the under arm or crotch of the legs.

HERE'S HOW TO RELIEVE IT

The germ that causes the disease is known as Tinea Trichophyton. It buries itself deep in the tissues of the skin and is very hard to kill. A test made shows it takes 15 minutes of boiling to kill the germ; so you can see why Athlete's Foot is so hard to relieve.

H. F. was developed solely for the purpose of relieving Athlete's Foot. It is a liquid that penetrates and dries quickly. You just paint the affected parts. It peels off the tissue of the skin where the germ breeds.

ITCHING STOPS QUICKLY

When you apply H. F. you may find that the itching is quickly relieved. You should paint the infected parts with H. F. night and morning until your feet are better. Usually this takes from three to ten days, although in severe cases be sure to consult a specialist.

H. F. should leave the skin soft and smooth. You may marvel at the quick way it brings you relief.

H. F. SENT ON FREE TRIAL

Sign and mail the coupon, and a bottle of H. F. will be mailed you immediately. Don't send any money and don't pay the postman any money; don't pay anything any time unless H. F. is helping you. If it does help you, we know you will be glad to send us $1 for the bottle at the end of ten days. That's how much faith we have in H. F. Read, sign and mail the coupon today.

PRICE $1.00
Sold by
Gore Products, Inc.
New Orleans, La.

UNDER OBSERVATION

THE Wizard of Science! Captain Future!

The most colorful planeteer in the Solar System makes his debut in this, America's newest and most scintillating scientifiction magazine—CAPTAIN FUTURE.

This is the magazine more than one hundred thousand scientifiction followers have been clamoring for! Here, for the first time in scientifiction history, is a publication devoted exclusively to the thrilling exploits of the greatest fantasy character of all time!

Follow the flashing rocket-trail of the *Comet* as the most extraordinary scientist the nine worlds have ever known explores the outposts of the cosmos to the very shores of infinity. Read about the Man of Tomorrow today!

Meet the companions of Captain Future, the most glamorous trio in the Universe!

Grag, the giant, metal robot; Otho, the man-made, synthetic android; and aged Simon Wright, the living Brain.

This all-star parade of the most unusual characters in the realm of fantasy is presented for your entertainment. Come along with this amazing band as they rove the uncharted spaceways—in each issue of CAPTAIN FUTURE!

And readers—please drop us a line and let us know what you think of this first issue! UNDER OBSERVATION will be our regular correspondence department—where you can air your views in public! Be sure to send those letters along!

—THE EDITOR.

To those who think
LEARNING MUSIC
is hard...

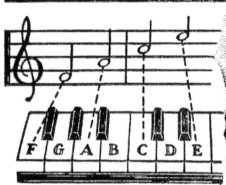

F G A B C D E

PERHAPS *you* think that taking music lessons is like taking a dose of medicine. It isn't any longer!

As far as you're concerned, the old days of long practice hours with their scales and hard-work exercises and expensive personal teacher fees are over and done with.

For, through a method that removes the boredom and extravagance from music lessons, you can now learn to play your favorite instrument entirely at home—without a private teacher—in an amazingly short time—at a fraction of the usual cost.

Just imagine . . . a method that has made the reading and playing of music so downright simple that you don't have to know one note from another to begin. Do you wonder that this remarkable way of learning music has already been vouched for by over 700,000 people in all parts of the world?

EASY AS CAN BE!

The lessons come to you by mail from the famous U. S. School of Music. They consist of complete printed instructions, diagrams, and all the music you need. It's actually fun to learn this simple way. One week you are learning a dreamy waltz—the next you are mastering a stirring march. As the lessons continue they prove easier and easier. For instead of just scales you are always learning to play by *actual* notes the classic favorites and the latest syncopation that formerly you only *listened* to.

And you're never in hot water. First, you are told how a thing is done. Then a picture shows you how, then you do it yourself and hear it. No private teacher could make it clearer or easier.

NEW FRIENDS—BETTER TIMES

Soon, when your friends say "please play something," you can surprise and entertain them with pleasing melodies on your favorite instrument. You'll find yourself in the spotlight—popular everywhere.

If you're tired of just looking-on at parties—if you've been envious of others entertaining your friends and family—if learning music has always been one of those never-to-come-true dreams, let the time-proven and tested home-study method of the U. S. School of Music come to your rescue.

Don't be afraid to begin your lessons at once. Over 700,000 people have studied music this modern way—and found it easy as A.B.C. Forget that old-fashioned idea that you need special "talent." And bear in mind no matter which instrument you choose, the cost in each case will average the same—just a few cents a day. No matter whether you are a mere beginner or already a good performer you will be interested in learning about this newly perfected method.

Our wonderful illustrated Free Book and our Free Demonstration Lesson explain all about this remarkable method. They show just how anyone can learn to play his favorite instrument by *not* in a short time and for just a fraction of what old slow methods cost.

Read the list of instruments below, decide which one you want to learn to play. Act NOW. Clip and mail this coupon today, and the fascinating Free Book and Free Demonstration Lesson will be sent to you at once. No obligation. Instruments supplied when needed, cash or credit. U. S. School of Music, 29412 Brunswick Bldg., New York City.

ACT NOW!

ON THIS BARGAIN OFFER.

THIS BEAUTIFUL DESK FOR ONLY $1.00

THE COMBINATION FOR AS LITTLE AS 10¢ A DAY

How easy it is to pay for this combination. Just imagine! A small good will deposit and terms as low as 10¢ a day to get this combination at once. You will never miss 10¢ a day. Become immediately the possessor of this combination. You assume no obligation by sending the coupon.

WITH ANY REMINGTON PORTABLE TYPEWRITER

A beautiful desk in a neutral blue-green—trimmed in black and silver—made of sturdy fibre board—now available for only one dollar ($1.00) to purchasers of a Remington Deluxe Noiseless Portable Typewriter. The desk is so light that it can be moved anywhere without trouble. It will hold six hundred (600) pounds. This combination gives you a miniature office at home. Mail the coupon today.

THESE EXTRAS FOR YOU

LEARN TYPING FREE

To help you even further, you get Free with this special offer a 24-page booklet, prepared by experts, to teach you quickly how to typewrite by the touch method. When you buy a Noiseless you get this free Remington Rand gift that increases the pleasure of using your Remington Deluxe Noiseless Portable. Remember, the touch typing book is sent Free while this offer holds.

SPECIAL CARRYING CASE

The Remington Deluxe Noiseless Portable is light in weight, easily carried about. With this offer Remington supplies a beautiful carrying case sturdily built of 3-ply wood bound with a special Dupont Fabric.

SPECIFICATIONS

ALL ESSENTIAL FEATURES of large standard office machines appear in the Noiseless Deluxe Portable—standard 4-row keyboard; back spacer; margin stops and margin release; double shift key; two color ribbon and automatic reverse; variable line spacer; paper fingers; makes as many as seven carbons; takes paper 9.5" wide; writes lines 8.2" wide, black key cards and white letters, rubber cushioned feet.

MONEY BACK GUARANTEE

The Remington Noiseless Deluxe Portable Typewriter is sold on a trial basis with a money-back guarantee. If, after ten days trail, you are not entirely satisfied, we will take it back, paying all shipping charges and refunding your good will deposit at once. You take no risk.

SEND COUPON. NOW!

Remington Rand Inc. Dept 169-13
465 Washington St., Buffalo, N. Y.

Tell me, without obligation, how to get a Free Trial of a new Remington Noiseless Deluxe Portable, including Carrying Case and Free Typing Booklet, for as little as 10¢ a day. Send Catalogue.

Name...

Address...

City...State...............

CAPTAIN FUTURE

Follow the quest of Curtis Newton, wizardman of science, as he scours the worlds of tomorrow in the hunt for the greatest interplanetary outlaw of all time!

A Book-Length Novel of Planet Conquest

By
EDMOND HAMILTON

Author of "The Three Planeteers," "The Prisoner of Mars," etc.

Illustrated
by
H. W. WESSO

and the SPACE EMPEROR

Captain Future's body became translucent. He was becoming—invisible! (Chapter XIV)

CHAPTER I

Doom on Jupiter

THE chill, uncanny breath of a dark menace millions of miles away pervaded the spacious, softly-lit office high in the greatest of New York's mighty towers.

The man who sat there at an ebonite desk was worried. Facing a broad window which framed the stupendous pinnacles of the moonlit city, he could feel that cold, malign aura. He shuddered at the thought of what he knew was happening even at this moment.

"It can't go on," he muttered sickly to himself. "That horror must be stopped, somehow. Or else—"

James Carthew, President of the

Earth Government which had ruled all humanity since the last World War, was not an old man. Fifty was considered the prime of life, in these days. But the appalling responsibilities of guiding the destinies of all mankind had aged this man before his time.

His gray-shot hair was thinning around his high forehead. There were deep lines of strain in his keen, powerful face, and his dark eyes were haunted by haggard weariness and lurking fear.

As the door of his office opened his thin hands gripped the edges of his desk convulsively.

North Bonnel, his slender, dark young secretary, entered.

"The liner from Jupiter just landed, sir," he reported. "I had a flash from the spaceport."

"Thank heavens!" Carthew muttered. "Sperling should be here in five minutes. He knows I'm waiting for his report."

Bonnel hesitated.

"I hope he's reached the bottom of that mystery out there. The special committee of Jupiter citizens called by televisor again this evening."

"I know—calling to protest again about conditions on Jupiter," Carthew said bitterly. "Each one of them trying to voice a louder complaint than the others."

"You can hardly blame them, sir," the young secretary ventured to say. "Things must be pretty horrible out there on Jupiter, with that hideous thing spreading as it is."

"Sperling will have found out what's causing it," the President asserted confidently. He looked at the perpetual uranium clock on his desk. "He ought to be arriving any second—"

A scream from somewhere in the lower levels of the great Government Tower cut him off. It was a woman's scream.

There were many girl clerks employed here in the huge Government Headquarters for Earth and its planet colonies. Even at night, some of them were always in the building. But what had frightened one of them into uttering that agonized scream?

James Carthew had risen to his feet behind his desk, his aging face paling with sudden apprehension. The secretary started violently.

"Something wrong, sir! I'd better see—"

He started toward the door. It was suddenly flung open from outside.

Young Bonnel recoiled wildly.

"My God!" he cried.

In the open door stood a hideous and incredible figure, a monstrosity out of nightmare.

It was a giant, hunched ape, hairy and abhorrent. Its squat figure wore a man's zipper-suit of white synthesilk. In the too-tight garment, the creature looked like a gruesome travesty on humanity, its brutish, hairy face a bestial mask, jaws parted to reveal great fangs. Its eyes blazed with a cold glitter as it started into the room. "Look out!" Bonnel yelled frantically.

A WHITE-FACED guard in the dark uniform of the Planet Police appeared in the door. He leveled his flare-gun swiftly at the monstrous ape.

"Wait—don't shoot!" James Carthew cried suddenly, as he looked into the monster's hairy face.

His warning was too late. The guard had seen nothing but an incredible, menacing creature advancing toward the President. He had squeezed the trigger.

The little flare from the pistol struck the ape's broad back. The creature's bestial face contorted in sudden agony. With a deep, almost human groan, it collapsed.

James Carthew, with a cry of horror, jumped forward. His face was paper-white as he bent over the creature.

The ape's eyes, strange *blue* eyes, had a dying light in them as they looked up at the President. The creature strove to speak.

From the hairy throat came a hoarse, gurgling rattle—dying words, thickened to a brutish growl, but dimly recognizable.

"Jupiter — the Space Emperor— causing atavism—" the thing gasped hoarsely in dying accents.

Captain Future—Wizard of Science

It sought to raise its head, its fading blue eyes weirdly human in agonized apprehension and appeal as they looked up at the President.

"Danger from—"

And then, as it sought to form another word, life ebbed swiftly, and the creature sank back, its eyes glazing.

"Dead!" Carthew exclaimed, trembling violently.

"My God, it talked!" cried the white-faced guard. "That ape—talked!"

"It's not an ape. It's a man!" said James Carthew hoarsely.

He got to his feet. Guards and officials were running alarmedly into the office.

"Get out—all of you," Carthew whispered, making a gesture with his trembling hand.

Horrified, still staring at the monstrous, hairy corpse on the floor, they withdrew and left the President and his secretary alone with the macabre corpse.

"Good God—those blue eyes—it couldn't be Sperling!" cried the shuddering young secretary.

"Yes, it's Sperling all right," James Carthew said softly. "I recognized him, by his eyes, a moment too late. John Sperling, our best secret agent—

transformed into that dead brute on the floor!"

"You sent him to investigate the horror on Jupiter, and he fell prey to it!" Bonnel exclaimed hoarsely. "He changed, like those others out there, from man to brute. Yet he was still man enough to try to get here and make his report!"

The pale young secretary looked beseechingly at his chief.

"What *is* it that's causing that horrible wave of monstrosities out on Jupiter? Hundreds of cases in the last month—hundreds of men changing into apish brutes!"

"Whatever it is, it's something bigger than just Jupiter," Carthew whispered haggardly. "Suppose this strange plague spreads to the other planets—to Earth?"

Bonnel blanched at the hideousness of the suggestion.

"Good God, that must not happen!"

The President looked down at the hairy body that a few weeks before had been the keenest, most stalwart man in the whole force of the Planet Police secret agents.

"Sperling may have written out a report," Carthew muttered. "Secret agents are not supposed to do so, but—"

HASTILY, the young secretary searched the clothing of the hairy creature. He uttered a little exclamation as he drew forth a paper.

It was covered with crude, almost illegible writing, like the scrawl of a child. It was headed, "To the President." Carthew read it aloud:

Ship only one day from Earth, but feel myself changing so fast, I fear I won't be able to talk or think clearly by then. Was stricken by the atavism on Jupiter, days ago. Tried to get back to Earth to report what I learned, before I became completely unhuman.

I've learned that the blight on Jupiter is being caused by a mysterious being called the Space Emperor. Don't know whether he's Earthman or a Jovian. How he causes this doom, I don't know, but it is some power he uses secretly on Earthman there. I felt nothing of it, until I noticed myself changing, becoming foggy-minded, brutish.

Can't write much more now—getting hard to hold pen—haven't dared to leave my cabin on this ship, I've changed so badly—mind getting foggier—wish I could have learned more—

The young secretary's eyes had horror and pity in them as James Carthew read the last words.

"So Sperling failed to learn anything except that this horrible flight was being deliberately caused by some h u m a n agency!" he exclaimed. "Think of him huddling in his cabin all the way back to Earth, becoming more brutish each day, hoping to reach Earth while he was still human—"

"We've no time to think of Sperling now!" Carthew explained, his voice high and raw. "It's the people out there on Jupiter, and on the other planets, we must think of now—the arresting of this terror!"

James Carthew was feeling the awful weight of his responsibility, in this moment. The nine planets from Mercury to Pluto had entrusted their welfare to his care. And now he felt the approach of a mysterious, dreadful peril, a dark and unguessable horror spreading like subtle poison.

The first reports of the blight had come from Jupiter, weeks before. Out on that mightiest of planets, whose vast jungles and great oceans were still largely unexplored, there flourished a sizeable Earth colony. Centering around the capital of Jovopolis were dozens of smaller towns of Earthmen, engaged in working mines, and timbering, and in great grain-growing projects.

From one of those colonial towns near Jovopolis had come the first incredible reports. Earthmen—changing into beasts! Earthmen inexplicably being transformed into ape-like animals, their bodies and minds becoming more brutish each day. A horrible retracing of the road of human evolution! The victims had become atavisms — biological throwbacks hurled down the ladder of evolution.

Carthew had hardly believed those first reports. But soon had come ample corroboration. Already hundreds of Earthmen had been stricken by the dreadful change. The colonists out there were becoming panicky.

Carthew had sent scientists, men skilled in planetary medicine, to fight the horrid plague. But they had been unable to stop the cases of atavism, or even learn their cause. And neither had the secret agents of the Planet Police been able to learn much. Sperling, ace agent of them all, had learned but little, despite his sacrifice.

"We've got to do something at once, to check this blight," Carthew declared shakenly. "We know now, at least, that these atavism cases are being caused deliberately, by this being Sperling called the Space Emperor."

"But if Sperling, our best agent, couldn't succeed, who in the world can?" Bonnel cried.

JAMES CARTHEW went to the window and stepped out onto the little balcony. He looked up at the full moon that sailed in queenly splendor high above the soaring towers of nighted New York.

There was a look of desperation in the President's aging, haunted face as he gazed up at the shining white face of the lonely satellite.

"There's only one thing left to do," he said purposefully. "I'm going to call Captain Future."

The secretary stiffened.

"Captain Future? But the whole world will know this is a perilous emergency, if you call *him!*"

"This *is* a perilous emergency!" exclaimed his superior. "We've got to call him. Televise the meteorological rocket-patrol base at Spitzbergen. Order them to flash the magnesium flare signal from the North Pole."

"Very well, sir," acceded the secretary, and went to the televisor.

He came back a little later to the balcony, where James Carthew was gazing in anxiety toward the moon.

"The flare is being set off at the North Pole," he reported.

They waited, then, in tense silence. An hour passed—and another. The uranium clock showed it was past midnight.

Far out beyond New York's towers, the moon was declining from the zenith. They could see the distant rocket-flash of liners taking off from the spaceport for far Venus or Saturn or Pluto.

"Why doesn't Captain Future come?" North Bonnel burst out, unable to keep silent longer. "That ship of his can get from the moon to Earth in a few hours—he should be here by now."

James Carthew's gray head lifted. "He will be here. He's never yet failed to answer our call."

"As a matter of fact, I'm here now, sir," said a deep, laughing voice.

It came from the balcony outside the window. A big, red-headed young man had miraculously appeared there, as though by magic.

"Curt Newton—Captain Future!" cried the President eagerly.

CURT NEWTON was a tall, well-built young man. His unruly shock of red hair towered six feet four above the floor, and his wide lithe shoulders threatened to burst the jacket of his gray synthesilk zippersuit. He wore a flat tungstite belt in which was holstered a queer-looking pistol, and on his left hand was a large, odd ring.

This big young man's tanned, handsome face had lines of humor around the mouth, crinkles of laughter around the eyes. Yet behind the bantering humor in those gray eyes there lurked something deep and purposeful, some hidden, overpowering determination.

"Captain Future!" repeated James Carthew to this big young man. "But where's your ship, the *Comet?*"

"Hanging onto the wall outside by its magnetic anchor," answered Curt Newton cheerfully. "Here come my comrades now."

A weird shape had just leaped onto the balcony. It was a manlike figure, but one whose body was rubbery, boneless-looking, blank-white in color. He wore a metal harness, and his long, slitted green unhuman eyes peered brightly out of an alien white face.

Following this rubbery android, or synthetic man, came another figure, equally as strange—a great metal robot who strode across the balcony on padded feet. He towered seven feet high. In his bulbous metal head gleamed a pair of photoelectric eyes.

The robot's left hand carried the handle of a square transparent box. Inside it a living brain was housed. In the front of the case were the Brain's two glittering glass lens-eyes. Even now they were moving on their flexible metal stalks to look at the President.

"You know my assistants," Curt Newton said shortly. "Grag the robot, Otho the android, and Simon Wright, the living Brain. We came from the moon full speed when I saw your signal. What's wrong?"

"We've need of you, Captain Future—dire need." James Carthew said haggardly. "You'll have to leave for Jupiter, at once."

"Jupiter?" The handsome young man's brows drew together. "Has something popped out there?"

"A terror is growing out there!" the President cried. "A black horror that you must stop, immediately. Listen—"

CHAPTER II

Out of the Past

THE name of Captain Future, the supreme foe of all evil and evildoers, was known to every inhabitant of the Solar System.

That tall, cheerful, red-haired

young adventurer of the ready laugh and flying fists was the implacable Nemesis of all oppressors and exploiters of the System's human and planetary races. Combining a gay audacity with an unswervable purposefulness and an unparalleled mastery of science, he had blazed a brilliant trail across the nine worlds in defense of the right.

He and his three unhuman comrades, the living Brain, the metal robot and the synthetic man, were the talk of the System. Everyone knew that the scientific wizards' home was in some obscure crater on the desolate moon. People looked up at the lunar orb at night and felt safer because they knew that Captain Future was there, watching and ready. They knew that should any sinister catastrophe threaten the System, he would come forth to combat it.

But who *was* Captain Future? What had been the origin of his trio of unhuman comrades? And how had he come to achieve his super-scientific powers?

That was a story that only the President knew. And it was perhaps the strangest story in the history of the Solar System.

Twenty-five years before, a young Earth biologist named Roger Newton had dreamed a great dream. His dream was to create life—artificial, intelligent living creatures who would be able to think and work to serve humanity. He had already made great strides toward that goal, and felt on the verge of success.

But a certain unscrupulous politician with sinister ambitions had heard of Roger Newton's potent discoveries. He had made several daring attempts to steal them. There was danger to humanity if those discoveries passed into such hands. So Newton decided to seek a safe refuge in which he could work secretly.

On a night in that June of 1990, the young biologist communicated his decision to his only intimates, his young wife Elaine, and his loyal co-worker, Simon Wright.

Restlessly pacing the big, crowded laboratory of their secluded Adirondack farm, his red hair disordered and his lean, sensitive young face and blue eyes worried, Roger Newton addressed them.

"Victor Corvo's agents will find us here sooner or later," he asserted. "Think of my discoveries in Corvo's hands! We must leave Earth—go to a place where he'll never find us."

"But where can we go, Roger?" appealed Elaine Newton anxiously, her soft gray eyes fretful, her small hand grasping his sleeve.

"Yes, where can we go?" echoed Simon Wright in his metallic, unhuman voice. "To one of the colonized planets?"

"No, Corvo's agents would be sure to find us in any of the planetary colonies, sooner or later," Newton replied.

"Then where is this refuge you speak of, if it's not on Earth or any of the planets?" demanded Simon Wright, his lenslike artificial eyes boring questionably into Newton's face.

Simon Wright was not a man. He had once been a man. He had once been a famous, aging scientist whose body was racked by an incurable disease. To save his brilliant brain from death, Newton had acceded to the old man's plea and had removed Wright's living brain from his body and had encased it in a serum-case in which it could live indefinitely.

THE case stood now on a table beside Newton and his wife. It was a transparent metal box a foot square. Made of a secret alloy, it was insulated against shock, heat and cold, and contained a tiny battery that could operate its compact perfusion pump and serum purifier for a year.

Set in its sides were the microphones that were Simon Wright's ears. In front was the resonator by which he spoke, and his artificial lens-eyes, mounted on little flexible metal stalks he could turn at will. In that box lived the greatest brain in scientific history.

"Where can we find refuge, if not on Earth or any of the planets?" Wright repeated in his rasping, metallic voice.

Newton went to a window and drew aside the curtain. Outside lay the peaceful, nighted hills, washed with silver by the effulgent rays of the full moon that was rising in glorious majesty.

The white disc of the great satellite, mottled by its dark mountain ranges and plains, shone starkly clear in the heavens. Newton pointed up to it, as girl and brain watched wondering.

"There is our refuge," Roger Newton said. "Up there, on the moon."

"On the moon?" cried Elaine Newton, her hand going to her throat. "Oh, no, Roger—it's impossible!"

"Why impossible?" he countered. "A good interplanetary rocket can make the trip easily. We have enough money from my father's estate to buy such a rocket."

"But the moon!" Elaine exclaimed, deep repulsion shadowing her eyes. "That barren, airless globe that no one ever visits! How could anyone live there?"

"We can live there quite easily, dear," her young husband replied earnestly. "We shall take with us tools and equipment capable of excavating an underground home, with a glassite ceiling open to the sun and stars. Atomic energy will enable us to heat or cool it as we need, and to transmute rock into hydrogen and oxygen and nitrogen for air and water. We can take sufficient concentrated food with

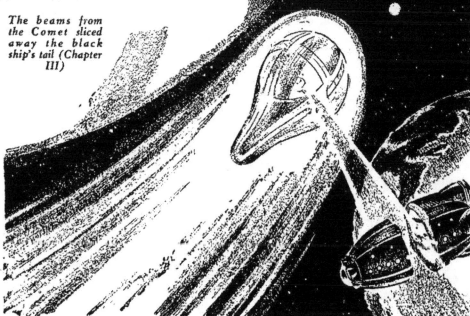

The beams from the Comet sliced away the black ship's tail (Chapter III)

us to last us for a lifetime."

"I believe your plan is good, Roger," said Simon Wright's metallic voice slowly. "Corvo is not likely to think of looking for us on the moon. We will be able to work in peace, and I feel sure we'll succeed there in creating a living being. Then we can return and give humanity a new race of artificial servants."

Elaine smiled bravely.

"Very well, Roger," she told her husband. "We'll go there, and maybe we'll be as happy on the moon as we have been here on Earth."

"We?" echoed the young biologist astoundedly. "But you can't go, Elaine. When I said 'we' I meant Simon and myself. You could not possibly live on that wild, lonely world."

"Do you think I would let you go there without me?" she cried. "No, if you go, I'm going with you."

"But our child——" he objected, a frown on his face.

"Our child can be born on the moon as well as on the Earth," she declared. And as he hesitated, she added, "If you left me here, Victor Corvo would find me and force me to tell where you had gone."

"That is true, Roger," interjected the Brain's cold, incisive voice. "We must take Elaine with us."

"If we must, we must," Newton said resignedly, his face deeply troubled. "But it's a terrible place to take anyone you love—a terrible place for our baby to be born——"

Ten weeks later, Newton, Elaine and Simon Wright — man, woman and Brain—sailed secretly for the moon in a big rocket crammed with scientific equipment and supplies.

Upon the moon, beneath the surface of Tycho crater, they built their underground home. There a son was soon born to the man and woman—a red-haired baby boy they named Curtis.

And there in the laboratory of the lonely moon home, a little later, Newton and Simon Wright created their first artificial living creature—a great metal robot.

GRAG, as they named the robot, stood seven feet high, a massive, man-shaped metal figure with limbs of incredible strength. He had super-sensitive photoelectric eyes and hearing, and a brain of metal neurones which gave him sufficient intelligence to speak and work, to think and to feel primitive emotions.

But though Grag the robot proved an utterly loyal, faithful servant, he was not of high enough mentality to satisfy Newton. The biologist saw that to create more manlike life he must create it of flesh, not of metal. After more weeks of work, they produced a second artificial creature, an android of synthetic flesh.

This synthetic man they named Otho. He was a rubbery, manlike creature whose dead-white synthetic flesh had been molded into human resemblance, but whose hairless white head and face, long, slitted green eyes, and wonderful quickness of physical and mental reactions, were quite unhuman. They soon found that Otho, the synthetic man, learned more quickly than had Grag, the robot.

"Otho's training is complete," Newton declared finally. His eyes shone with triumph as he continued, "Now we'll go back to Earth and show what we've done. Otho will be the first of a whole race of androids that soon will be serving mankind."

Elaine's face lit with pure happiness.

"Back to Earth! But dare we go back, when Victor Corvo is there?"

"Corvo won't dare bother us, when we return as supreme benefactors of humanity," her husband said confidently.

He turned to the two unhuman beings.

"Grag," he ordered, "you and Otho go out and remove the rock camouflage from the rocket, so that we can begin to make it ready for the return trip."

When the huge metal robot and the rubbery android had gone out through the airlock chamber to the lunar surface, Elaine Newton brought her infant son into the big laboratory.

She pointed up through the glassite ceiling which framed a great circle of starry space. There amid the stars bulked the huge, cloudy blue sphere of Earth, half in shadow.

"See, Curtis," she told the baby happily. "That is where we're going—back to the Earth you've never seen."

Little Curtis Newton looked up with wise gray baby eyes at the great sphere and stretched his chubby arms.

Newton heard the airlock door slam. He turned surprisedly. "Grag and Otho—are you back so soon?"

The voice of Simon Wright rasped with sudden alarm.

"That's not Grag and Otho—I know their steps," the living Brain cried. "It's men!"

Elaine uttered a cry, and Newton paled. Four men in space suits, carrying long flare-pistols, stood in the doorway.

stored. But he never reached it. Jets of fire from the pistols of Corvo's men hit him in mid-air and tumbled him into a scorched, lifeless heap.

Elaine Newton screamed, and thrust her baby onto a table, out of range of the guns. Then she leaped to the side of her husband.

"Elaine, look out!" cried the Brain.

She did not turn. The flare from Corvo's pistol struck her side, and she toppled to the floor beside her husband.

Little Curtis Newton, upon the table, began to whimper. Corvo ignored him and strode past the two still forms toward the square metal

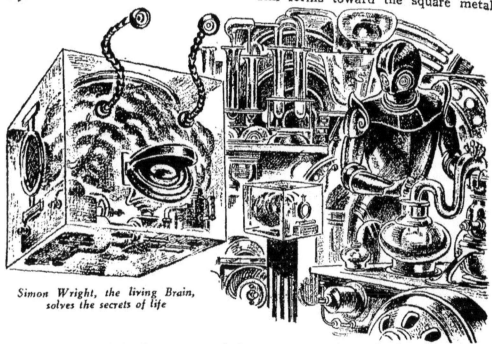

Simon Wright, the living Brain, solves the secrets of life

The face of their leader was revealed as they took off their helmets. It was a hawklike face, darkly handsome.

"Victor Corvo!" Newton cried appalledly, recognizing the ruthless man who had coveted his scientific discoveries.

"Yes, Newton, we meet again," said Corvo exultantly. "You thought I'd never find you here, but I finally tracked you down!"

Newton read death in the man's triumphant black eyes. And the sight of his wife's bloodless face and horrified eyes galvanized the young biologist into desperate action.

He sprang toward a locker in the corner in which his own flare-guns were

serum-case that held Simon Wright's living brain. He looked triumphantly into the glittering lens-eyes.

"Now to finish you, Wright," he laughed, "and then all the powers gathered in this laboratory belong to me."

"Corvo, you are a dead man now," answered the Brain in cold, metallic accents. "Vengeance is coming—I hear it entering now—terrible vengeance—"

"Don't try to threaten me, you miserable bodiless brain!" Corvo jeered, "I'll soon silence you—"

Two figures burst into the laboratory at that moment. Corvo and his men spun, appalled, unable to believe their eyes as they stared at the two incredible shapes who had entered.

The huge metal robot and the rubbery android! They stood, their unhuman eyes surveying the scene of death.

"Grag! Otho! Kill!" screamed the Brain's metallic voice. "They have slain your master. Kill them! Kill them!"

With a booming roar of rage from the robot, a fierce, hissing cry from the synthetic man, the two leaped forward.

In less than a minute, Corvo and his three men lay horribly dead, their skulls smashed to pulp by the robot's metal fists, their necks broken by the android's rubbery arms. Then Grag and Otho stood still, gazing around with blazing eyes.

"Set me down by your master and mistress!" ordered Simon Wright urgently. "They may still live!"

The robot put the Brain down by the two scorched forms. Wright's lens-eyes rapidly surveyed the bodies.

"Newton is dead, but Elaine is not dead yet," the Brain declared. "Lift her, Grag!"

With ponderous metal arms, the huge robot raised the dying girl to a sitting position. In a moment she opened her eyes. Wide, dark and filled with shadows, they looked at the Brain and robot and android.

"My—baby," she whispered. "Bring me Curtis."

It was Otho who sprang to obey. The android gently set the whimpering infant down beside her. The dying girl looked down at it tenderly, heartbreaking emotion in her fading eyes.

"I leave him to the care of you three, Simon," she choked. "You are the only ones I can trust to rear him safely."

"We'll watch over little Curtis and protect him!" cried the Brain.

"Do not take him to Earth," she whispered. "People there would take him away from you. They would say it is wrong to let a human child be reared by a brain and robot and android. Keep him here upon the moon, until he grows to manhood."

"We will," promised the Brain. "Grag and Otho and I will rear him here safely."

"And when he is a man," whispered Elaine, "tell him of his father and mother and how they died—how his parents were killed by those who wished to use the gifts of science for evil ends. Tell him to war always against those who would pervert science to sinister ambition."

"I will tell him," promised the Brain, and in its toneless metallic voice was a queer catch.

The girl's hand moved feebly and touched the whimpering infant's cheek. Into her dying eyes came a strange, far-seeing expression.

"I seem to see little Curtis a man," she whispered, her eyes raptly brilliant. "A man such as the System has never known before—fighting against all enemies of humanity—"

SO Elaine Newton died. And so her infant son was left in the lonely laboratory on the moon, with the Brain and the robot and the synthetic man.

Simon Wright and Grag and Otho kept their promise, in the years that followed. They reared little Curtis Newton to manhood, and the three unhuman tutors and guardians gave the growing boy such an education as no human had ever received before.

The Brain, with its unparalleled store of scientific knowledge, supervised the boy's education. It was the Brain who instructed Curtis Newton in every branch of science, making him in a short period of years into a complete master of all technical knowledge. And together the bodiless Brain and the brilliant, growing youth delved far beyond the known limits of science and devised instruments of unprecedented nature.

The robot instilled some of his own incredible strength and stamina into the boy, by a system of super exercises rigidly maintained. In mock struggle, the red-haired youth would pit himself against the great metal creature who could have crushed him in a second had he wished. Gradually, thus, Curt's strength became immense.

The android endowed the growing lad with his own unbelievable swiftness of physical and mental reactions. The two spent many hours on the barren lunar surface, engaged in strange games in which the lad would try to match the android's wonderful agility.

And as he grew older, Curt Newton started secret voyages through the Solar System, in the little super-ship Simon Wright and he had devised and built. The four secretly visited every world from scorched Mercury to Arctic Pluto, and so he came to know not only the Earthman colonies of each world, but much of the unexplored planetary wildernesses also. And he visited moon and asteroids that no other man had ever landed upon.

Finally, when Curtis Newton had grown to full manhood, Simon Wright told him how his father and mother had died, and of his mother's dying wish that he war always against those who would use the powers of science for evil ends.

"You must choose now, Curtis," the Brain concluded solemnly. "You must decide whether you will make your purpose in life the championing of mankind against its exploiters and oppressors, or whether you will seek happiness for yourself in normal, comfortable life.

"We three have given you the education and training you would need for such a life-long crusade. And we three will stand by you and fight at your side, if you take up that cause. But we cannot decide for you. You must do that for yourself."

Curt Newton looked up through the glassite ceiling at the starry vault of space in which bulked Earth's cloudy sphere. And the big, red-haired young man's cheerful face grew sober.

"I believe it's my duty to take up the cause you speak of, Simon," he said slowly. "Men such as killed my parents must be crushed, or they'll destroy the nine worlds' civilization."

CURTIS NEWTON drew a long breath.

"It's a mighty big job, and I may go down to defeat. But while I live, I'll stick to it."

"I knew you'd decide so, lad!" exclaimed the Brain. "You will be fighting for the future of the whole Solar System!"

"For the future?" repeated Curt. The humor came back into his gray eyes. "Then I'll call myself—Captain Future!"

That very night, Curt had flown from the moon to Earth and had secretly visited the President, offering the service of his abilities in the war against interplanetary crime.

"I know you've no faith in me now," he had told the President, "but a time may come when you'll need me. When that time comes, flash a signal flare from the North Pole. I'll see it, and come."

Months later, when a mysterious criminal was terrorizing the inner planets and the Planet Police were helpless, the President had remembered the red-haired young man who had called himself Captain Future, and as a desperate last hope had summoned him.

Captain Future and his three unhuman comrades had smashed the menace in a few weeks. And since then, time after time the signal flare had blazed from the North Pole—and each time Curt Newton and his comrades had answered. Each time, the fame of the mysterious foe of evil had become greater throughout the Solar System, as he destroyed one supercriminal after another.

But now, Captain Future had been called to face the greatest and deadliest antagonist he had ever confronted. The mysterious being who was striking down the Earthmen of Jupiter with a fearful horror that changed men into primeval beasts!

CHAPTER III

Ambush in Space

OUT beyond the orbit of Mars, out past the whirling wilderness of the asteroidal belt, flew a queer little ship. Shaped oddly like an elongated teardrop, and driven by muffled rocket-tubes whose secret design gave it a power and speed far beyond those of any other craft, it was traveling now at a velocity that lived up to its name of *Comet*.

Inside the *Comet*, in the transparent-walled room at the nose where its controls were centered, Grag the robot sat on watch. The great robot sat utterly rigid and unmoving, his metal fingers resting upon the throttles that controlled the flow of atomic energy to the rocket-tubes, his gleaming photoelectric eyes staring unswervingly ahead.

Curt Newton stood beside the robot, his hand resting familiarly on Grag's metal shoulder as he too peered ahead, toward the largening white sphere of Jupiter.

"Twenty more hours at this speed will bring us there, Grag," the big young man said thoughtfully.

"Yes, master," answered the robot simply in his booming mechanical voice. "And then what?"

Curt's eyes twinkled.

"Why, then we'll find this Space Emperor who's behind the terror out here, and take him back to Earth. That's all."

"Do you think it will be so easy, master?" asked the robot naively.

Captain Future laughed aloud.

"Grag, irony is wasted on you. The truth is that it's going to be a pretty tough job—the toughest we ever faced, maybe. But we'll win out. We've got to."

His face sobered a little. "This thing is big—big enough to wreck the Solar System if it isn't stopped at once."

He was remembering James Carthew's haggard face, the desperate appeal in his trembling voice.

"You'll do your best out there on Jupiter, Captain Future?" the President had pleaded. "That horror—men retracking the path of evolution to brutehood—it mustn't go on!"

"It won't go on if I can stop it," Curt had promised, his voice like level steel. "Whoever or whatever this Space Emperor is, we'll track him down or we won't come back."

Curt was thinking of that promise now. He knew well how difficult it was going to be to fulfill it. Yet the prospect of the perilous struggle ahead exhilarated him strangely.

Peril was like a heady wine to Curt's adventure-loving soul. He had met it in the poisonous swamps of Venus, in the black and sunless caverns of Uranus, in the icy snow-hell of Pluto. And always, when the danger was greatest, he had felt that he was living the most.

Grag broke the silence, the robot still looking ahead with his strange photoelectric eyes toward Jupiter.

"Jupiter is a big world, master," he boomed thoughtfully. "It took us long to catch the Lords of Power when they fled there."

Curt nodded, remembering that relentless hunt for the outer-planet criminals who had sought to hide on the giant planet. That had been the end of a blazing battle and chase that he and his three comrades had taken part in and that had reached from far Pluto to this mighty world ahead.

"It may take us even longer to find this Space Emperor, but we'll do it," he said resolutely.

There was silence, except for the droning of the cyclotrons in the *Comet's* stern, and the muffled purring of the atomic energy they produced, as it was released by the rocket-tubes. Then into the control-room came the synthetic man.

"You are late, Otho," boomed the robot, turning severely toward the android. "It was your turn to take over a half hour ago."

Otho's lipless mouth opened to give vent to a hissing chuckle. His green eyes gleamed mockingly.

"What difference can it make to you, Grag?" he inquired mockingly. "You are not a man, and so you do not need rest as we men do."

GRAG'S voice boomed angrily. "I am as much like a man as you are!" he declared.

"You, a metal machine?" taunted Otho. "Why, men are not of metal. They are of flesh, like myself."

The gibing, hissing voice of the android awakened all Grag's rudimentary capacity for indignation. He turned his unhuman metal face appealingly toward Captain Future.

"Am I not as near human as Otho, master?" he appealed.

"Otho, quit teasing Grag and take over," Curt Newton ordered sternly.

Yet there was a merry spark in Cap-

The cataract of brilliant crystals was now pouring steadily toward them
(Chapter IV)

tain Future's gray eyes as the android hastily obeyed.

Curt loved these three unhuman companions of his, the great, simple robot, the fierce, eager android and the dour, austere Brain. He knew they were more loyal and single-hearted than any human comrades could have been.

Yet he derived a secret amusement from these ceaseless quarrels between Otho and Grag. Both the robot and the android liked to be thought of as human or nearly human. And the fact that Otho was more manlike was a continual irritation to big Grag.

"I can do almost everything that Otho can do," Grag was saying to him anxiously. "And I am far stronger than he is."

"A machine is strong," sneered Otho, "but it is still only a machine."

"Come along with me, Grag," Curt told the robot hastily as he saw that the big metal creature was really angry.

The robot followed him back into the main-cabin that occupied the middle section of the *Comet*.

Simon Wright's lens-eyes looked up inquiringly at them. The Brain's transparent square case rested on a special stand, which embodied an ingenious spoolholder that automatically unreeled the long micro-film scientific work the Brain was consulting.

"What is wrong?" rasped Wright.

"Otho was just deviling Grag again," Curt told him. "Nothing serious."

"He is not *really* more human than I am, is he, master?" appealed the big robot anxiously.

"Of course not, Grag," answered Captain Future, his eyes twinkling as he laid his hand affectionately on the metal shoulder. "You should know enough by now to ignore Otho's taunts."

"Aye," rasped Simon Wright to the robot. "It is nothing to be proud of to be human, Grag. I was human, once, and I was not as happy as I am now."

"Go back and check the cyclotrons, Grag," Curt told the robot, and the great metal creature stalked obediently through the cabin into the power-room at the stern.

Captain Future's gray eyes looked inquiringly into the glittering glass ones of the Brain.

"Have you found any clue yet, Simon?"

"No," the Brain answered somberly. "Not in all the records of human science can I find any hint of how that ghastly method of causing this strange doom — this a t a v i s m — c o u l d be achieved."

"Yet it has been done — it is being done now," Curt muttered. "And that means that this time we are up against an antagonist who somehow has gone far beyond known science — further than we ourselves have gone!"

With brooding, unseeing eyes, the red-haired adventurer stared around the cabin, his mind far away.

The cabin was a marvel of compactness, with facilities for research in all fields of science. There was a chemistry alcove, with containers of every element known to science; an astronomical outfit, including an electro-telescope, electro-spectroscope, and a file of spectra of all planets, satellites, and stars above the fifth magnitude.

There were samples of the atmosphere of every planet, satellite and asteroid. And a botanical division contained specimen plants and vegetable drugs from various worlds.

BESIDES this equipment, there were many instruments which Captain Future and Simon Wright had devised, unknown to conventional science. A small locker contained every valuable scientific book or monograph ever published, reduced to micro-film. It was one of these micro-film spools the Brain had been consulting.

"I know of every biologist of note in the System today," the Brain was saying. "Not one of them could have discovered the secret of reversing evolution."

"Could such an epochal discovery have been made by a wholly unknown scientist?" Curt demanded.

"That seems unlikely," the Brain replied slowly. "There is some great mystery about this which I cannot understand, lad."

Curt's tanned face hardened.

"We're going to understand soon," he affirmed. "We've got to, to stop this thing."

Thoughtfully, he reached into a locker for a little hemispherical musical instrument. Absently, he touched its strings, bringing forth queer, shivering, haunting tones.

The instrument was a twenty-string Venusian guitar, two sets of ten strings each strung across each other on a metal hemisphere. Few Earthmen could play the complicated thing, but Captain Future had a habit of plucking haunting tones from it when he was lost in thought.

Wright's eye-stalks twitched annoyedly.

"I wish you'd never picked up that thing," the Brain complained. "How can I concentrate on reading when you're making that dismal whining?"

Curt grinned at the Brain.

"I'll take it into the control-room, since you don't appreciate good music," he said jestingly.

TWENTY hours later saw the little teardrop ship decelerating in velocity as it hurtled toward the world now close ahead.

Jupiter now loomed gigantic before them. It was a huge, spinning white sphere, attended by its eleven circling moons, belted with the clouds of its deep atmosphere, and wearing like an ominous badge the glowing crimson patch of the Fire Sea which men had once called the Great Red Spot. A world that was hundreds of times larger than Earth, a world whose fifty great jungle-clad continents and thirty vast oceans were still almost wholly unexplored.

Only on the continent of South Equatoria, Curt knew, had Earthmen settled. There they had cleared the steaming, unearthly jungles enough to build towns and operate plantations and mines, using the Jovian inhabitants for labor. But only a small part of even South Equatoria was known to them. The rest was unexplored, brooding jungle, stretching northward to the Fire Sea.

Curt Newton held the controls, and his three unhuman comrades were in the control-room with him as he expertly fingered the throttles. They flashed close past the gray sphere of Callisto, outermost of Jupiter's four biggest moons, and plunged on toward the giant planet.

"You're going to land at Jovopolis?" rasped Simon Wright inquiringly.

Captain Future nodded.

"That's the capital of the Earth colony, and there, I think, must be the heart of this menace."

Suddenly a bell rang sharply from the panel of complicated gauges and scientific tell-tales.

"The ship-alarm!" Curt exclaimed. "There's some other craft near us in space!"

"There it is behind us!" Otho cried out. "It's an ambush!"

Curt glanced back through the rear curve of the control-room's transparent wall. A dark little space-cruiser had just darted out from behind Callisto, and from its bows a big flare-gun was loosing a flare of atomic energy that sped toward the Comet.

No other space-pilot in the System could have moved quickly enough to escape that leaping flare. But Captain Future had reflexes trained since boyhood to superhuman speed.

The Comet lurched sideward from a blast of its starboard tubes, just enough to let the flare shoot past it. Before the attacker on their tail could fire again, Curt Newton had acted.

His tanned hand slammed down a burnished red lever beside the throttles. Instantly an astounding thing happened.

From the Comet's tubes shot a tremendous discharge of tiny, glowing particles. Almost instantly they formed a huge, glowing cloud around the little teardrop ship, hiding it from view and streaming back in a vast, shining tail.

The Comet had become, to all appearances, what it was named after—a comet! This was Curt Newton's method of camouflaging his ship when he wished to avoid discovery in space, or when he wished to confuse an enemy craft. It was operated by a powerful discharge of electrified atoms, or ions, produced in a special generator and released through the regular rocket-tubes.

"I'm banking around on them!" Curt called to the android. "Stand by to use our proton beams on them, Otho!"

"I'll blast them out of space!" exclaimed the android fiercely as he leaped to the breech of the proton-guns.

"No, I want those men alive if we can get them!" Captain Future snapped. "Try to cripple them by blasting their tail—that will force them down on Callisto."

As Curt swung the *Comet* sharply around, the black attacking ship rose viciously to meet it, letting go another burst of atomic energy from its flare-guns.

"So you still want to play, do you?" grinned Curt. "That's fine!"

CAPTAIN FUTURE had avoided the leaping flares by a lightning roll of the *Comet* that did not change its direction of flight for more than a moment.

Now he sent the little ship, still wrapped in its glowing cloud, swooping down upon the enemy, before it could turn.

"Now—let go our beams, Otho!" Captain Future cried.

The android obeyed. The pale proton beams lanced from the *Comet*, grazed past the tail of the black enemy.

"Missed them!" hissed Otho in bitter disappointment.

"They're trying to escape, master!" boomed Grag, pointing a metal arm.

The black enemy craft, its occupants apparently unnerved by the closeness of the proton beams, was diving sharply to flee away through space.

"It's easier to start a fight than to quit it, my friends," muttered Curt, jerking open two of his throttles. "Here's where you find that out."

Like a streak of glowing light, the *Comet* dived after the fleeing enemy. Pursued and pursuer rushed down through the dizzy depths of space at nightmare velocity.

Curt felt his pulse pounding with excitement as he guided his craft in that terrific swoop. To Captain Future, this was living—this wild whirl and flash of battle out here in the awesome solar spaces where he felt most at home.

"Try again now, Otho!" he cried a moment later.

The *Comet* had pulled almost abreast of the other swooping ship. The android now loosed their proton beams again.

The beams sliced away a third of the black ship's tail. Crippled, its rocket-tubes blasted and useless, it slowed in its wild rush until it was merely floating. Then it began to drift with ever increasing speed toward nearby Callisto.

"That got them!" Captain Future exclaimed, his gray eyes snapping with excitement. "They'll drift in to Callisto and we'll land there with them, and capture whoever's in that ship."

"You think they were sent by the Space Emperor—the mysterious figure behind the Jupiter horror—to ambush us?" rasped Simon Wright inquiringly.

"They must have been!" Otho declared. "The Space Emperor, whoever he is, didn't want Captain Future coming to Jupiter to investigate him."

Curt Newton interrupted, his gray eyes lit.

"But this may give us a lead right to the Space Emperor! If we can capture the men in that ship and make them talk—"

The black enemy craft was now drifting in a spiral around Callisto, ever approaching nearer to that barren-looking gray moon. Curt kept the *Comet* trailing the other ship, but far enough away to be out of range of its flare-guns, and with the ion-discharge apparatus now cut off.

"But lad," said Simon Wright's harsh voice, "how could the Space Emperor know that Captain Future was coming to Jupiter? The only person there whom the President would notify of our coming would be the Planetary Governor."

"Yes," said Curt meaningly, "and that may give us another lead to him. But right now our best chance is to wring information out of the men in that ship."

Otho, the synthetic android, is a master of disguise

Curt's mind was vibrant with eager hope. His mysterious foe had struck at him already, even before he reached Jupiter. But it might be that the attack of the unknown plotter was going to recoil on his own head.

"We near Callisto's surface, master!" came the booming voice of Grag.

Captain Future's gray eyes lit with a reckless gleam. "Get ready for a scrap then, Grag!"

Down through the thin atmosphere of Callisto the black ship was sinking, falling faster and faster. Still the *Comet* clung to its trail, grimly following it down toward the barren surface of the big moon. . . .

CHAPTER IV

World of Creeping Crystals

AT ever increasing speed the small black space-cruiser and its grim pursuer sped down toward the surface of Callisto. This was the sunward side of the big moon, and in the pale sunlight it presented a drear and desolate landscape.

A forbidding desert of drab gray rock, rising into low stony hills, it was infinitely repellent. The air here was barely breathable, as on all the larger moons, but because of its barrenness and also because of the grotesque, dangerous forms of life known to exist on its surface, few Earthmen had ever visited this world.

Now the black ship was only a mile from the glaring gray rock surface. It hurtled downward at slowly increasing speed.

"They won't crash with much force," Curt observed. "Callisto's gravitation is not strong. It'll be enough to shake them up and stun them for a moment, though, and we'll jump them before they make trouble."

"I'd enjoy seeing their ship hit hard enough to splash them all over Callisto," hissed the emotional android.

Captain Future grinned.

"You're too bloodthirsty, Otho."

Otho stared at him puzzledly. "I can't understand you humans some times," he complained.

Curt chuckled. Then he turned his attention below, ready for action.

The black ship was falling toward the rocky plain. A moment later it struck the stony desert, bounced violently, then hit the ground again with a sharp impact and lay still.

Instantly Captain Future sent the *Comet* speeding downward in a gliding swoop that brought it to a jarring landing close to the other ship. He jumped up from the controls.

"Come on, Grag!" he shouted. "Otho, you stay here at our proton-beams, just in case."

"Be careful, lad," cautioned the Brain.

Curt paused to adjust the gravity equalizer he wore on his belt. Every interplanetary traveler owned one of these clever devices. Its "gravity charge" of magnetic force of selected polarity and strength made its wearer feel exactly as light or heavy as he was on Earth.

Then Captain Future and the big metal robot emerged from the *Comet* into pale sunlight and a thin, pungent atmosphere that rasped the lungs. Curt led the way toward the black craft on a run, the barren desert's sterile surface reminding him strongly of the drab lifelessness of Mercury's Hot Side.

The black, torpedo-shaped space-cruiser lay a little on its side on the gray rock. There was no sound from inside it, indicating that the men within had been temporarily stunned by the crash. Curt and the robot reached the circular door.

"You'll have to open this door, Grag," Captain Future said rapidly. "Use your drills."

"Yes, master," boomed the big robot.

Grag's big metal fingers were removable. The robot rapidly unscrewed two of them and replaced them with small drills which he took from a kit of scalpels, chisels and similar tools carried in a little locker in his metal side.

Then Grag touched a switch on his wrist. The two drills which had replaced two of his fingers whirled hummingly. He quickly used them to drill six holes in the edge of the ship's door.

Then he replaced the drills with his fingers, hooked six fingers inside the holes he had made. He braced his great metal body, then pulled with all his strength at the door.

They could hear the men inside stirring as they recovered from the shock of crashing. But the colossal strength of the huge robot now ripped the door bodily off its heavy hinges. Instantly Captain Future leaped inside, the robot following.

TWO men sprang fiercely to meet them. They were hard-bitten, brutal-faced Earthmen, one with a bald head and pale eyes, the other a shock-haired giant. The bald one held a flare-pistol and fired swiftly at Captain Future.

Curt swerved, with a fierce, low laugh, as the man pulled trigger. Before the bald one could fire again, Captain Future had leaped in and seized his gun-hand. They struggled tensely.

In this moment of conflict, Curt's mind reverted to his super-fast games with Otho on the moon, as a boy. How slow seemed this swearing man beside the blurring speed of the android!

And how puny seemed the man's strength compared to the giant power of the mighty robot against whom he had pitted himself in boyhood!

The bald man suddenly went limp. Curt Newton, with his unerring knowledge of anatomy, had pressed and paralyzed a vital nerve center at the base of his skull.

"That will hold *you*, my friend," Captain Future exclaimed. He turned quickly. "You have the other one, Grag?"

"Yes, master," boomed the big robot calmly.

Grag had grabbed the other Earthman in his huge metal arms before he could use his gun, and was holding him as helpless as a baby. Captain Future touched the same vital nerve-center of this man, and he too went limp and helpless.

"Now," Curt said grimly to the two, "you will tell me just who you are and why the Space Emperor sent you out here to ambush me."

"The Space Emperor? I never heard of him," answered the bald-headed Earthman loudly. "I'm Jon Orris and this is my partner, Martin Skeel. We're honest traders, going to Saturn."

"Traders, in a ship that looks to me like a stolen police-cruiser!" Curt Newton commented contemptuously. His gray eyes snapped. "Silence is better than such a clumsy lie."

"Try to make us talk then, Captain Future!" snarled Orris, defiant.

"Shall I make them, master?" asked Grag eagerly, clenching his great metal fist ominously.

"Not that way, Grag," Curt said quickly. He stiffened. "Listen! I hear Otho coming."

He sprang to the open door of the ship. Out in the pale sunlight, Otho was running toward him. The rubbery android carried the handle of Simon Wright's brain-case.

"What's wrong?" Curt demanded, sensing trouble.

The Brain answered.

"Crystals coming, lad. Look yonder."

Curt spun and peered westward, where the Brain's eyes had turned. His lips tightened at what he saw.

Over the brink of low rock hills there, a slender, shining mass was slowly flowing. It was like a brilliant cataract of diamonds, dazzling in the sun as it flowed slowly down the rock hill toward the two parked ships.

Curt recognized that slowly approaching mass as one of the grotesque, dangerous life-forms that existed on Callisto. This strange, bizarre variety of life had developed in inorganic crystalline forms, as semi-intelligent, mutualistic crystal colonies. These crystal colonies had limited powers of movement, which enveloped and killed any luckless living thing unable to evade their slow approach.

"The things can always sense any living creature who lands on their world," Simon Wright was rasping. "They'll reach us in a quarter hour."

Curt Newton's gray eyes lit.

"That gives me an idea! Grag, drag out our two prisoners."

The big robot obeyed. He emerged from the black ship in a moment, half-carrying the two paralyzed, helpless men.

Curt pointed out the distant, approaching crystalline cataract to Orris and Skeel.

"I guess you two know what those Callistan crystals do to anything they catch," he said grimly. "If we take off and leave you here paralyzed as you are now, they'll reach you in about fifteen minutes."

The two men paled with horror.

"You wouldn't do that, Captain Future!" gasped the bald-headed Orris wildly.

"I would, unless you tell what you know of this horror that's going on at Jupiter!" Curt snapped.

HIS bluff worked. Sight of the crystals approaching had broken the nerve of the two as nothing else could.

"I'll tell you—but I don't really know much!" Orris stammered. "The Space Emperor told us to steal a Planet Police cruiser. We were to wait here in ambush for you and blast you out of space. We had to do what he said."

"Why did you? Who is the Space Emperor?" Curt demanded, feeling a harp-string suspense as he awaited the answer.

Orris shook his bald head shakily.

"I don't know who he is. Nobody knows who the Space Emperor is. I don't even know if he's *human*," he added fearfully. "He's always concealed in a big, queer black suit, and he speaks out of it in a voice that don't sound human to me. He does things no human *could* do!

"Skeel and I have criminal records," he continued hastily. "We fled out here to Jupiter after we got into a murder scrape on Mars. Somehow the Space Emperor found out we were wanted by the Planet Police. He threatened to expose us to them unless we obeyed his orders. We had to do it! He's forced other fugitive criminals like ourselves to do his bidding, by the same threat."

"How does he cause that reverse evolution in Earthmen?" Curt demanded.

"I don't know that. I've never seen him do it, if it's he who does it," Orris answered, dread in his pale eyes. "I do know that the Jovians worship the Space Emperor, and obey his every order. He's stirred them up to wild unrest to do his bidding."

"The Jovians worship the Space Emperor?" echoed Simon Wright's metallic voice. "That is strange——"

"There's the devil of a lot about this story that's strange!" Captain Future declared crisply. "If you're lying——"

"I'm not!" Orris declared fearfully, glancing nervously toward the approaching cataract of crystals.

"Where were you to report to the Space Emperor when you'd succeeded in destroying me?" Captain Future demanded.

"He was to meet us tonight in our cabin in Jovopolis," Orris replied. "It's beyond the Street of Space Sailors, at the edge of the city."

Skeel, the other man, interrupted.

"Aren't you going to let us go now?" he pleaded hoarsely. "Those crystals will be here in a few minutes!"

Curt paid no attention to the approaching stream of dazzling crystals which had awakened panic in the two would-be murderers. A quick plan had been born in the red-haired adventurer's mind.

"Otho, I want you to make yourself up as a double of this man Orris," he told the synthetic man.

"What is your plan, lad?" rasped Simon Wright keenly.

NEWTON'S gray eyes snapped. "The Space Emperor will come to that cabin on the edge of Jovopolis tonight, to receive the report of these two men. Well, one of them is going to report with Captain Future as his prisoner—only it won't be really Orris who reports, but Otho!"

"I see!" muttered the Brain. "The Space Emperor will be thrown off guard by Otho's disguise, and we may be able to capture him."

"Hurry, Otho!" Curt exclaimed. "Those crystals are getting close!"

"I am hurrying, Chief," the synthetic man replied.

Otho was clawing in the square make-up pouch that hung at his belt beside his proton-pistol. He brought out a small lead flask with a sprayer attachment.

From the flask, the android sprayed a colorless chemical oil onto his own face and head. Then he waited.

In a moment a strange change came over Otho's face. His rubbery, white synthetic flesh seemed to lose its elastic firmness and to soften like melting wax.

Otho's synthetic flesh was so constituted that an application of the chemical oil would soften it and make it as plastic as putty. It would harden again in a few minutes, but before it hardened it could be molded into any desired features.

Now that his flesh was softened to plasticity, Otho himself began molding it. With firm, deft fingers the android pressed and touched the softened white flesh of his face. Modeling his features into different ones, as a sculptor might model a new clay mask from an old one!

As he worked, Otho's green eyes steadily watched the panicky, brutal face of the man Orris. And swiftly, Otho's face *became* the face of Orris, in every line and feature. The android, through long practice, could remake his face into an exact replica of any other face in a few minutes.

A minute after he had finished, the flesh of his face began hardening again into elastic firmness.

"Now for the make-up," Otho muttered, clawing in his square pouch again.

"Hurry!" urged Captain Future.

With a tiny hypodermic, Otho injected a drop of fluid into each eye which changed their color from green to a pale hue. Thin stain from a tube changed his new face from dead-white to a space-tanned color. A little fringe of artificial brown hair around his new tanned, bald head completed the amazing disguise.

Otho darted into the ship of Orris and Skeel. He returned in a moment clad in a zipper-suit of drab synthe-silk like that worn by Orris. Then the android turned to Curt Newton.

"Is it good enough?" he asked in a voice that was an uncanny replica of the voice of Orris.

"It's perfect!" Curt declared. Before him were *two* Orrises—indistinguishable from each other.

"Good God, that creatures made himself into *me!*" gasped Orris horrifiedly.

"Lad, it's time we left," rasped Simon Wright's warning. "The crystals are coming too near."

Curt whirled. The cataract of brilliant crystals was now pouring steadily across the rocky plain toward them. The gleaming, faceted crystalline things advanced inexorably, motivated by an electric force in their strange inorganic bodies that gave them the power of attraction and repulsion to each other.

With a clicking, murmuring, rustling sound, the brilliant flood moved at the rate of a few feet a moment, each separate gleaming crystal jerking a few inches forward by exerting repulsion upon those behind it. They were but a hundred feet away.

"Grag, wreck the cyclotrons of this ship!" Captain Future ordered. "Then we'll be off."

AS the big robot sprang into the black craft to obey, Orris and Skeel voiced wild protest.

"You're not going to leave us here to be killed by those things!" they cried.

Curt bent over the two helpless men and touched their nerve-centers, lifting the paralysis that held them. As they staggered up, Grag came out of the ship.

"It is wrecked, master," boomed the robot. "That ship will not fly space again."

"You two men can run now, and you can easily keep away from the crystals here," Curt told Orris and Skeel. "I'll notify the Planet Police at Jovopolis and they'll send a ship out to pick you up."

His eyes flamed.

"If I did what I'd like to, I'd let the crystals have you! You've helped to spread a horror that's blacker than murder!"

The two criminals stared wildly at the clicking, advancing flood of crystals now only fifty feet away, and then broke into a crazy run in an opposite direction, stumbling frantically away across the drab gray desert.

"Quick, to the Comet before those things cut us off!" Curt cried.

Grag snatched up the handle of Simon Wright's square brain-case. He and the disguised Otho and Captain Future ran hastily toward their ship.

The clicking crystals were only yards from them as they passed the head of their cataract. Tumbling inside the Comet, Curt leaped to the control-room, and in a moment had the little teardrop ship zooming upward with a muffled roar of tubes.

He looked back down and saw the baffled crystals flowing over the disabled black ship, smothering it until it seemed encrusted with blazing diamonds, searching its interior for any living thing. The two criminals who had fled were already far away across the rocky surface of Callisto, and would be safe until the Planet Police came for them.

Captain Future had an eager gleam in his gray eyes as he steered upward.

"Now for Jovopolis," he said tautly, "and the Space Emperor!"

CHAPTER V

Power of the Space Emperor

JUPITER, like all the other outer planets, had once been considered impossible as a habitation for Earthmen. Before interplanetary exploration actually began, it had been thought that the giant world would be too cold, its atmosphere too poisonous with methane and ammonia, its gravitation too great for human life.

But the first Earthmen who visited Jupiter found that the great planet's interior radioactive heat kept it at tropical warmth. The methane and ammonia, they discovered, existed only in the upper atmospheric layers. The lower layers were quite breathable. And the invention of the gravity equalizers had solved the problem of the powerful gravitation.

Down through the darkness toward the night side of this great world, splitting the deep atmosphere with a shrill, knife-edged sound, plunged the Comet.

Captain Future held the controls, with Grag and the disguised Otho and Simon Wright beside him. And the red-haired adventurer was tense with fierce hope as he peered downward.

"Here we are," Curt muttered finally, easing back a throttle. "We're west of South Equatoria."

"Not far west, I think," rasped Simon Wright, from the special pedestal upon which his brain-case rested.

Beneath them lay a vast, heaving sea, bathed in silvery light by the three moons now in the sky. It was one of the thirty tremendous oceans of the monarch planet, and endless watery plain whose moonlit surface heaved in great billows toward the sky.

Curt had leveled off, and now the *Comet* screamed eastward low above the tossing silver ocean. Under the brilliant rays of Ganymede and Europa and Io, the waste of waters stretched to the far horizons in magnificent splendor.

Moon-bats those weird Jovian birds that for some mysterious reason never fly except when the moons shine, were circling high above the waters. Their broad wings shone in the silver light with uncanny iridescence, due to some strange photochemical effect.

Schools of flame-fish, small fish that glowed with light because of their habit of feeding on radioactive sea-salts, swam just under the surface. The triple head of hydra, a species of big sea-snake always found twined in curious partnerships of three, reared above the waves. Far northward a "stunner", like an enormous flat white disc of flesh, shot up out of the moonlit sea and came down with a thunderous shock that would stun all fish immediately beneath and make them easy prey.

The *Comet* drove on low above the silver-lit ocean teeming with strange life. Under the three big, bright moons, the teardrop ship cleaved the atmosphere like a meteor, hurrying toward the perilous rendezvous with mystery that Curt Newton was determined to keep.

"Lights ahead, master," boomed Grag, the robot's photoelectric eyes peered keenly.

"Yes, it's South Equatoria," Curt said. "Those are the lights of Jovopolis."

Far ahead a low black coast rose from the moon-lit ocean. A little inland lay a big bunch of lights, dominated by the red-and-green lamps of the lofty spaceport tower.

Beyond the city lights stretched the black obscurity of the big plantations and the deep jungles beyond. And in the horizon the sky was painted by a dazzling aurora of twitching, quivering red rays—the crimson glare flung up by the distant Fire Sea.

"Only Saturn has more wonderful nights than this," Curt said, feeling even in his tensity the weird beauty of it.

"You're not going to land openly in Jovopolis?" Simon Wright questioned Curt.

Captain Future shook his red head at the question.

"No, we'll drop down secretly at the edge of the spaceport."

THE *Comet* glided with muffled rocket-tubes over the moonlit mud flats along the shore, against which the great lunar tide of the Jovian ocean was hurling itself in mighty combers. Silent as a shadow, the little teardrop ship approached the spaceport, avoiding the docks and sinking down at the unlighted edge of the field.

Curt Newton cut the cyclotrons and stood up. He had already set his gravity equalizer, so that he did not feel the full power of the crushing Jovian gravitation.

"Otho and I must hurry," he said tensely. "We must be at Orris' hut when the Space Emperor comes there."

"Can't I come too, master?" asked big Grag.

"You could never pass as a man," jeered Otho. "One glimpse of your metal face would give us away."

Grag turned angrily toward the android, but Captain Future intervened hastily between the two.

"You must stay with Simon and guard the *Comet*, Grag," he said. "We'll be back soon if we catch the one we're after."

"Be careful, lad," muttered the Brain. "This Space Emperor is the most dangerous antagonist we've ever encountered."

Curt smiled pleasantly.

"A foeman worthy of our steel eh? Don't worry, Simon. I'm not underestimating him!"

*The two men saw the immaterialized robot
floating up through the roof of the cavern
(Chapter XX)*

CURT and Otho emerged from the
Comet and started toward the
bright-lit Street of Space Sailors that
ran eastward from the spaceport. The
Jovian night lay soft and heavy upon
them, the warm air laden with fetid
scents of strange vegetation. The
three bright moons cast queer mul-
tiple shifting shadows around them.

Curt knew the Street of Space
Sailors well. It was usually roaring
with lusty life, for in its dubious taverns gathered Earthmen who knew
swampy Venus and desert Mars and
icy Pluto, men who would be here for
only a few days and who made the
most of them before they went back.

But now the street was less crowded
than usual. A pall seemed to lie over
the motley interplanetary throng, and
fewer rocket-cars came and went than
was usual. There were many space-
bronzed Earthmen drinking in the dis-
reputable taverns, but they drank in
unnatural silence. It was evident to
Curt's keen eyes that the dark shadow
of the plague lay over this city.

In the street were many Jovians,
the planetary natives of this world.
They were manlike, man-size creatures, but their green-skinned bodies
were squatter than the human, their
heads were small, round and hairless,

with large, circular dark eyes, and their arms and legs ended in queer flippers instead of hands or feet.

Their clothing was a scanty black leather harness. They seemed to watch the passing Earthmen with unfriendliness and distrust.

"The Jovians don't seem to care much for Earthmen any more," muttered Otho.

Curt's gray eyes narrowed slightly.

"According to what Orris told us, it's the Space Emperor who's stirred them into unrest."

"Look out!" yelled a wild voice suddenly from somewhere in the throng ahead. "He's got it!"

"Atavism—get away!" roared other voices.

Curt saw men darting away from an Earthman who had been wandering dazedly along the street, but who now was beating his breast, frothing at the lips, his glazed eyes glaring bestially around.

All shrank from the man thus suddenly stricken by the dread evolutionary blight. For a moment there was a frozen silence except for his growling cries. Then whistles shrilled and a rocket-car dashed along the street.

Haggard-faced hospital orderlies grabbed the struggling man who had just been stricken, pulled him into the car, and dashed away.

The tense silence lasted for an eternal moment, in which men stared sickly at each other. Then, as though desirous to get away from the spot, the motley throng moved rapidly on.

"So *that* is what it is like to be stricken by the horror!" hissed Otho.

A dangerous light flared in Captain Future's gray eyes, and his big form tensed.

"I think I'm going to enjoy meeting the black devil who's causing this," he said between his teeth.

They moved on along the Street of Space Sailors, out of the lighted section to the dark end of the avenue. Before them lay the black, vague fields beyond the city. Curt's keen eyes glimpsed a dark little metalloy cabin, that stood a little beyond the street end, beside a clump of towering, moonlit tree-ferns.

"Orris' cabin," he muttered, his hand dropping to his proton-pistol. "Come on, Otho."

HE listened at the door of the cabin, then pushed it open and entered the dark interior. The place was deserted.

Curt pulled the cord that uncovered the glowing uranite bulb in the ceiling. The illumination revealed a slovenly metal room, with a bunk in one corner, some zipper-suits and a couple of Jovian leather harnesses on hooks. The wide windows were screened against those pests of the planet, sucker-flies and brain-ticks.

Captain Future slipped his pistol inside his jacket. Then he stretched himself out on the bunk in the corner.

"The Space Emperor should be here soon," he told the android crisply. "When he comes, tell him you captured me, drugged me, and brought me here. Maneuver to get between him and the door."

Otho nodded his disguised head in understanding. There was a fierce, throbbing glitter in his eyes.

"No more talk now," Curt ordered tensely.

Lying sprawled stiffly on the bunk in perfect simulation of a drugged stupor, Curt watched through half-closed eyes. The android walked nervously back and forth, as though awaiting someone.

Eager suspense gripped Curt's mind. He, Captain Future, who had met and conquered so many evil ones in the past, was about to confront the most formidable adversary he had yet faced. His reckless soul almost exulted in the prospect.

Curt heard a sudden, low exclamation of astonishment from Otho. He opened his eyelids a trifle more, and received a surprise that was like an electric shock.

A black, weird figure now stood inside the cabin with them. The door had not opened, for Curt had been watching it. It was as though this dark visitant had come silently through the *walls*.

The Space Emperor! The mysterious figure who was turning Jupiter into a planetary hell! Curt knew that he looked upon his unknown antagonist.

The Space Emperor wore a grotesque, puffy black suit and helmet of mineraline, flexible material. The helmet had small eye-holes, but the eyes inside could not be seen. His real appearance was perfectly concealed by that puffy suit. It was impossible even to tell whether he was an Earthman or Jovian.

"You—you're here!" stammered Otho, in Orris' voice, putting into it and into the expression of his disguised face the same dread that Orris had shown in speaking of the Space Emperor.

Out of that helmet came a voice that rasped the fibers of Captain Future's spine. It was not a human-sounding voice. It was more like the deep voice of a Jovian, yet instead of being soft and slurred it was heavy, strong, vibrating with power.

"I'm here, yes," the Space Emperor said. "Did you and Skeel succeed in killing Captain Future?"

"We did better than that," Otho said, with assumed pride. "We captured him and I brought him here— see!"

Otho pointed toward the bunk upon which Curt Newton lay sprawled in apparent coma.

"Skeel was killed in the fight," Otho went on, "but I got Captain Future, all right. I gave him a shot of *somnal* to keep him quiet, and brought him here for you."

"You fool!" came the deep voice of the Space Emperor, shaking now with rage. "Why did you not kill him out there at once? Don't you know that this Captain Future is deadly dangerous as long as he is alive?"

The Space Emperor advanced a little in his rage, his dark figure not walking but moving with a queer, smooth glide across the metal floor.

Otho, pretending to shrink aside in fear, edged slowly to get between the dark visitant and the door.

"I thought you'd want him alive," Otho was apologizing abjectly. "I can kill him now, if you want me to."

"Kill him, at once!" throbbed the Space Emperor's voice. "This man has spoiled great plans before. He is

not going to spoil mine!"

CURT NEWTON had been gathering his muscles for action. Now, as the last word vibrated, the red-haired adventurer launched himself upward in a flying spring at his enemy.

Straight at that dark, erect figure plunged Curt. He expected to knock the mysterious plotter to the floor, overcome him. But Curt received the greatest surprise of his life.

For Captain Future felt himself plunge *through* the Space Emperor as though the latter did not exist! Just as though the Space Emperor were but an immaterial phantom, Curt hurtled through his solid-seeming body and crashed against the wall with stunning force.

"So!" cried the criminal's deep voice. "One of Captain Future's traps!"

Otho had charged in almost the same instant as Curt. And the disguised android also had plunged *through* the dark figure.

Curt had his proton-pistol out, as the black form started to glide swiftly across the room. Astounded, dazed as he was by the incredible thing that had happened, Captain Future did not lose his presence of mind for a moment.

He pulled trigger, and a pale thin beam lanced from the slender pistol toward the gliding dark figure.

Curt's proton-pistol was more deadly than any of the atomic flare-guns used by other men. It could be set either to stun or kill, and it was set to kill now. But its concentrated jet of protons merely drove through the Space Emperor without harming him in the least.

"At last you meet someone with powers greater than your own, Captain Future!" the hidden voice taunted.

The dark figure glided away. The solid-seeming shape passed through the solid metal wall. Then it was gone.

Otho stood still, numbed by the incredible sight. But Captain Future leaped toward the door, galvanized into action.

He burst out into the moon-shot darkness and swept the obscurity with his eyes. There was no sign of the Space Emperor. He had disappeared completely.

"He got away, that devil!" Curt cried, anger and self-reproach flaring in his voice.

"He wasn't real at all!" Otho exclaimed dazedly. "He was only a shadow, a phantom!"

"A phantom couldn't talk and be heard!" Curt snapped. "He's as real as you or I."

"But he came and went through the wall—" the android muttered bewilderedly.

Captain Future's tanned face frowned in thought, as he tried to comprehend his enemy's secret.

"I believe," he announced, "that the Space Emperor is using some secret of vibration to make himself effectively immaterial whenever he wishes."

Otho stared.

"Immaterial?"

Curt nodded his red head slowly.

"It's always been considered theoretically possible that if the frequency of atomic vibration of an object or man were stepped up higher than the frequency of ordinary matter, that object or man could pass *through* ordinary matter, just as two electric signals of different frequency can pass through the same wire at the same time."

"But if that were the case, he would sink right down through the ground to the center of gravity of the planet!" Otho objected.

IMPATIENTLY, Captain Future shook his head.

"Not if he set his gravity equalizer at zero. And he could use reactive force-push of some kind to achieve that gliding lateral motion. Of course, he couldn't breathe ordinary air, but inside that suit would be an air-supply whose atomic frequency would be changed along with his body."

"But how could he talk, and see, and hear us?" Otho wanted to know.

"That I can't understand yet myself," Captain Future admitted ruefully. "The whole thing embodies a science that is not human science. No Earthman scientist has ever yet achieved such a vibration set-up."

"Then where did he get the secret, and the secret of the evolutionary horror?" the android demanded. "There's supposed to have been a great civilization on Jupiter in the dim past. Now there's nothing here now but these half-civilized Jovians who have no science. Do you think the Space Emperor could be a Jovian?"

Curt shook his head. He felt baffled, for the moment. The sinister mystery around the dark plotter had deepened.

And his pride in his scientific knowledge had received a bad blow. He had run up against someone who apparently possessed scientific secrets beyond even his own attainments.

"We've got to find out *who* the Space Emperor is before we can even hope to get him," he declared. He looked at Otho. "You can make up as a Jovian, can't you?"

Otho stiffened.

"You know there isn't a planetary being in the System I can't disguise myself as, when I want to," he boasted.

"Then go ahead and assume Jovian disguise," Curt said quickly, "and go back into the crowded quarter. Mingle with the Jovians there. Try to find out what they know about the Space Emperor, and above all, if he is a Jovian or an Earthman."

Otho nodded understandingly.

"Shall I come back here if I learn anything?"

"No, report back to the *Comet*," Curt ordered. "I'm going to the Governor. There's a lead there somewhere to the Space Emperor. For the Governor, remember, would be the only person here notified that we were coming to Jupiter—and yet the Space Emperor knew of our coming and set an ambush for us!"

In surprisingly few minutes, Otho had shed the disguise of Orris and had assumed the likeness of a native Jovian.

The android had used the oily chemical spray to soften the synthetic flesh of his face, hands and feet. Then he had molded his head and features into the round head and flat, circular-eyed face of a Jovian, and his hands and feet into the flipper-like extremities of the planetary natives.

He smeared green pigment from his make-up pouch smoothly over all his body. A skillful hunching of his rubbery figure gave him the squat appearance of a Jovian. And finally, he donned one of the black leather harnesses hanging beside the zipper-suits on the wall of the cabin. Earthmen often wore those scanty harnesses in the damp, hot jungles of Jupiter, for the sake of coolness and freedom.

When Otho spoke, it was in the soft, slurred bass voice of a Jovian.

"Will I pass?" he asked Curt.

Captain Future smiled.

"I wouldn't recognize you myself," he said. "Get going, and watch yourself."

Joan Randall

Otho slipped out of the cabin, and was gone. In a moment, Curt emerged also into the moonlit night.

The red-headed space-farer strode rapidly toward the silvered metal mass of buildings of the city, heading toward the central section where was located the seat of colonial government.

Somewhere there, he was certain, was a key to the mystery that had shrouded this planet in a spell of dark horror.

CHAPTER VI

Monsters That Were Men

THE governor's mansion stood in parklike grounds of big tree-ferns and banked shrubbery. It was a large rectangular structure, built of gleaming metalloy like all the rest of the Earthman city. Tonight, its many wide windows were glowing with light.

Curt approached it silently through the dark grove. Brilliant rays of the three big moons struck down between the fronds of the towering tree-ferns and glistened on his determined face. Perfume of beautiful but forbidding "shock flowers" was heavy in his nostrils. High above glided moon-bats, those weird, iridescent winged creatures of Jupiter that appear only when one or more moons are in the sky.

He reached a terrace on the west side of the big metal mansion. Soundlessly, Captain Future advanced to an open window that spilled forth the bright white glow of powerful uranite bulbs. He peered keenly into the office inside, and at once recognized the governor of the Earth colony, from the President's description.

Sylvanus Quale, the colonial governor, sat behind a metal desk. Quale was a man of fifty, with a stocky, powerful figure, iron-gray hair, and a square face that had a stony impassivity. He looked as inscrutable as a statue, his colorless eyes expressionless.

Captain Future saw that Quale was talking to a girl in white nurse's uniform.

"Why didn't Doctor Britt bring the report from Emergency Hospital himself, Miss Randall?" Quale was asking.

"He's worn out and on the verge of collapse," she replied. Her eyes were shadowed as she added, "This terrible thing is getting too much for us."

Curt saw that the girl was strikingly pretty, even in the severe white uniform. Her dark, wavy, uncovered hair framed a small face whose brown eyes and firm lips gave an impression of cool steadiness and efficiency. Yet deep horror lurked in her eyes.

"Mr. Quale, what are we going to do?" Curt heard her appeal to the governor. "There are over three hundred cases of the blight in Emergency Hospital now. And some of them are getting—ghastly."

"You mean they're still changing, Joan?" Quale asked, forgetting official formality in his deep thoughtfulness.

The girl nodded, her face pale.

"Yes. I can't describe what hideous monsters some of them have become. And only days ago they were men! You must do something to stop it!"

Curt stepped into the office through the open window, silently as a shadow.

"I hope there is something that I can do to stop it," he said quietly.

Joan Randall turned with a little startled cry, and Sylvanus Quale half rose to his feet as he saw the big, red-haired, gray-eyed young man who stood inside the room, gravely facing them.

"Who—what—" the governor stammered, reaching toward a button on his desk.

"You needn't call guards," Curt told him impatiently. "This ring will identify me."

Curt Newton held out his left hand. On that hand he wore a ring with a curious, large bezel. At its center was a little glowing sphere of radioactive metal, representing the sun. This was surrounded by nine concentric circular grooves, in each of which was a small jewel.

The jewels represented the nine planets. There was a tiny brown one for Mercury, a larger pearly gem for Venus, and so on. And the jewels *moved* slowly, circling the little glowing sun. Motivated by a tiny atomic power plant, they moved exactly in accordance with the planets they represented. This unique ring was known from Mercury to Pluto as the identifying emblem of Captain Future.

"Why, you're Captain Future!" Sylvanus Quale exclaimed startledly.

"Captain Future?" echoed Joan Randall, staring with sudden eagerness at this big, red-haired adventurer.

"President Carthew notified you that I was coming here?" Curt asked the governor.

QUALE nodded quickly. "He televised me when you started."

"Did you tell anyone else I was coming?" Curt asked keenly.

He watched Quale narrowly as he awaited an answer. If the governor admitted having told no one, it meant—

But Quale was nodding.

"I told Eldred Kells, the vice-governor, and Doctor Britt, chief planetary physician, and some others here. I wanted to reassure them—they're all so panicky."

Curt felt momentarily thwarted. It looked as though his possible lead to the Space Emperor had faded out.

Disguising his disappointment, he told Quale briefly about the ambush and the two criminals now marooned on Callisto.

"I'll send a Planet Police cruiser out to pick them up," Quale promised quickly.

At that moment a door opened. A tall, blond man of thirty in a white zipper-suit entered the office. His strong face was worn and lined by too-great strain.

"What is it, Kells?" Sylvanus Quale demanded.

Eldred Kells, the vice-governor, was staring wonderingly at Curt. Then, as he glimpsed the red-haired man's ring, Kells' worn face lighted with hope.

"Captain Future—you're here!" he cried. "Thank God! Maybe you can do something to end this horror."

Kells turned quickly back to his superior.

"Lucas Brewer and young Mark Cannig are here, sir. They just flew down from Jungletown. I gather that things are getting pretty horrible up there."

Quale turned to Captain Future.

"Brewer is president of Jovian Mines, a small company that owns a radium mine north of Jungletown," he explained. "Mark Cannig is his mine-superintendent."

"I remember hearing of this Brewer

before," Curt said, frowning. "On Saturn, three years ago."

Kells returned in a moment with the two men he had named.

Lucas Brewer, the mine owner, was a grossly fat man of forty, with dark, shrewd little eyes and a puffy face that wore the pitiless look of those who live too well.

Mark Cannig, his mine-superintendent, was a dark, handsome young fellow with a rather nervous look. He glanced eagerly at Joan Randall but the pretty nurse avoided his gaze.

"Quale, you've got to do something!" Lucas Brewer said emphatically as he entered. "This thing is getting—"

He stopped suddenly, as his eyes rested on Captain Future. An expression of recognition came into his eyes.

"Why, is that—" he started to say.

"It's Captain Future, yes," Quale said. "I told you he was coming, remember."

Curt saw something of apprehension creep into Brewer's small eyes. And it seemed to him that there was a sudden uneasiness also in the face of young Mark Cannig.

Curt hated promoters of Brewer's type. He had met them before on many planets. They were ruthless tricksters whose greed brought misery to colonizing Earthmen and planetary natives alike.

"I've heard a lot about you, of course, Captain Future," Brewer was saying hesitantly.

"And I heard something about you and your business activities on Saturn a few years ago," Curt said disgustedly.

HE asked suddenly, "Why did you come here from Jungletown tonight?"

"Because things are getting so bad up at Jungletown!" Brewer declared. "We've got over five hundred cases of the blight there. The hospital's hopelessly overcrowded, and I wanted to urge Quale to do something to stop this horrible thing. Anyone up there may be the next stricken by that horror. Why, I might be next!"

Captain Future stared contemptuously at the fat promoter. But Eldred Kells immediately answered him indignantly.

"We can't stop the plague until we know what's causing it," defended the haggard vice-governor.

"Where did the thing start?" Curt asked him.

Quale answered.

"Up at Jungletown, several hundred miles north of here. It's a new boomtown. Sprang up after radium and uranium deposits were located nearby. The place is pretty close to the southern shore of the Fire Sea, and there are some thousands of Earthmen engineers, prospectors and the like who make it their base.

"The first cases were of a few radium prospectors," Quale went on. "They stumbled out of the jungle, already horribly transformed into ape-like creatures. Since then, more people have been stricken every day. Most of the cases have been at Jungletown, but there have been a large number down here at Jovopolis, and others elsewhere."

"We're completely in the dark about the cause of this awful disease," Eldred Kells added hopelessly.

"It's not a disease," Curt told them forcefully. "It's being deliberately caused."

"Impossible!" exclaimed Lucas Brewer. "What man would do such a fiendish thing?"

"I didn't say it was a man doing it," Captain Future retorted. "The one who is causing it calls himself—the Space Emperor."

He watched their faces closely as he spoke the name. Brewer looked blank. Young Mark Cannig shifted uneasily. But Kells and the governor only started wonderingly.

"Have any of you ever heard that name?" Curt demanded.

All of them shook their heads negatively. Curt came quickly to a decision.

"I want to see the victims you have here in Jovopolis," he declared. "I'd like to study them. You spoke of an Emergency Hospital you're keeping them in?"

Sylvanus Quale nodded.

"We converted our Colony Prison into an emergency hospital. It alone could hold those—creatures. Miss Randall and I can take you there."

Curt's big figure strode with the governor and the nurse out of the office and through the halls of the mansion. They emerged into the soft, heavy night, which was now illuminated by only Europa and Io.

The two bright moons cast queer forked shadows down among the tall, solemn tree-ferns as they went through the grounds. The buildings housing the colonial government bordered the square around the governor's mansion. The Emergency Hospital, formerly a prison, was a massive structure with heavy blank walls of synthetic metal.

As they entered the vestibule, in which nervous-looking orderlies were on guard, an aide rushed in after the governor.

"There's an urgent televisor call for you from Jungletown, sir," he told Sylvanus Quale breathlessly.

"I'll have to go back and answer it," Quale said to Captain Future. "Miss Randall will show you the atavism cases."

THE girl led the way from the vestibule into a long, lighted main hall of the prison. She went to the heavy, solid metal door of the first cell-block. There she touched a switch outside the door, and they heard its bolt shoot back.

They stepped into the cell-block. It was a windowless barracks with solid metal walls, lighted by a half-dozen glowing uranite bulbs in the ceiling. Cell doors were ranged along either side of the corridor which they had entered.

"These are cases of varying dates," the pale girl told Curt. "Some of them are recent and are only apelike, but others are—you can see for yourself."

Curt went down the row of doors, peering through the gratings into the cells.

The cells contained a nightmare assortment of ghastly horrors. In some were huge ape-like creatures standing erect and beating with hairy fists at their doors, roars of rage coming from their throats.

In others were creatures that were even more bestial, quadrupedal hairy brutes with pouched bodies and blazing feral eyes and wide jaws bristling with fangs. Still other cells held scaled green reptilian monsters shuffling forward on four limbs and crawling with their talons to reach Curt and Joan Randall.

Captain Future was shaken by a storm of fierce wrath such as he had never felt before. Never before, on any of the nine worlds, had he encountered a horror like this. He felt in the presence of something utterly unclean and monstrous.

"God help the devil who did this if I get my hands on him," he gritted.

Joan Randall, who had followed him down the corridor, looked up into his face.

"If it was an Earthman who caused this, I have a suspicion as to his identity, Captain Future," she said.

She had taken from a pocket a little badge which she showed him. It bore the initials "P. P."

"I'm a Planet Police secret agent," the girl explained. "There have been several of us here since this horror began."

"Whom do you suspect?" Curt demanded quickly.

Before the girl could answer, there came a startling interruption. It was the click of the cell-block door bolt.

"Someone has locked us in!" Joan cried.

Curt sprang toward the door. It was immovable, the bolt having been shot home by the electric control outside.

"It's a trap!" he declared.

He drew his proton-pistol, aimed it at the door, and released a lightning-like lance of force. But the heavy slab of artificial metal resisted the flash of force. It was scorched but unharmed.

"Is there any other way out of here?" Captain Future demanded.

"No. This was a prison, remember," Joan answered. "Ventilation is indirect, and the whole place is soundproofed and rayproofed."

"What the devil is that?" Curt exclaimed.

A loud, simultaneous clicking had sounded, and every cell-door along the corridor had suddenly slid open.

Joan went deathly white.

"The cells have been unlocked!" she cried. "They are controlled from a switch out there, and someone has opened that switch!"

She uttered a little scream.

"Look, they're coming out—"

With the opening of the cell-doors, the hideous creatures inside the cells were beginning to emerge.

Out into the corridor shuffled a great, hairy ape-thing, then another, then a shambling, blazing-eyed quadrupedal beast, and then one of the shuffling, taloned reptilian monstrosities.

Captain Future felt Joan Randall shrink against him, terrified. The monsters emerging into the corridor, monsters that had once been men, had sensed the presence of the man and girl and were starting down the hall toward them.

CHAPTER VII

Otho Takes the Trail

BACK at the Street of Space Sailors, Otho the android moved slowly through the crowded, noisy quarter. Perfectly disguised as one of the green, squat Jovians, the synthetic man walked with the shuffling movement characteristic of the planetary natives. He concentrated upon maintaining an appearance of sulky silence.

Inwardly, Otho was intensely alert to everyone about him. The android was absolutely loyal to Captain Future. His devotion to the laughing, red-headed adventurer was the strongest trait of his fierce, unhuman nature, stronger even than his love of action and combat. He was determined to find out what he could for Curt, no matter what the cost.

He kept an eye out for other Jovians. His task was to mix with the planetary natives and find out what they knew about the Space Emperor. Otho had no doubt of success. His supreme, cocky self-confidence was bolstered by his knowledge of the Jovian language and customs, gained on former trips to this planet with Captain Future.

So intently was the android looking out for other Jovians with whom he might strike up acquaintance, that he bumped into a big, hulking Earthman prospector in the crowd.

"Git outa my way, greenie!" roared the angry Earthman, and gave Otho a cuff that sent him spinning aside.

The fierce-natured android's body tensed for a spring at the other. Then he realized that for a Jovian to attack an Earthman would cause a riot and give him away.

"I did not mean to bump you, Earthman," Otho said humbly, in the Jovian language.

"Why don't you greenies stay out in your jungles and keep out of this colony?" the prospector demanded roughly, and then moved on.

Otho had noticed that three Jovians stood at the side of the street, and that they had been watching the incident. In a flash, the android saw how he could make capital of it.

He moved over to the three squat planetary natives, and spoke to them in a voice whose slurred bass tones he kept throbbing with resentment.

"I am only trying to find the way out of here," Otho told them, "yet these Earthmen will not even allow me to walk freely through the city."

The Jovians looked at him. One of them was a very large individual, with strong intelligence in the stamp of his unhuman green face and his dark, round eyes.

"Are you a stranger in this country?" he asked Otho. "I have never seen you in our northern villages."

"I am not from the north," Otho answered quickly. "I come from a village which lies far east of here in the jungle. My name is Zhil."

"And I am Guro, chief of my people," the big Jovian told Otho, pride in his deep, bass tones.

At that moment there was an interruption to their talk. Out of a doorway farther down the street burst another Earthman who had suddenly fallen victim to the dreaded blight.

"Atavism!" went up the familiar, dreaded cry from scores of voices. "Call the police!"

"Keep away from him or you'll catch it!" yelled others in horror.

IN very few moments, a rocket-car had come and the growling, frothing Earthman had been overcome and taken away. And, as Otho had noticed before, the throng in the street hastened fearfully away from the place as though hoping to escape possible contagion.

"The curse of the Ancients spreads fast," said Guro solemnly to his two Jovian companions and Otho.

"Yes, the time grows near," one of the other two green natives declared.

Otho felt a dawning surprise. What did they mean by the curse of the Ancients?

He knew that the Jovians believed the mighty, mysterious ruins in the jungle had once been the cities of a race of demi-gods they called the Ancients. But what had that legend to do with this avatism terror?

Otho decided upon a bold attempt. He had to find out what these Jovians knew about the Space Emperor, and for that reason he risked exposure by his next words.

"Our dark leader told us the truth," Otho said solemnly, looking at the others.

Guro's round eyes expressed surprise.

"Then you of the eastern villages have seen and heard the Living Ancient also? He has appeared to you as he has to us?"

The Living Ancient? So that was what the Jovians called the Space Emperor? Otho wondered what the name could mean.

"Yes, he has appeared to us," he told Guro. "He brought his message to us also."

That could cover almost anything, Otho thought. Yet he was puzzled over the calling of the Space Emperor the *living* Ancient. Was it possible their enemy was a Jovian?

"Then you will also be ready to rise and sweep away the Earthmen when the Living Ancient gives the word?" Guro asked.

So his guess had been right! Otho almost gave himself away by a slight start of surprise which he could not wholly suppress.

A rising of the Jovians against the Earthmen? Was that the mainspring of the mysterious Space Emperor's gigantic plot? But how could such an attack of the natives hope to succeed? Their weapons were very primitive. And how was the spread of the atavism terror connected with it?

The thoughts flashed swiftly through the android's mind in a moment. But he did not hesitate in answering Guro.

"Yes, we too are ready when the word comes," he told Guro fervently.

"Good!" muttered the big Jovian. "And the word will come soon. The wrath of the mighty Ancients grows ever greater against the Earthmen, making more and more of them into brute beasts. Soon the Living Ancient will give us the word."

Otho thought quickly, and then spoke in the same fervent tones.

"I was to bring word to the Living Ancient of our preparations," he told Guro. "He commanded us to send such word when we were ready. But I do not know where to find our mighty leader."

"The Living Ancient is to appear to us tomorrow night in a spot near my own village," Guro told him in a bass whisper. "That spot is the Place of the Dead."

"I know that," lied Otho. "But how shall I hope to find it, when I do not know the land here in the north?" Otho asked doubtfully. "I have never been this far toward the Fire Sea before."

Guro reassured him.

"You will have no trouble finding it, for we shall take you there ourselves. We are returning northward now, and you can come with us. Two nights hence you can go with us to the Place of the Dead, and deliver your message to our leader when he appears."

OTHO thanked him quickly. It was apparent that Guro and the other two Jovians had completely accepted him.

"We leave now," Guro told him. "The mission that brought us here is finished. Our lopers wait in the jungle beyond this city."

Otho shuffled with the three Jovians, following Guro's lead through the rowdy, noisy streets of the interplanetary colonial city. They were not molested, and presently they were out of the metalloy streets of Jovopolis, and moving along the road that led between the great grain fields of the Earthmen.

The android's mind was racing. He must notify Curt Newton of what he had learned and where he was going. But though he had his pocket televisor concealed inside his leather harness, he dared not try to use it while Guro and the others were so close to him.

The three Jovians and the disguised

"We need your loper for this stranger. You will stay here until we send back another," Guro told the Jovian who had waited with the animals. Then he told Otho, "Mount, Zhil."

Otho had never ridden one of the lizardlike creatures before, but the android, afraid neither of man nor devil, swung up unhesitatingly into the rude leather saddle.

The creature turned and hissed angrily at him, its small eyes flaring red. Otho saw the other Jovians kick their mounts to quiet them, and he did the same. The creature calmed down.

Grag, the metal robot, has superhuman strength

android shuffled on along the road between the mingled brilliance of the two moons now in the sky. Soon they reached the end of the grain fields, and entered the moon-drenched jungle whose wilderness stretched unbroken toward the Fire Sea.

Just inside the jungle waited another Jovian, with four "lopers," as the Jovians called their queer steeds. The lopers were large, lizardlike creatures, with scaled, barreled bodies supported by four bowed legs that gave them incredible speed. Their necks were long and snaky, ending in reptilian heads from whose fangless mouths ran the leather reins by which the rider controlled his mount.

"Now, northward!" Guro called in his deep bass voice, and uttered a loud cry to their mounts.

Next moment, Otho was clinging for his life. It was as though the creature had exploded forward.

All four of the lopers were rushing at a nightmare pace along a dim trail through the moonlit jungle. Their speed was incredible, yet the motion was so gliding that Otho soon adjusted himself to it.

Guro and the other Jovians were riding around him. There was still no chance to call Captain Future on the pocket televisor, so the android gave up the idea for the time.

"It is a long ride," Guro called to

him over the rush of wind, "but we shall be with my people by tomorrow night, and you will go with us to the Place of the Dead."

"I am eager to see the Living Ancient again," Otho called back, and reflected that he was not lying about that.

The moonlit jungle through which they rode along narrow, dim trails was dense and wild. Huge tree-ferns reared their glossy pillared trunks nearly a hundred feet. Big stiff brush-trees towered almost as high. Slender "copper trees" whose fibers contained a high copper content gleamed metallically in the light of the moons.

Snake-vines hanging from the tall trunks swayed blindly toward the quartet as they sped past. Sucker-flies swarmed around them, and deadly brain-ticks were visible on leaves. Somewhere off in the jungle, a siren-bird was charming its prey with weird song. Now and then a tree-octopus flitted hastily through the fronds above like a white ghost.

OTHO was enjoying this wild, rushing ride through the moonshot Jovian jungle. The android had, more than any human could have, the capacity for taking things as they came.

Whether he was battling through blinding red sandstorms on desert Mars or wading poisonous Venusian swamps, climbing down into the awful chasms of mighty-mountained Uranus or braving the terrible ice-fields of Pluto, he did not usually bother to look far ahead.

But now the necessity of getting word to Captain Future weighed upon his mind. Several hours of unceasing riding passed without his getting a chance to use his pocket televisor. One or other of the three Jovians was always near him.

Finally Guro pulled in on his reins and their lopers came gradually to a halt, as the others did likewise.

"We stop here to eat," Guro announced. "The lopers must have a little rest. We start again at dawn."

They dismounted, and the four liz-ard-like creatures stretched out upon the soft black ground of the little clearing in which they had halted.

"I will get food," Guro declared, and strode out of the clearing into the brush.

The other two Jovians were seeing to the girths of their saddles. Otho saw his opportunity, and crouched down quickly as though relaxing, drawing out his watchlike pocket televisor.

He touched its call-button hastily. He was not sure that the little instrument, designed for short distances, could reach as far back as Jovopolis. Tensely he waited for an answering buzz.

There was no answer. Otho felt something as near despair as his fierce, resolute nature could experience. Again he jabbed the call-button, and again.

Then came a faint answering whirr from the little instrument, an indication that his call-signal had been heard.

"This is Otho speaking," he whispered tensely into the tiny thing, not turning on its visi-wave. "I am going with Jovians northward. The Space Emperor is to be—"

A shadow fell across the moonlit ground in front of him. And a deep voice sounded.

"What are you doing?" it demanded.

The android turned swiftly. Behind him stood Guro, a bunch of brilliant flame-fruit in his hand. He stared down at Otho with suspicious eyes.

CHAPTER VIII

The Trail

INSIDE Jovopolis' former prison, Captain Future rapidly set his proton-pistol, then triggered quickly at the horde of monsters advancing down the corridor of the cell-block toward Joan and himself.

The thin white beam from his weapon struck some of the creatures in the front of the savage mob. They collapsed as though struck by lightning, stunned by the potent beams.

The others hesitated. But as more and more of them emerged from the unlocked cells, they came forward again.

"Captain Future, it must have been the Space Emperor you spoke of who trapped us like this!" cried Joan Randall.

"Yes," gritted Curt, "and that means that the Space Emperor is one of those men who were with us in Quale's office. Only they knew we had come here!"

His mind was seething. Which of those men had followed them here and trapped them? Which one was the Space Emperor?

Could it be Quale himself, he wondered? Or Lucas Brewer, or Kells, or young Cannig?

As his mind grappled with that problem, he was firing again at the advancing monsters. Again the creatures retreated from the beam that had stunned a dozen of their number.

A fight started between an ape-thing and a scaly green reptilian creature. Snarling, hissing, clawing each other, the two nightmare brutes soon had involved others in the battle. Their ferocity was bestial, terrifying.

"What are we going to do?" cried Joan Randall. The girl's face was deathly pale.

Curt smiled grimly.

"Don't worry, we'll get out somehow. I've been in worse spots than this."

Somehow the confidence of this tall, red-haired young man was reassuring to Joan, even in the face of inevitable death.

"If these walls are rayproof, there's no chance to call Grag and Simon on my pocket televisor," he was muttering. "I could make us invisible, but it wouldn't last long and wouldn't do us any good."

"Invisible?" cried the girl, astounded even in this moment of terror.

"Yes, I could do it," Curt smiled. "But it only lasts ten minutes or so. We've got to think of something else."

"Captain Future, they're coming again!" Joan exclaimed fearfully.

The evolutionary monsters had broken off their battle, and now were once more beginning to shuffle down the white-lit corridor toward the man and girl.

Captain Future's beam licked forth hungrily. Again, the creatures hesitated as some of them fell stunned. Curt had not set the beam at full strength. He didn't want to kill these creatures who had been men once and might become normal if a cure were found for them.

Curt's clear gray eyes swept the interior of the cell-block again, in search of some way out. It seemed hopeless to think that they could escape or get any call for help through these soundproofed, rayproofed walls.

Then his gaze fastened on the glowing uranite bulbs in the ceiling of the corridor. At once, his eyes lit up.

"I've got it!" he exclaimed. "The only way for us to get out is to destroy the lock of the door. And there's a chance that we can do that."

"Your pistol's ray can't get at the lock," the girl reminded him, her voice hopeless. "The electric mechanism is encased in the wall beside the door."

A QUADRUPEDAL monster hurtled through the air at that moment. Curt's beam caught him and he fell unconscious in a mass at their feet.

"My pistol won't reach the lock," Captain Future admitted, as coolly as though nothing had happened, "but maybe I can get at it with something else. Here, take my pistol and hold those creatures off while I work."

He did not ask the girl whether she could do it. He calmly assumed her courage, and this trust on the part of the red-haired adventurer steadied Joan's nerve.

She took the proton-pistol, and each time one of the growling, roaring monsters moved forward, she pulled the trigger.

Meanwhile, Curt was bunching himself for a spring. He might have used his gravity equalizer, he thought fleetingly, but there was no time. With all his force, he leaped upward. The metal ceiling was only a few feet above his head. His superb muscles shot him up toward it, and his hand grasped one of the glowing uranite bulbs.

He fell back to the floor, sliding the glowing bulb out of its socket. The thing was merely a glass bulb containing a few ounces of the glowing, powerful white radioactive powder called uranite.

Hastily, Curt took from his tungstite belt-kit a thin little glass tube. It contained a restorative gas he always carried with him. Deliberately, he broke both ends of the sealed tube, allowing the gas to escape. This left him a tiny glass pipette.

He broke the uranite bulb, then deftly filled the little pipette with the glowing radioactive powder. As he worked, he glanced up every few moments to make sure that Joan Randall was managing to hold off the monstrous mob, smiling at her encouragingly.

"Now I'll try it," he told her, when the pipette was full of the uranite powder. "Hope it works. If it doesn't we're stuck here."

Quickly Captain Future went to the door of the cell-block.

He applied one open end of the pipette of uranite to the crack between door and wall, just where the lock was located.

Then, with extreme care to make sure that he did not inhale any of the super-powerful radioactive powder, he applied his lips to the other end of the pipette and blew.

The radioactive powder was blown in a little jet into the crack between the door and frame. Wherever a grain of the glowing stuff struck the metal, it sizzled and hissed, eating into the surface like a red-hot poker applied to an ice-cube.

"If I was able to blow any of the powder into the lock, it ought to eat away the delicate mechanism there and the magnetic control of the bolt will be released," he told the girl.

"I—I don't think I can hold them back much longer," came Joan's shaken voice heard over the babel of growls.

Captain Future could hear the powerful uranite eating into the metal between door and wall. Had he got any of the grains into the lock? He waited, his nerves taut.

SUDDENLY he heard a sharp click. The bolt of the door shot back, released when the magnetic pull of the lock was ended by destruction of the electric lock-circuit.

"Come on, Joan!" cried the spacefarer, seizing the girl by the arm.

They burst out into the main hall of the prison and raced down it, monsters emerging after them.

In a moment they were safe in the vestibule.

"That was too close for comfort!" Captain Future declared. His big figure swung toward the startled orderlies. "Has anyone come through this vestibule in the last half hour?"

They shook their heads. Curt's tanned face frowned, but in a moment he spoke again to the orderlies.

"You'd better use sleep-gas to get those creatures back into the cellblock," he said. "And you'll have to fix the lock."

As the orderlies hastened to restore order, Curt turned to the pale girl.

"Joan, tell me — is there anyway someone from outside could have got to that door-switch without coming through this vestibule?"

Joan nodded quickly.

"Someone who knew the building could come into the main hall through the Prison Warden's offices, which are unoccupied since this was made into a hospital."

"Then that's how the Space Emperor, whoever the devil is, came and trapped us!" Captain Future said.

He asked the girl another question.

"Just before we were locked in there, you were saying that you suspected some Earthman here as possibly being the one behind this terrible blight?"

"Yes, Lucas Brewer," said the girl. "Brewer seems to have some queer, mysterious influence over the Jovians. They work in his radium mine as laborers, and they won't work for any other Earthman, no matter what pay is offered them."

The girl continued.

"You said that the Space Emperor, the one who is causing the horror, is worshiped by the Jovians. That's what makes me suspect it is Brewer."

Curt frowned in deep thought.

"That's certainly grounds for suspecting Brewer. And also, we *know* now that the Space Emperor is one of the four men who were in Quale's office when we left it, and Brewer is one of those four."

His chin hardened.

"I think I have some questions to ask Mr. Brewer. Come along!"

CHAPTER IX

Laboratory Magic

THEY hastened back beneath the two brilliant jovian moons toward the metalloy mansion of the governor.

Sylvanus Quale and Eldred Kells were bending over a map when Curt and the girl entered the white-lit office.

"Why — what's happened?" exclaimed Quale, his colorless face startled as he looked inquiringly at the disheveled two.

"The Space Emperor tried to scrag us and nearly succeeded, that's what happened," rasped Captain Future. His gray eyes were searching their faces as he told what had occurred.

"Where are Brewer and young Cannig?" he demanded.

"They've left—gone back to Jungletown in their rocket-flier," Quale replied.

"Why did they go?" Curt demanded, his big figure stiffening.

"That message that called me back here to my office was from Captain Gurney, the police marshal up there at Jungletown," Quale explained. "He reported that the atavism cases are getting out of control up there, and also that the unrest of the Jovians up there seems to be increasing."

The governor paused.

"Brewer said that he and Cannig ought to return to look after his company's mine," he continued. "He insisted on going."

"That's right," confirmed Eldred Kells, the blond vice-governor. "I tried to get them to stay, but couldn't."

Curt was thinking. Either Brewer or Cannig could have slipped into the Emergency Hospital to spring that death-trap, before leaving.

"Kells is going up to Jungletown at once, to see how bad conditions are there," Quale told Curt.

"I'll go too," Joan Randall said quickly. "If the number of victims is increasing so, I'll be needed at the hospital there."

The girl secret agent flashed Captain Future a glance as she spoke. Curt realized she intended to continue her observation of Brewer and Cannig, if possible. [*Turn page*]

Kells hesitated at her going along. "Jungletown is rather a tough, wild town for a girl to go into," he declared. "But it's true you'll be needed up there. Come along, and we'll start at once."

Captain Future made no comment as the man and girl left the office. A few moments later, the roar of their rocket-flier was heard as they took off from the nearby hangar.

Curt turned toward the governor.

"Quale, as governor here you know something about these legends of a mighty Jovian civilization that is supposed to have existed on this planet in the remote past?"

The governor looked surprised.

"Why, yes, I've heard the superstitious stories the Jovians tell," he admitted. "And the few archaeologists who have looked at those queer ruins in the jungle say that they really were once the cities of a highly civilized race. But why do you ask, Captain Future?"

"Has anyone ever unearthed any of the scientific secrets of that vanished Jovian race?" Curt demanded.

Quale was a little startled. "Why, no. It's true that some have hoped to find the hidden secrets of that mysterious race. One young archaeologist who was through here some weeks ago was sure he could. But no one has ever done so."

"What was the name of that young archaeologist?" Curt asked quickly.

"His name was Kenneth Lester," Quale replied. "He told me he'd been studying the Jovian legends and believed he was on the trail of solving the whole mystery of the vanished race. He went from here up to Jungletown, and then on northward into the jungles toward the Fire Sea."

Captain Future's eyes narrowed.

"Where's Lester now? What did he say he'd found when he came back?"

The governor shook his head.

"Lester never came back. Nothing more was ever heard from him, though he'd promised to notify me of any discoveries he made. He had no experience with those jungles, and undoubtedly he perished up there in them."

Captain Future remained silent for a moment, wrapped in thought. The governor looked attentively at the big, red-haired young man.

"That's all I wanted to know," Curt said finally. "One more thing, though —I would like to have one of the most recent atavism cases from your hospital, for study by Simon Wright and myself, in order that we can try to find a cure for this thing."

A QUARTER hour later, in a borrowed police rocket-car, Captain Future reached the edge of the dark Jovopolis spaceport where the *Comet* waited. He carried out of the car an unconscious Earthman with a brutalized, flushed face—the atavism victim the governor had allowed him to bring from the hospital.

Inside the little ship, Grag the robot greeted him with noisy, booming relief. Simon Wright's lens-eyes focused at once on the big young adventurer's taut face.

"Did you succeed in trapping the Space Emperor, lad?" the Brain asked quickly.

"He nearly trapped me, damn him!" Curt exclaimed ruefully. "Isn't Otho back yet?"

"No, he hasn't been here," Wright declared.

Curt uttered an impatient exclamation.

"I wanted to get on up to Jungletown at once. Now we'll have to wait for that crazy android who's probably busy getting himself into trouble."

Concisely, he told Simon Wright all that had happened, while Grag listened also.

"So I believe," Curt finished, "that the Space Emperor has actually discovered the secret of making matter temporarily immaterial, by a step-up in frequency of its atomic vibration. The thing's possible, isn't it, Simon?"

"It's possible theoretically, though no known scientist has ever done it," rasped the Brain. "Furthermore, not one of your four suspects is a scientist."

"I know!" Curt exclaimed. "And that's what makes me think the Space Emperor has discovered the scientific secrets of the vanished race of this world. The secret of vibration-step up is probably one of them, and the atavism weapon another.

"And what's more," Curt declared, "I believe this Kenneth Lester, the missing archaeologist, ties into it somewhere. This Lester was highly certain, according to Quale, that he could find the secrets of the vanished race. Then he disappeared."

Grag had listened with attention, trying to follow Curt's explanation. Now the big robot asked a question.

"If the Space Emperor can make himself immaterial whenever he wants to, how can we catch him, master?"

"We can't catch him if he's immaterial, that's the devil of it," Captain Future told the robot. "Our only chance is to grab him while he's in his normal state."

He turned to the Brain.

"I want to investigate this Lucas Brewer first. As soon as Otho comes, we'll go up to Jungletown and I'll see what I can find out about that fat swindler. While we're waiting for Otho," he went on, "we can start study of this atavism victim I brought with me. It's urgent that some cure for the blight be found as soon as possible, or this whole colony will be wiped out."

Grag unfolded the metal table from the wall of the little compact laboratory that occupied the whole midship of the *Comet*. The robot laid the stricken, drugged man upon it.

Captain Future hung a curious lamp over the unconscious man. It was a long cylindrical glass tube that could project "tuned" X-rays which made either bone, blood or solid flesh tissue or nerve-tissue almost invisible, at will.

Curt set the rays to block out the whole skin, skull, and outer tissues of the victim's head. Then he donned the fluoroscopic spectacles that were part of the equipment, and slipped similar spectacles over the eye-lenses of Simon Wright.

They could now look deep into the head of the victim as though he were semi-transparent.

"I believe," Curt said tersely, "that this evolutionary blight is caused by a deep change in the ductless glands.

We know that slight malfunctioning of the pituitary gland will produce acromegaly, in which the victim becomes brutish of body and mind. Suppose that the pituitary is really the secret control of physical evolution?"

"I understand," said Simon, his lenses glittering. "You think that acromegaly, which has always been considered a mere disease, is really a case of mild atavism?"

CURT nodded his red head keenly. "That's it, Simon. And if a man found a way to paralyze the pituitary gland completely, then the resulting atavism would not be just mild but would become worse each day, the victim reverting farther each day to the brute!"

"Let's look at the pituitary gland and see," said Simon Wright.

Intently, they scrutinized the big gland that was attached to the base of the victim's brain by a thin stalk.

"See the dark color of the gland!" Captain Future exclaimed. "That's abnormal—the pituitary of this man has been subjected to some freezing or paralyzing radiation!"

He straightened his big figure, and there was a gleam in his gray eyes as he took off the fluoroscopic glasses.

"What we've got to do is to devise some way of starting the paralyzed pituitaries of the stricken man," he said. "Do you think we could find a counter-radiation that would do it?"

"I doubt it, lad," muttered Simon Wright. "It seems to me that our best chance would be to devise a chemical formula that could be injected directly into the victims' bloodstream and which would reach their glands in that way."

"Then we'll try out different formulae on this victim—" Curt started to say. He suddenly stopped.

His keen ears had just caught the faint whir of the buzzer in his pocket-televisor. He snatched out the little instrument and touched the call-button to signal that he had heard.

"This is Otho speaking!" came a rapid whisper from it. "I am going with Jovians northward. The Space Emperor is to be—"

Suddenly the android's whisper

broke off. Curt waited, his tanned face a little alarmed in expression.

He dared not call the android back, without knowing what had happened. Minutes passed in silence. After a quarter-hour, Otho's whisper came again, a little louder.

"One of these Jovians nearly caught me calling you, but I convinced him I was just talking to myself," Otho chuckled.

"You crazy fool, be careful!" Captain Future spoke angrily into the instrument. "Do you want to get yourself killed? What the devil are you up to, anyway?"

"I'm going to stay with these Jovians until I find out where the Space Emperor is to appear before them," Otho's answer came back. "It's to be tomorrow night, at some spot called the Place of the Dead, in the north jungles. As soon as I find out where the place is, I'll come back and tell you."

"We'll have the *Comet* at Jungletown," Curt told the android quickly through the instrument. "We're going there now."

"Give my regards to Grag and tell him that I am sorry he is sitting in the ship and doing nothing," Otho's voice teased, before he was silent.

Grag moved his metal head furiously.

"Is it my fault that I have been sitting here?" boomed the robot. "I wanted to go with you, and you took him instead!"

Curt gave the massive robot a powerful shove toward the control-room.

"Get in there and start the ship without more grumbling or I'll disconnect your speech-apparatus!" he warned Grag. "We're flying north to Jungletown, in a hurry."

"What about our patient—do we take him too?" asked the robot.

Curt nodded.

"Simon can keep hunting for a cure and test his formulae on that poor fellow. I've got to attend to more urgent business."

As Captain Future turned back to the Brain, his gray eyes had an expectant gleam.

"So the Space Emperor is to appear up in those northern jungles tomor-row night? And Lucas Brewer had to fly north tonight. The trail leads to Brewer, Simon!"

CHAPTER X

Beneath Jovian Moons

JUNGLETOWN throbbed with roaring life tonight, under the two bright moons. Even the dreadful shadow of the horror that had stricken down hundreds, even the knowledge that the Jovian aborigines hordes were ominously restless could not slacken the gusty, lusty tempo of life in this wild new town.

This was a typical planetary boom town, such as sprang up wherever a great new strike was made, be it on desert Mars or mountainous Uranus or Arctic Pluto. To these boom towns thronged adventurous Earthmen from all over the System, prospectors and gamblers, merchants and criminals, engineers and drug-peddlers, dreamers and knaves and fools.

The great strike of uranium and radium northward had been responsible for the birth of Jungletown. It had grown with mushroom speed, till now it was a straggling mass of some thousands of metalloy houses, huddled together in the big clearing that had been blasted out of the mighty fern-jungles.

Captain Future peered keenly toward the town from where he stood with his comrades beside the *Comet*. They had landed the ship near the dark edge of the jungle, unobserved.

"The atavism cases haven't slowed this place down much," Curt muttered as he stared.

"These boom towns aren't afraid of man or God or devil," rasped Simon Wright dourly. "Murder and robbery walk in them hand and hand. Remember the one on Neptune's moon?"

"That town where those criminals laid the atomic trap for us?" said Curt. He chuckled softly. "I remember!"

"Hear that queer throbbing, master?" Grag boomed suddenly to Curt.

Captain Future and his companions stood with the solemn, murmurous black jungle towering at their backs. Out of it came heavy exhalations of rotting vegetation and the spicy scent of flowers.

The heavy tread of "stampers" was audible from its depths, and the rustle of a tree-octopus. Balloon-beasts floated overhead in the moonlight, the membranous gas-sac that held them aloft glimmering. And little sucker-flies hummed viciously around, while big death-moths fluttered in their strange dying flight that lasts for days.

In front of them, beyond the black, raw fields, lay the moonlit metal roofs and blazing, noisy streets of the town. Even from here the vibration of brassy music could be heard. And above the town, the whole northern sky flamed brilliant, quaking crimson from the great glare of the mighty Fire Sea beyond.

Curt was listening tensely. Then he heard the sound the robot's artificial hearing had detected. It was a dim, deep throbbing that came from the dark jungles northwest of the town, and that he felt rather than heard. It seemed to roll up from the ground on which they stood, in a steady, heavy rhythm.

"It's Jovian ground-drums," Simon Wright rasped.

Curt nodded tightly.

"There's no doubt about it. They're out there somewhere northwest of the town."

Captain Future had heard the "ground-drums" before—unknown instruments by which Jovian aborigines caused a percussive vibration in the ground which could be heard for far.

"That means trouble, lad," the Brain said harshly. "The Jovians ordinarily never do any ground-drumming where Earthmen can hear them."

"I'm going into the town and hunt up Ezra Gurney, the Planet Police marshal here," he told the Brain. "You can stay here and work on the atavism cure, Simon."

"Yes, of course," rasped the Brain.

"I go with you this time, master?" Grag asked anxiously.

"No, Grag, you'd attract too much attention in the town," Captain Fu-ture told the big robot. "I'll call you if I need you."

Then Curt strode across the dark fields toward the town. The two moons looked down on his big figure, and the shaking glare of crimson in the sky tinged his keen face redly.

CURT entered the chief street of Jungletown, a narrow, unpaved one bordered on both sides by metalloy structures of hasty construction. Gambling places, drinking shops, lodging houses of ill appearance, all stood out under a blaze of uranite bulbs. Music blared from many places, and a babel of voices dazed the ears.

He shouldered through a motley, noisy crowd that jammed the street. Here were husky prospectors in stained zipper-suits, furtive, unshaven space-bums begging, cool-eyed interplanetary gamblers, gaunt engineers in high boots with flare-pistols at their belts, bronzed space-sailors up from Jovopolis for a carousal in the wildest new frontier-town in the System.

Curt noticed that only a few of the green Jovians were in the streets. The flipper-men made no remonstrance when drunken Earthmen cuffed them out of the way, but their silence was queerly ominous.

"Anybody want to buy a Saturnian 'talker'?" a big space-sailor with an owl-like bird on his shoulder was shouting.

"Anybody want to buy a Saturnian 'talker'?" the bird repeated, exactly mimicking its master's voice.

"Biggest bar on Jupiter!" a telespeaker outside the roaring drinking place was calling. "Martian gold-wine, Mercurian dream-water—any drink from any planet!"

As Curt passed a big gambling-hall noisy with the click of "quantum wheels," a hand grasped his hand. It was a thin-bodied, red-skinned native Martian, whose breath was strong with Jovian brandy as he appealed to Curt in his shrill, high voice.

"Help me out, Earthman!" he begged. "I've been stranded here a year and I've got to get back to Mars to my family."

Curt chuckled.

"You've not been on Jupiter more than a month or your skin would have bleached out. You've no family for you belong to the Syrtis people of Mars, where the children are raised communally. But here's something for a drink."

The Martian, startled, took the coin and stumbled hastily away from the big redhead.

Then as Curt passed a tavern from which came wild, whirling music with the pulsing Venusian double-rhythm in it, he heard a sudden uproar break loose inside.

"Marshal or no marshal, you can't tell Jon Daumer what to do!" roared an Earthman's bellowing voice.

"I'm telling you, and I'm not telling you again," answered a steely voice. "You and your friends get out of town and get out now."

Captain Future recognized that hard second voice. He pushed quickly into the tavern.

It was a big, bright-lit metal hall, hazy with the acrid smoke of Venusian swamp-leaf tobacco. A mixed throng jammed the place. There were prospectors, gamblers and engineers, some of whom had been drinking at the long glassite bar, others of whom had been dancing with hard-faced, painted girls.

All eyes were now watching the tense drama t a k i n g place. A big, heavy-faced Earthman in white zipper-suit, with three other mean-eyed men behind him, confronted a grizzled, iron-haired man who wore the black uniform of the Planet Police and a marshal's badge.

Ezra Gurney, the gray-haired marshal, was looking grimly at the quartet who faced him.

"I'm giving you and your three fellow-crooks just one hour to leave Jungletown, Daumer," he warned.

Curt saw Daumer crimson with rage.

"You've not proved that we have broken any laws!" the man bellowed at Gurney.

"I don't need any more proof than what I've got," said Ezra Gurney. "I know you four have been getting prospectors drunk and robbing them of their radium. You're leaving!"

DAUMER'S face stiffened. He and his companions dropped their hands toward the hilts of their flare-guns.

"We're not going, Gurney," he said ominously.

Curt Newton stepped suddenly from behind Gurney. His tall, red-headed figure confronted Daumer and his companions.

"Take your hands off those guns and get out of town as Marshal Gurney says," Curt ordered the four men coldly.

Daumer was first amazed at the stranger's audacity. Then he uttered a guffaw of laughter that was echoed by the motley crowd.

"Listen to this Mr. Nobody that's telling me what to do!" he exclaimed. The crowd roared in appreciative mirth.

"Captain Future!" cried Ezra Gurney suddenly as he glimpsed Curt's face.

"Captain Future?" echoed Daumer blankly. His eyes dropped frozenly to the big ring on Curt's finger.

"It's him!" he whispered through stiff lips.

The laughter of the crowd was struck to silence as by a blow. In frozen, unbelieving stillness, they stared at Curt.

The greatest adventurer in the Solar System's history, the mysterious, awesome figure whose legend dominated the nine worlds, stood in their midst. As they realized it, they could only stare rigidly at this big, red-haired, gray-eyed man whose name and fame had rung around the System.

"We're—going, Captain Future," Daumer said hoarsely, his brutal face pallid.

"See that you take the first ship off Jupiter," Curt lashed, his bleak gray eyes boring into the faces of the four men.

Daumer and his companions were out of the place in a moment. Curt and Ezra Gurney followed them.

No man or woman in the crowded hall moved, as Captain Future and the grizzled marshal walked out to the street. But as they reached the noisy, thronged thoroughfare, they heard a great babel of excited voices from behind them blast forth in the tavern.

"Thanks for steppin' in to help me out, Captain Future, but you spoiled a swell fight," said Ezra Gurney testily.

Curt grinned.

"I see you're as bloodthirsty as ever, Marshal. I thought maybe that fracas in the Swampmen's Quarter on Venus two years ago would have quieted you down."

Gurney looked at him with shrewd old eyes.

"What brings you to Jupiter is this atavism business, isn't it?"

Curt nodded grimly.

"That's it. What do you know about it, Ezra?"

"I know it's hell's blackest masterpiece," said Ezra Gurney somberly. "Captain Future, I've been out on the planetary frontiers for forty years. I've seen some evil things on the nine worlds in that time. But I never saw anything like this before."

His weatherbeaten face tightened.

"This town is sitting on top of hell, and no one knows when it'll bust loose. The atavism cases are increasing daily, and the Jovians are acting queer."

"You called Quale tonight about the Jovian unrest increasing?" Curt said, and Ezra Gurney nodded emphatically.

"Yes, I told Quale the truth, that the Jovians are working up to something big. You can hear their grounddrums out in the jungle all the time now."

They had turned off the crowded street into the small metalloy structure that housed Planet Police Headquarters.

"Ezra, what do you know about Lucas Brewer's radium mine?" Captain Future asked.

Gurney looked at him keenly.

"There's something queer about it. Brewer is able to get the Jovians to work for him as laborers, something nobody else can do. That gives him a big advantage, with labor as scarce as it is here. He's getting rich producing radium, up there."

"How does he explain the fact that the Jovians work for him and no one else?" Curt demanded.

"He says he treats 'em right," Gurney answered skeptically. "I know he pays 'em a lot of trade-goods—shipments go up to his mine all the time. But the green critters won't work for nobody else, no matter what pay is offered them."

THE big red-haired man considered that, his tanned face thoughtful. He asked another question.

"Do you know anything about the disappearance of Kenneth Lester, a young planetary archaeologist, up here?"

"Not a thing," Ezra confessed. "He went up into the jungles weeks ago. Then he flew back down here to send a letter off, and went back north. No more word ever came back from him and he's never been found."

"I'm going out and make a secret investigation of Lucas Brewer's mine," Captain Future declared, getting up. "Lend me a rocket-flier?"

Gurney's face grew anxious.

"That's a dangerous place to monkey around. Brewer's got guards all around the mine. Says he's afraid of radium-bandits."

Curt grinned, and there was no trace of alarm in the big young adventurer's cheerful face.

"I'll take my chances, Ezra. What about that rocket-flier?"

Ten minutes later, in a small, torpedolike Planet Police flier, Curt flew up above the blazing, turbulent streets of Jungletown and headed northward.

Black, brooding jungle unreeled beneath, an endless blanket of dark obscurity. Ahead, the whole northern sky flamed shaking scarlet from the glare of the Fire Sea.

Dark, low ranges of hills showed far ahead, standing out blackly against the quivering red aurora.

Curt hummed a haunting Venusian tune as he flew on, keenly eyeing the blank blackness of jungle. He sensed himself closer on the trail of the Space Emperor, and the thought of coming to grips with his unknown adversary brought a cheerful gleam to his eyes.

At last he saw what he was looking for—a little cluster of lights far ahead and below. At once, he swooped downward in the flier, hovered hummingly above the dense dark tangle of jungle, and then landed expertly in a small clearing.

In a few minutes, Curt was slogging steadily through the moon-drenched jungle of tree-ferns toward the lights.

Tree-octopi flitted overhead. Bulbous balloon-beasts sailed slowly by high above the ceiling of foliage. Once Captain Future's foot crashed down into the mouth of an underground tunnel made by "diggers." They were big, bloodthirsty burrowers who seldom appeared above ground.

Sucker-flies swarmed around him, cunningly injecting a tiny drop of anaesthetic to deaden their sting. And once Curt fancied he heard the distant, flowing passage of a "crawler," one of the most weird and dreaded of Jovian beasts.

He came finally to the edge of a mile-wide blasted clearing in which lay the mine. Out there in rock quarries scores of Jovians clad in protective lead suits were digging radium ores, working by the brilliant light of uranite bulbs, and superintended by Earthmen overseers.

Further away lay the field-office of the mine, and the warehouses, smelters and other buildings. Their windows glowed with light.

"Looks innocent enough," Captain Future muttered, "but there's something damned queer about it. Who ever heard of Jovians doing dangerous labor like that, for any Earthman?"

He loosed his proton pistol in its holster.

"I think we'll see whether the corpulent Mr. Brewer is here or not. And first, a look inside those warehouses—"

Curt started along the edge of the clearing, keeping inside the shadow of the jungle. He had gone but a few rods when a faint sound behind him made him whirl quickly.

A dark Earthman guard stepped out of the shrubbery, his flare-pistol leveled menacingly at Curt's head.

"Spy, eh?" rasped the guard. "You get it now!"

And he loosed a blazing flare from his gun that shot straight toward Curt's face.

CHAPTER XI

Brain and Robot

GRAG was worried. The big robot paced restlessly, back and forth inside the *Comet*, in ponderous stride. Every few minutes he went to the door and peered out.

He had run the ship into the jungle outside Jungletown. The boom-town lay out there, beneath the thin wash of red light from the setting sun. The lights were coming on in its streets, the uproar commencing as night came once more.

"Something has happened to our master," the robot boomed as he came back from the door to the midship laboratory. "He said he would be back soon. That was last night. A whole day has passed, and he has not come back."

Simon Wright's eye-stalks turned irritatedly toward the robot.

"Will you quit worrying?" the Brain demanded. "Curtis isn't a boy any more. He can take care of himself, better than any man in the System. You seem to think you're still his guardian and nursemaid."

Grag answered.

"I think you worry about him as much as I do."

From the Brain's vocal opening came something that might have been a rasping chuckle.

"You are right, Grag. We all three worry about him, you and I and Otho. We cannot forget the long years of his babyhood and boyhood on the moon, when we alone protected him."

"But there is no need to worry, really," Simon went on. "He'll be back soon now surely. And in the meantime I can't go on with the synthesizing of this new formula without your help."

"I am sorry, I will help now," Grag said simply.

Simon was about to prepare still another chemical formula which he hoped would prove capable of reviving the paralyzed pituitary glands of the blight's victims, and bring abou their recovery. He had tested several such formulae already on the stricken Earthman who still lay here in drugged sleep, but without success.

Now, from the pedestal upon which his chromium case rested, Simon called out the exact measures and actions which must be combined, and Grag performed them with an exactitude of which only a robot was capable, pouring, mixing, weighing and heating as the Brain directed.

Simon and Grag had worked thus together for many years. Otho was too restless and impatient to make a perfect partner for the Brain. But Grag, with his superhuman patience and precision, was an ideal partner.

The formula was finally finished. Darkness had come, by then. Simon directed the robot as he injected the pinkish fluid into the drugged Earthman's veins.

Then, after some minutes, the Brain had Grag turn on the X-ray lamp, and peered into the drugged man's skull for long minutes through the fluoroscopic glasses.

"It works!" he rasped finally. "We've found a cure, Grag!"

"But the man looks just the same," objected the robot, staring down dubiously at the drugged, brutish victim.

"Of course—he won't recover all in a minute," Simon snapped. "But now that his pituitary gland is functioning again, his body and mind will again come back to human semblance in a period of days."

Grag stalked to the door and looked out. The flare of light and noise from rioting Jungletown rose against the red, distant glare of the Fire Sea.

Three moons were in the sky, and the fourth was rising. But the anxious robot did not see by their light the big, red-haired figure he yearned to see.

"Still master has not come back," he boomed. "And neither has Otho come. Something has happened."

"You may be right, at that," Simon muttered. "It shouldn't have taken Curtis all this time to go out to that mine and back."

"Perhaps he did not go there?" Grag suggested. "Perhaps he went somewhere else?"

Simon thought.

"We'd better find out," the Brain finally declared. "Curtis went into the town to see Marshal Ezra Gurney, so Gurney ought to know just where he went."

"Pick me up, Grag," the Brain continued. "We're going to find the marshal."

Quickly, the robot grasped the handle of the Brain's transparent case in his metal fingers. Then he strode out of the *Comet* and stalked with mighty strides across the moonlit fields toward the flaring, noisy towns.

They could hear the chatter of deep and shrill voices from the streets. The heavy throb of the Jovian grounddrums seemed louder tonight.

"Avoid the streets," Simon ordered the robot who carried him. "Keep behind the buildings, in the shadows, until we see Gurney."

Grag obeyed, stalking behind the rows of metalloy structures, pausing at breaks between them so that he and Simon could peer into the bright,

[Turn page]

crowded streets in search of the marshal.

But neither the Brain nor the robot could spot the veteran peace-officer. As they continued their search an intoxicated Earthman came staggering back from the street toward the shadows from which Grag and Simon were watching. He stopped suddenly as he glimpsed them in front of him.

The drunken man tipped his head back and looked up unbelievingly with bleared eyes at the blank metal face and gleaming photoelectric eyes of the huge robot.

"Go 'way," he muttered thickly. "I know you're not real."

"Shall I silence him, Simon?" asked Grag in his deep voice.

"No, he is only a drunken fool," rasped the Brain.

As the intoxicated one heard the voices from the robot and the transparent brain-case he carried, he uttered a wild shriek.

"They're *real!*"

And with the cry, he stumbled wildly back out into the street.

"Police!" he yelled. "Where's the Planet Police?"

Ezra Gurney came along the street quickly in answer to that cry, and the drunken one grabbed his arm.

"There's a couple of—monsters—back there," he babbled wildly, pointing.

Gurney was about to reply in disgust, when Simon Wright's rasping voice reached him.

"Marshal Gurney! This way!"

Gurney started at the sound of the metallic voice, then pushed the drunk away and hastened back into the shadows. He uttered an exclamation as he glimpsed the big robot and the Brain he carried. He knew Captain Future's aides well.

"Simon Wright! And Grag!" he exclaimed. "What's wrong now?"

"Curtis hasn't come back," Simon told him quickly. "Did he go to the Brewer mine last night?"

"That's where he said he was goin'," Gurney declared. "An' he's not back yet? That don't look so good."

"Is Brewer in town now, or out at the mine?" Simon demanded keenly.

"I don't know but we can soon find out," the marshal answered. "His company office is over in the next street, and if he's in town he'll be there."

THEY started through the shadows, keeping out of the moonlight of the four silver satellites, toward the next street.

It was a sober business thoroughfare rather than a carnival street, bordered by small metalloy offices. Gurney led the way to the door of one whose windows glowed with light.

As Gurney walked in, followed by the huge robot with the glittering-eyed Brain, a man alone in the room uttered a startled cry.

"Good God, what are those creatures?"

It was Mark Cannig. His eyes bulged as he stared at Grag and Simon Wright.

"They're Captain Future's pals," Gurney replied sharply. "Is Brewer here?"

"No—I don't know where he is," Cannig answered uneasily.

The nervousness of the young mine superintendent did not miss Simon Wright's keen lens-eyes. Then the Brain glimpsed something lying on the floor near the wall.

"Pick that up, Grag," he directed sharply, looking toward it.

Grag obeyed, and held the little object so the Brain could inspect it closely.

It was a small badge with the letters "P.P." on it, and a number on its back.

"That's a Planet Police secret-agent emblem," Gurney said sharply. "And the number is Joan Randall's number."

He turned on Cannig.

"When was she here?"

Cannig flushed uneasily.

"I don't know if she was here or not. I just came myself."

"Call the hospital and find out if she's there, Marshal," Simon Wright suggested raspingly.

Gurney went to the televisor on the desk and made the call. His face was grim as he straightened.

"She left the hospital an hour ago and didn't come back. They don't know why she hasn't, either.

"I don't know where she is!" Cannig exclaimed. "I don't know anything about that badge."

"In other words, you just don't know nothin'," Ezra Gurney said sarcastically.

There was a rush of feet, and into the room came a flying figure. It was a green Jovian, moving with amazing speed, his round, dark eyes blazing.

"Get out of here, greenie," ordered the Marshal. "We're busy."

"You're no busier than I've been," answered the Jovian in a hissing, familiar voice. "And I've got news."

"Otho!" exclaimed Simon instantly, as he recognized the android's voice through his disguise. "What have you learned?"

"I've learned the exact spot where the Space Emperor will appear to these benighted Jovians tonight, an hour from now!" Otho declared, "I was supposed to be there with them, but I slipped away to bring Captain Future the news."

His eyes swept the room. "But where is Captain Future?"

"We don't know!" Simon Wright exclaimed. "It's beginning to look as though something has happened to him, and to Joan Randall too!"

CHAPTER XII

Secret of the Mine

CURT NEWTON'S physical and mental reflexes were a shade faster than those of any other man in the System. He could not quite match the blurring speed of the android who had taught him quickness, but his reactions were almost as instantaneous. As the Earthman guard fired his flare-gun at Captain Future, the big red-head was already diving beneath the whizzing flare in a low, swift tackle. Curt had started moving in the second before the guard could pull his trigger.

He knocked the man crashing from his feet. Before the fellow could utter a cry, Curt smashed his fist hard

upward to the chin. The guard's head snapped back and he went limp and senseless.

Captain Future straightened, tensely listening. The scuffle and the whizzing shot had not aroused alarm among the laboring Jovians and alert overseers out in the radium diggings.

But dawn was coming. Already the sky was reddening. Hastily, Curt dragged the senseless guard into the jungle and tightly bound his hands and feet with strips from his jacket.

"You shouldn't be so free with your little flare-gun," Captain Future told the man pleasantly as he groggily opened his eyes. "You might hurt somebody one of these days."

The guard looked up at this big red-haired young man grinning down at him, and uttered a vicious curse.

"Such language!" Curt deprecated. "By the way, don't attempt to cry out, or I'll have to knock you out again."

"What do you want here?" the guard snarled to him.

"I want to know just what the estimable Mr. Brewer is carrying on at this mine," Captain Future told him. "There's something funny about this place, and you can tell me what it is."

"I can, but I won't," the guard declared. "What are you, anyway, a Planet Police agent?"

Curt held up his left hand so that the man could see the big, odd ring he wore.

"Captain Future!" muttered the man appalledly. He looked up at the big red-head in sudden fear. Then his lips compressed. "You're not getting anything out of me, anyway."

"So you don't want to talk?" Curt said mildly. "Very well, then I shall make very sure that you don't talk, or shout either."

And coolly, he efficiently gagged the bound guard with more strips that he tore from the man's own zipper-jacket.

By this time, the Jovian day had fully dawned, the sun throwing a pale flood of light across the clearing of the mine. From his hiding place in the dense jungle, Curt studied the place.

He saw at once that he could not hope to venture out during the daylight. The scores of Jovians were still working out there, and with them were the half-dozen or more armed overseers.

"Have to wait for night," Curt muttered to himself. "Lucky the days are so short here on Jupiter."

Curt settled down to wait. The big red-haired man had learned patience from Grag, and he exercised it now. As he waited through the five hours of the Jovian day, he watched every move out in the mine.

He saw nothing of either Lucas Brewer or Mark Cannig. But the work went on steadily under the direction of the overseers. Hour after hour, the Jovians labored at digging the radium-bearing rock and hauling it in hand-trucks to the smelter.

Curt would have liked to call Simon Wright by his pocket-televisor, to tell them where he was and what he was doing. But he feared that his call might happen to be picked up if someone in those mine-offices was using a televisor, and decided not to risk it.

NIGHT finally came down, the dramatically sudden Jovian night that clapped down after only a few moments of twilight. Callisto and Europa and Ganymede were in the heavens, moving toward conjunction, while Io hurtled up to join them.

Curt made sure of the bound guard's safety, then rose to his feet to venture out into the clearing. But he stopped a moment, peering.

"Now what goes on?" he muttered to himself. "Are they quitting for good?"

The Jovians who had worked through a shift of ten hours during night and day were now dropping their tools, and streaming with the overseers toward the mine-office.

The green natives discarded their protective lead suits as they left the radium diggings. They clustered in the moonlight outside the office.

Captain Future moved hastily around the edge of the clearing until he had the smelter-structure between him and the office-building. Then he moved out, silently as a shadow.

From behind the smelter, he watched. And he saw that the over-seers were now distributing some objects from big boxes to the Jovians who crowded eagerly forward.

"Paying them off in trade goods," Curt muttered to himself. "But what—"

Then his keen eyes made out what the Earthmen were passing out to the Jovians. And his big crouching figure stiffened as though he had received an electric shock.

"So *that* is how Brewer induces the Jovians to work for him!" he muttered, his eyes suddenly blazing.

The things that the overseers were passing out to the green natives as reward for their labor were—flareguns.

Guns! The one thing that Earthmen were utterly forbidden to sell or give to the planetary natives! The strictest laws forbade it on every world in the System.

Captain Future felt like rushing out to stop the distributing of the weapons. But he knew well that it would be suicide to try it. Those Jovians, armed with the deadly flare-guns, would destroy any man who tried to take the weapons from them.

"Have to wait," Curt told himself fiercely. "But by Heaven, Brewer will have to account for plenty!"

As the Jovians received the weapons, they streamed away from the mine into the jungles eastward. From those moonlit jungles, the ground-drums had begun to throb. The deep, pulsing rhythm was now loud to Curt's ears, as though it came from nearby.

Finally all the Jovians had received weapons and hurried away into the moon-shot fern-forest. The overseers went into the office-building.

Curt drew his proton-pistol and crept forward. He gained the screen door of the lighted offices, then poise there, listening.

"Don't like giving those damned greenies guns," one of the Earthmen inside was saying. "They're too cursed eager to get them."

"What difference does it make to us?" another demanded. "They're only going to use the guns in a war with another tribe, Brewer says."

"That's what Brewer says," the

man muttered, "but I'm not so sure about it."

"Neither am I, gentlemen," spoke a throbbing voice from the doorway.

THE six Earthmen whirled, astonished. In the door bulked Curt Newton's big, broad-shouldered figure and red head, a little grim smile playing on his lips, and his slender proton-pistol leveled at them.

With an oath, one Earthman reached for the flare-gun at his belt. Captain Future's proton-beam licked forth, and the man fell stunned.

"I could kill you with this beam as easily as stun you," Curt said pleasantly. "Don't make me do it."

"It's Captain Future!" exclaimed one of the men, going pale as he recognized the unique ring on Curt's finger.

"You men," Curt told them, "are going to spend a long time out on the prison moon of Pluto for violating interplanetary law! Supplying natives with guns is risky business."

"I didn't want to do it!" the first overseer defended desperately. "Brewer made us. He's been getting rich that way, for the greenies will labor for guns when they won't for anything else."

"How did you get the guns up here from Jovopolis without detection?" Captain Future demanded.

"They were shipped in as trade-goods," the man explained hastily. "But each box had a false bottom, under which were the guns."

"You'll have a chance to testify to all that when the time cames," Curt said grimly. "In the meantime, I must ask you to sit down in those chairs and keep your hands up. I am going to make sure that you remain here while I am busy elsewhere."

Helplessly, the men sat down, their hands raised. Curt tore flexible metal cords from the shutters at the windows. Swiftly, he went about using them to bind the men to the chairs.

He worked with his pistol in one hand, keeping behind the seated men. In a few minutes, he had all of them securely lashed.

"Be sure and wait till I come back, gentlemen," he grinned at them, and then started a rapid search of the office and other buildings.

He was hoping to find some evidence that would definitely establish whether or not Lucas Brewer was the Space Emperor. But he could find nothing.

Time was flying. The throb of ground-drums from the moonlit jungles westward seemed louder. Curt rapidly made up his mind.

"The Space Emperor was to appear to the Jovians tonight in these jungles, according to Otho," he muttered to himself. "So that's where all those Jovians who left here must have gone."

He hastened out into the moonlight, and hurried across the clearing toward the jungle.

"If I can be there when the Space Emperor shows up, and if I can get him when he isn't in an immaterial state—"

He plunged into the jungle, following the Jovians westward along dim trails, able to hear their excited voices as they pressed on.

Somewhere ahead, he knew, lay the meeting place Otho had spoken of, the locale that the Jovians called the Place of the Dead. From there, the ground-drums were throbbing. And there, if he was lucky, he would come to grips with the dark super-criminal who was terrorizing a world.

CHAPTER XIII

Place of the Dead

BOOM! Boom! Through the moonlit Jovian jungles throbbed the heavy, rhythmic vibration, one that was felt rather than heard.

Ground-drums of the flipper-men, beating in the night like the dark heart of the savage Jupiter! *Boom! Boom! Boom!*

Captain Future looked up tensely through the canopy of tree-fern fronds high above. Callisto, Ganymede, Europa and Io were converging near the zenith, four brilliant moons nearing wonderful conjunction.

"The hour of the four moons meeting must have been the appointed time," he muttered to himself.

A moment later, his big figure tensed as he hurried on along the dim trail he was following through the forest.

"What's that?"

A dim, deep chanting sound came through the jungle in a murmurous wave, rising and swelling strangely in the night and then dying away.

For more than an hour, Curt had followed the Jovians through the unearthly wilderness. The green natives had pressed on at high speed, as though afraid that they would be late for the great gathering.

They had unerringly followed narrow trails that wound tortuously through the ferns. And they had kept the angry red glow of the Fire Sea always on their right.

The jungle was weird tonight! The drenching radiance of the four moons made it a fantastic fairyland of deep black shadows and dappled silver light. High overhead stretched the great tree-ferns' masses of feathery fronds, tipped with spore-pods. Gleaming bright in the moons towered the metallic copper-trees. The blindly swaying snake-vines hung like dark pendulous serpents from the branches.

In the choked spaces between the great fern-trunks bloomed supernally lovely shock-flowers, tempting, wonderful blossoms ready to give the unwary toucher a stinging electric shock from the biochemical "battery" inside their calyxes. Giant night-lilies flourished in the shadows, their yard-wide white petals slowly closing and unclosing. Down from the upper canopy when it was stirred by the breeze floated shining clouds of spore-dust, silvering all things below.

Curt could glimpse iridescent moon-bats gliding on motionless wings above the fern-tops, and bulbous balloon beasts floating slowly by. From beneath his feet more than once came the queer rasping sound of "diggers" burrowing. There was no sign of the dreaded "crawlers" about, and for that the big redhead felt thankful.

"Must be almost there," he told himself as the throbbing and chanting from ahead grew louder.

A tension such as he had seldom felt was mounting inside Captain Future as he hurried on. He felt himself on the verge of a second encounter with the Space Emperor.

But what would be its result? Would he be able to catch the Space Emperor off guard in his normal material state, or was there no chance of that?

"Getting close," Curt muttered. "Take it easy, my boy—"

Boom! Boom! The ground-drums were throbbing so near now that he could feel the vibration strongly beneath his feet. Tensely, he crept on.

The jungle was thinning ahead. He stopped a moment later, sank down behind a clump of shock-flowers.

Captain Future looked out upon an uncanny scene. It was a mile-wide circular clearing in the jungle, in which only scattered tree-ferns and shrubs and vines grew.

IN this clearing, bathed in the wonderful silver radiance of the four moons, lay the crumbling ruins of what had once been a great city.

City of Jupiter's unguessable past, mystery metropolis that long and long ago had fallen to wreck and had been swallowed by the jungle! Cyclopean masses of crumbled black masonry of grotesque architecture, towering solemnly out of the shrubs and clinging vines.

There had been paved streets and courts, Curt saw, but they were broken and covered by creeping moulds and fungi. There had been curving colonnades, but of them there remained nothing but a few broken, lonely black stone pillars.

"Place of the Dead," he whispered to himself. "It's well-named."

Captain Future had looked upon dead planetary cities before. He had seen the wonderful lost city on Tethys, moon of Saturn, whose history no man knows. He was familiar with those mysterious wrecks which are found everywhere in the deserts of Mars.

But he had, he felt, never looked upon a place more somber and darkly sentient than this ruined and forgot.

ten metropolis that brooded, beneath Jupiter's brilliant moons. The spirit of a mighty past reached out from it to lay cold fingers on the heart.

Captain Future glimpsed, far toward the center of the ruined city, a large circular plaza in which thousands of the Jovians were gathered in a tightly packed mass. Almost all seemed to possess flare-guns. They were facing toward a low, half-preserved black structure which partly hid them from Curt's view. It was from there that emanated the deep, rumbling throb of the b o o m i n g ground-drums.

"Have to get closer," Curt muttered tensely. "If the Space Emperor's already there—"

Stealthily, he slipped out of the jungle into the vast circle of ruins. Like a shadow, he worked toward the low and half-ruined stone structure that lay between him and the plaza of the gathered Jovians.

Keeping always within the shadows of brooding masonry masses, moving soundlessly over the broken paving, the big adventurer a d v a n c e d. He breathed more easily when he reached the deep shadow of the low building. From the plaza on the other side of it came loudly the deep throb of the ground-drums and the steady, swelling chanting of thousands of bass Jovian voices.

Boom! Boom! Boom! quivered the deep vibrations, shaking the ground under him.

Full of deep fanaticism, laden with a strange note of overwhelming sadness and despair, the chanting of the natives swelled frenziedly.

Curt knew the Jovian tongue well, but this chant was apparently in an archaic form that he could not understand.

HE flattened himself on the broken paving and inched forward until he could peer out into the moonlit plaza from behind the corner of the crumbling building. His eyes photographed the strange scene before him in a second.

Directly in front of the ruin behind which he crouched were the two great ground-drums. They consisted of deep pits that had been dug by the Jovians in the black ground, thirty feet deep and shaped like hollow cones with the apex at the surface.

A group of Jovians at each pit held a heavy fern-trunk with a flattened end, which they raised a little and then allowed to fall heavily, producing by the concussion the throbbing vibrations in the ground.

Captain Future saw between the ground-drum pits a great black stone globe carved with the outlines of continents and seas. It was set with scattered silver stars that he guessed immediately marked the location of other cities of the Ancients. He saw something else on the surface of the globe that made him start. He peered closer.

"If that's what it is—" he whispered tautly to himself, and then forgot his discovery as he heard a sound.

It was the distant, almost inaudible sound of a rocket-flier landing. The Jovians appeared not to have heard it through the boom of ground-drums and the chanting, but Curt's superkeen ears had detected it.

He waited, his pistol in his hand. After a few minutes, as the four moons overhead gathered together in a dazzling cluster, the chant of the Jovians ceased and the fern-trunks were withdrawn from the ground-drum pits. An air of tense expectancy seemed to grip the thousands of green men.

"Zero hour," Curt thought. "The four moons have—met!"

CHAPTER XIV

The Living Ancient

A STIR ran through the crowd of Jovians, and there was a movement near the far edge of the grotesque, moonlit crowd.

"He comes! The Living Ancient comes!" sped the rustling Jovian cry.

"The Living Ancient?" Curt wondered. "So that's what he calls himself?"

Into the packed plaza from the jungle on the far side of the city was coming a dark shape.

Curt raised his proton-pistol. If he could blast the Space Emperor before he became immaterial—

He saw that it was indeed the Space Emporer, the same figure he had battled in Orris' cabin in Jovopolis. A grotesque shape in his dark suit with its tiny eye-holes.

The Space Emperor was material, Curt saw at once. For he was *carrying* someone—the bound figure of a girl in a white synthe-silk uniform, whose dark, wavy hair fell back from her moonlit white face.

"Joan Randall!" Captain Future gasped. "That devil has seized her and brought her here for some reason!"

Curt's whole plan of action was upset by the disastrous surprise. He knew the Space Emperor was now material and vulnerable. But he could not blast him down while he held Joan.

The Space Emperor uttered a few words in his deep voice. Out of the worshipful Jovian crowd, two green natives sprang in obedience. They took the bound girl from their sinister ruler's arms.

As the Jovians stepped back with Joan, Curt's pistol was poised to blast the super-criminal. But the Space Emperor had touched something at his belt as the Jovians stepped back. And now the Space Emperor moved glidingly forward, *through* the two Jovians.

"Too late!" Captain Future hissed, with a feeling of blind anger.

Too late! The Space Emperor had made himself immaterial, and no proton-beam could harm him.

A great cry arose from the Jovian horde as they saw the dark figure glide forward through their comrades, like an unreal phantom. It was a cry of fanatic worship.

The Space Emperor glided forward, until he reached the paving between the ground-drum pits. There he turned to face the Jovian throng, his back toward Captain Future.

Curt could see now that the dark criminal moved, in his immaterial state, by the reactive push of a force-tube attached to his belt. There was a small switch beside it, that he guessed was the control of the Space Emperor's de-materializing apparatus. Apparently, the device that would return him to a normal state had also been changed into an immaterial state.

The two Jovians laid down Joan Randall's helpless form a little to one side of and behind the Space Emperor. Then they stepped back into the throng.

The deep, heavy voice of the black figure rolled out, speaking to the masses of Jovians in their own language.

"I bring to you again the command of the great Ancients, of whom I am the last living one," vibrated his voice.

A sigh of awe swept through the horde of green natives as they heard.

"You know that the spirits of the Ancients are wroth with the Earthmen who have come to this world," the black figure continued. "You have seen our curse fall upon many of them and change them into beasts."

"We have seen, lord," came a great responding cry from the Jovians.

"It is the curse of our anger that has made them change so," went on the Space Emperor. "Before you leave here, you shall see me put that curse upon this Earth girl."

CAPTAIN FUTURE'S big body went rigid. The super-plotter was going to use the dread atavism weapon on Joan—

"The time is almost here," the dark criminal was saying loudly, "when you must gather and sweep the Earthmen from this world to appease the anger of the Ancients. Are you ready for that?"

"We are ready, lord," answered a big Jovian fervently from the throng. "We have obtained many of the Earth guns from the Earthman at the radium mine, in exchange for our labor. All through the jungles now, the villages of our people only await the great signal of the ground-drums to attack the Earthmen."

"That signal will be given to you soon, perhaps within hours!" the Space Emperor declared. "I will lead you when the moment comes and we will sweep first upon the Earthman town they call Jungletown, and then upon the other Earthman cities until all are taken. Then *I*, the last of the Ancient, shall rule this world for your good."

"You shall rule, lord," answered the Jovians in a reverent, humble chorus.

Captain Future was clawing in his belt, working to extract something from that flat, capacious tungstite container.

"There's only one chance to get Joan away before that devil inflicts the blight upon her," he whispered fiercely to himself. "The invisibility charge—"

Captain Future extracted from his belt the little mechanism he wanted. It was a disclike instrument that was one of the greatest secrets of Curt and Simon Wright.

He took it, pressed a stud upon it, holding it above his head. He felt the unseen force that streamed down from it flood through every fiber of his body with stinging shock.

Quickly, Captain Future saw his own body becoming a little misty and translucent. For Curt was disappearing!

The little instrument was one which could give any matter a charge of force that caused all light to be refracted around it, thus making it invisible. But the charge only lasted temporarily, for ten minutes. Then the charge dissipated, and such matter became visible again.

Captain Future, as he became slowly invisible, felt an utter darkness close in around him. With all light refracted around him, he was now in complete darkness. He could see nothing whatever! For no light could reach his eyes. By that he knew finally that he had become completely invisible.

Curt started soundlessly around the corner of the ruined building, moving in an absolute and rayless blackness.

Captain Future could move in this darkness that now encompassed him, almost as well as by sight. His super-keen senses of hearing and touch, and his long practice in this, enabled him to do what no other man could have done.

He crept around the crumbling ruin. He knew that, had he been visible, he would be standing in full view of the Jovian thousands. He could hear the Space Emperor, still speaking in his heavy, disguised voice, exhorting the green natives.

CURT crept toward that voice. Moving with utter care, he crept on until he neared Joan. He could hear her frightened breathing. He clapped his invisible hand over her mouth and felt her body quiver in wild alarm.

"It's me—Captain Future," he murmured in the faintest of whispers in her ear. "Lie still, and I'll untie you."

He felt Joan stiffen, then relax. He groped at her bonds, which he discovered were tough metal cords.

Curt could not untie the cords, nor break them. Frantically he clawed in his belt, and brought out a sharp little tool. Slowly, so as to make no twanging sound, he cut the cords.

"Don't get up," he murmured to the girl. "I'll drag you slowly back around the ruin. If the Jovians notice

[*Turn page*]

you, we'll have to run for it."

He gripped Joan's shoulders firmly. Then, with infinite care to make no sound, he drew the girl back from the loudly declaiming Space Emperor.

In the darkness, Curt was tensely listening for signs of discovery. But he heard no sound of alarm from the Jovian throng. Intently listening to their leader, Curt guessed that they were not watching the half-hidden shape of the girl.

Captain Future's hopes were soaring when he heard a wild cry from a Jovian in the throng.

"See! A spirit of the Ancients appears to us now!"

At the same moment, faint light began to penetrate the rayless blackness in which Curt moved.

He looked down at himself. His ten minutes of invisibility had expired. He was becoming visible again!

CHAPTER XV

Doom of An Earthman

THERE was a taut silence in the little office of Jovian Mines in Jungletown, as Simon Wright and Grag and the disguised Otho realized the situation.

Mark Cannig stood before the incredible trio of comrades, fear evident in his eyes. The young mine superintendent's face was flushed and queer, as though he labored under strong emotion.

"You know what happened to Joan, Cannig," rasped the Brain. "You'd better talk, quickly."

"I tell you I don't know anything," asserted Cannig desperately, his voice thick and hoarse.

"We can make you talk, you know!" hissed Otho ominously, his eyes blazing. "Where is the girl? And where is Captain Future?"

Grag took a ponderous step forward toward the young man, and half-raised his enormous metal hands.

"Shall I squeeze the truth out of him, Simon?" boomed the great robot questioningly.

Mark Cannig appealed wildly to Ezra Gurney who stood beside the un human trio.

"Marshal Gurney, you can't let them harm me!" cried the young man hoarsely.

Ezra Gurney's weatherbeaten face was grim and his blue eyes cold.

"I'm with them on this, Cannig," he said uncompromisingly. "You've done something to that girl, and you're going to tell what."

Cannig made a bolt for the door. But before he reached it, Otho had moved with blurring speed to intercept him.

The android hauled him back despite his struggles and yells.

"He's guilty as hell or he wouldn't have tried to get away!" cried Ezra Gurney.

"What's going on in here?" demanded a startled voice from the door.

Sylvanus Quale stood there, and behind him was the vice-governor, Eldred Kells. The governor's colorless face was amazed as he looked in at the strange tableau presented by the brain and robot and android, and to the two Earthmen.

Quale and Kells strode inside. And at once Cannig appealed hoarsely to the governor.

"Captain Future's comrades are planning to torture me!" he cried.

"It wouldn't be a bad idea, at that," Gurney said.

The marshal told the governor what had happened and showed him the Planet Police badge they had found upon the floor.

"Captain Future and Joan both missing?" Quale exclaimed. His face grew strange. "I was afraid things were going wrong up here at Jungletown. That's why I just flew up here to check."

"Do you suppose that Cannig could be the Space Emperor?" Eldred Kells exclaimed excitedly.

"I'm not—I'm not!" howled Cannig, his face distorted and his cry almost unrecognizable.

"Where's Lucas Brewer?" Quale demanded of him, but he did not answer.

"Brewer may be out at the mine, he may be lying low somewhere he in Jungletown," Gurney answered. "I've an idea hell is going to pop tonight."

"And meanwhile we're wasting time here!" Otho hissed fiercely.

"You'd better talk fast, Cannig," rasped Simon Wright to the young superintendent. "Grag and Otho will do some unpleasant things to you if you don't."

CANNIG'S nerve seemed to break. His voice babbled hoarsely of a sudden.

"I'll tell you what I know! I don't know anything about where Captain Future is, but Joan was taken from here tonight by the Space Emperor, because she saw us together."

"You've been an accomplice of that criminal, then?" Simon rasped instantly.

Mark Cannig nodded, slowly and dazedly.

"Yes," he muttered. "There's no use denying it now."

"Who is the Space Emperor, Cannig?" the Brain demanded quickly.

"I don't know," Cannig choked. "I never knew who he was."

"Tell the truth!" Otho hissed, his voice threatening.

"I'm telling the truth!" choked Cannig dazedly. "I was just a pawn of the Space Emperor, like Orris and Skeel and a few others. The Space Emperor never appeared to me except inside that concealing suit. And he was almost always immaterial. He didn't take any chances."

Cannig seemed struggling for words, his glazed eyes wild and his voice thick and stumbling.

"He told me he would soon hold supreme power on Jupiter, and that I would share that power if I helped him. I agreed, like a fool. Then when the atavism cases began, I realized that he was causing that horror.

"He said he'd found powers beyond any Earth science, and that one of them was the atavism force. He was using it on Earthmen at random, to create a demoralization of horror and influence the superstitious Jovians, through whom he meant to win power over the whole planet. He inflicted the blight with an invisible beam.

Victims didn't feel it at the time, but a few days later the horrible change began."

"And you were helping him?" cried Eldred Kells, looking at the young man in utter loathing.

"I had to obey him. I was afraid of him!" Cannig cried hoarsely. "That black devil has been more and more menacing to me of late, because of the protests I made to him against the horror he was causing."

"Did he say just when he intended to lead the Jovians against the Earthman towns?" Simon Wright demanded.

Mark Cannig nodded dazedly.

"Yes, he said that—"

Cannig stopped, the words trailing from his lips, his eyes glazed and strange. He passed a hand unsteadily over his face.

"He said that—" he started to continue, in the same stumbling voice.

But again, his thick voice trailed off. He looked from one to another of them with blank, empty eyes.

"Why," he said hoarsely, "I feel—"

"Look out!" yelled Ezra Gurney an instant later.

MARK CANNIG'S flushed, strange face had suddenly stiffened into an animal-like snarl, his lips writhing back in a bestial grin from his teeth, his eyes blazing with new feral light.

Growling like a suddenly enraged beast, he wrenched himself from Otho's grasp with a superhuman surge of strength, and launched himself at the throat of Sylvanus Quale.

"Grag—get him!" cried Simon Wright.

The robot seized the maddened Cannig, and tore him from Quale. The stricken man struggled ferociously, frothing at the lips, until Grag's metal fist knocked him senseless.

Cannig went down, unconscious. Yet even in unconsciousness there were bestial lines in his flushed face.

"Good God!" muttered Ezra Gurney. "The blight has got him!"

For a moment there was a strained silence. And in that silence there came to them from northward the distant, persistent throbbing of the Jovian ground-drums.

Boom! Boom! they throbbed, in faraway, ominous quivering vibration that was felt rather than heard.

"Cannig said that he'd been afraid of the Space Emperor lately," Simon rasped. "He had reason to be. His protests against the atavism horror had made the black devil suspicious of him, and the thing was turned on *him*."

"And he didn't know that poison was working in him till it hit him just now!" exclaimed Ezra Gurney, aghast.

"But what of master, Simon?" asked Grag anxiously of the Brain.

The robot's unswerving devotion to Captain Future ruled him now as always.

"We're going to find Curtis," Simon declared. "We'll go first to Brewer's mine, where you said he'd gone, Ezra."

"I'll go with you!" Ezra Gurney declared instantly.

"You can take Cannig up to the hospital," the Brain rasped to the staring Quale and Kells. "And tell them up there I now have a cure for the atavism horror which I'll use on the victims when we get back."

"A cure?" echoed Quale unbelievingly.

"Come on—what are we waiting for?" Otho interrupted. "Let's go."

THE three unhuman comrades and Ezra Gurney hastened out into the night. By dark back-streets they hurried to the jungle-edge where the *Comet* waited.

Presently, with Grag at the controls, the little teardrop ship was hurtling northward over the moonlit jungles. Otho removed his Jovian disguise as they flew on.

Gurney directed their course. Presently the little cluster of lights at the Brewer mine came into view, and with a rush, the *Comet* landed beside the lighted offices.

A half-dozen men bound in chairs met their eyes as they entered the office. The men, now thoroughly surrendering to the inevitable and hoping for judicial mercy, told them of Captain Future's visit and the flare-gun traffic with the natives.

"Giving the Jovians guns!" Ezra Gurney cried wrathfully. "By heaven, Brewer will spend the rest of his life in prison out on Cerberus for this."

He went to the televisor and called Planet Police Headquarters in Jungletown.

"Send a flier up here to pick up some prisoners. I'll wait until you come," the marshal said. "And if you see Lucas Brewer anywhere, arrest him at once!"

"We're not going to wait here," Simon told the marshal. "Curtis isn't here. That means he's gone to the Jovian meeting where the Space Emperor was to appear, the meeting of which Otho brought us news."

"The place is only a little west of here!" Otho cried. "It's a ruin the Jovians call the Place of the Dead."

"Let us go, then," boomed Grag anxiously.

"Go ahead—I'll see you when I've taken these men back to Jungletown," Gurney told them. "And save that girl, if you can!"

The *Comet*, with only the three weird comrades aboard it now, split the night like a shooting star, plunging westward over the moon-drenched jungle.

The throb of the ground-drums had ceased for the time being, and that fact was like an ominous warning to the three.

"There's the place!" Otho cried, his green eyes peering intently ahead. "That big clearing—"

"There's a fight going on there!" boomed Grag suddenly. "Look!"

The sinister flash of a deadly beam was visible amid a group of struggling figures in the moonlit ruins.

CHAPTER XVI

Prison Pit

CAPTAIN FUTURE realized that his concealment was gone. The invisibility-charge was now dissipating by the second, and he was already almost solidly visible.

The Jovian throng was uttering a chorus of cries and surging toward him. The dark shape of the Space Emperor had turned, and from the mysterious plotter came a low cry.

"Captain Future—here!"

Then the Space Emperor uttered a deep shout to the Jovians.

"Seize the Earthman spy!"

The green natives surged forward with wild bass yells of rage, incited by that shout.

Curt sprang erect, drew his pistol and triggered at the sinister black figure. Now that he was discovered, he would at least make one more attempt to destroy the dark plotter.

The attempt was as futile as he had known it must be. The proton-beam splashed through the immaterialized form of the Space Emperor without harming him.

"Run!" Curt was calling fiercely to Joan Randall as he fired. "I'll hold them off—"

The pale ray of his pistol leaped like a thing alive, and knocked down Jovians in their tracks. The weapon was only set at stunning force now. Even in this desperate moment, Curt could not bring himself to kill these misguided natives.

Joan had gained her feet. But the girl had not tried to make an escape.

"I'll not leave you, Captain Future!" she cried pluckily.

"Don't be a fool!" Curt cried, his gray eyes blazing. "You can't—"

"Captain Future!" screamed the girl. "Behind you—"

Curt whirled. But too late. Jovians who had rushed around to get at him from behind now leaped up upon him.

For moments Curt stood erect, struggling with superhuman strength, his red head and straining face towering out of the mass of green flippermen who sought to pull him down. The proton-pistol had been torn from his hands but his big fists beat a devil's tattoo on the faces of the natives.

But the struggle was hopeless. He felt himself pulled down by the smothering mass of enemies. His belt, too, was torn from him and flung aside like the pistol.

Then he was hauled to his feet, held by the flipper-hands of so many Jovians that escape was impossible. He saw Joan, similarly held, nearby.

"Why the devil didn't you get away when there was a chance!" Curt panted to the girl. "Now we're both in for it."

The Space Emperor, a dark, erect shape of mystery, glided forward until he towered in front of Curt and Joan.

"So the famous Captain Future meets defeat at last," mocked the mysterious criminal.

Curt felt an emotion as near despair as he ever could feel. Yet the big redhead let no trace of it enter his voice as he stared contemptuously at the black figure.

"Just who are you inside that suit?" he demanded. "Quale? Kells? Lucas Brewer?"

The Space Emperor jerked, as though startled by Curt Newton's guesses.

"You'll never know, Captain Future!" he declared. "You're going to die. Not a quick, easy death, but the most horrible one that any man could die."

THE uncanny plotter raised his voice in a command to the Jovians who held the man and girl.

"Drop them into one of the ground-drum pits!" he ordered.

Captain Future struggled suddenly, used every trick of super ju-jutsu that Otho the android had taught him. But it was futile.

He and Joan were dragged to one of the deep pits that had been used for the ground-drums. They were lowered into the big dirt pit by the Jovians, and then released.

Curt dropped over twenty feet, and struck the dirt floor of the pit. Joan was crumpled beside him.

"I'm not hurt," she gasped. Then horror came into her eyes. "Is he going to leave us in here to starve to death?"

"I'm afraid it's something a devil of a lot worse than starvation," the big redhead answered tightly.

He looked up. The dirt walls of the pit sloped upward toward each other, and at the small opening at the top he could see Jovians armed with flare-guns looking down at them.

The dark, helmeted head of the Black One became visible at the top, against the brilliant moonlight. The super-criminal leaned down toward them.

Curt saw that the Space Emperor was again material, since in his hand he carried a small, flat metal lantern-like thing, with a big translucent lens in its face.

"You wanted to find out how I produce the atavism effect, Captain Future," mocked the plotter. "Now you are going to have your curiosity gratified."

He held out the little lanternlike apparatus as he spoke.

"This apparatus produces a super-hard vibration that paralyzes the pituitary gland of any living creature and allows atavism to occur," rumbled the black figure. "Allow me to demonstrate it for you."

"Back, Joan!" yelled Captain Future, sweeping the girl behind the shelter of his own big form, against the wall.

It was too late. The lens in the thing the Space Emperor held had glowed palely for an instant, and a dim, almost wholly invisible ray had flickered from it and bathed the heads of Curt and Joan. They felt a momentary sensation of shivering cold.

Joan screamed in horror. Curt felt a blind, raging fury. He had not felt anything but that momentary sensation of cold, but he knew that the deadly work had been done. The pituitaries of Joan and himself were paralyzed, and inevitably the atavism would begin in them—

"You will suffer the change now, Captain Future!" mocked the sinister black shape. "Down in that pit, you and the girl will become hideous creatures within a few days. And I am leaving a few of my faithful Jovians here to watch and make sure that you stay in the pit to suffer."

Curt kept his voice steady, by a supreme effort, as he looked up at the mocking figure.

"I have never promised death to a man without keeping my promise," he said in chill, even voice. "I am promising it to you now."

He said nothing more. But something deadly in his tones made the Space Emperor stiffen.

"Not you or any other Earthman can harm me, protected as I am by immateriality," the criminal retorted. "And you forget that you, and the girl too, will soon be raving, hideous brutes!"

The Space Emperor withdrew. They could hear the Jovians above being dismissed by the plotter. A number of Jovians remained on guard above the pit, however. They could hear the excited bass voices overhead.

JOAN RANDALL was staring at Captain Future with dark eyes wide with dazed horror. It was as though the girl could not yet realize what had happened.

"We—becoming beasts down here," she c h o k e d hoarsely. "Changing more horribly, day by day—"

Curt's big figure strode to her, and he grasped her shoulders in strong hands and shook her.

"Joan, get a grip on yourself!" he commanded harshly. "This is no time to get hysterical. We're in a devil of a bad jam and it will take all our brains and nerves to get us out."

"But we can't get out!" sobbed the girl. "Those Jovians above would kill us if we could manage even to get out of this pit. And even if we did, we'd still change and change—like those horrors in the hospital—"

She buried her face in her hands. Curt soothed her and spoke encouragingly.

"There's a strong chance we can escape the atavism if we can escape from here and get back to Jungletown quickly," he told her. "Simon Wright should have found a cure by now. He was working on it when I left."

She raised a tear-smeared face.

"I'm—sorry," she said unsteadily. "It isn't just dying that I'm afraid of, but changing—"

"We're not going to die or change either!" Curt declared forcefully. "It will take hours, perhaps days, before the paralysis of the pituitaries begins to affect us in the slightest. That gives us a reasonable time to try to get away."

His gray eyes flashed as he added, "And we've got to do that, not for our own sakes alone, but to prevent a terrible thing from happening. That black devil is inciting the Jovians to attack all the Earthman settlements, and that attack may take place within hours!"

His big fists clenched.

"I've an idea now of a way in which the Space Emperor could be conquered—the only way. But it'll do no good as long as we're trapped down here."

"You wouldn't be here if you hadn't tried to rescue me," Joan said in self-reproach.

"Joan, how did it happen that the Space Emperor kidnaped you?" Captain Future asked. "Did you see who he really is?"

"I don't know who he is," the shaken girl replied, "but I know someone whom I think does know."

She explained unsteadily.

"Earlier tonight I slipped out of the hospital in Jungletown and went down to spy on Lucas Brewer and Mark Cannig in their offices. I peered in through a window.

"I saw Mark Cannig, in the offices, talking to the Space Emperor! He was, just as you had described him, concealed in that dark suit. Then as I watched, Cannig glimpsed me at the window and rushed out. I tried to escape but someone struck me a blow that knocked me unconscious. When I awoke I was bound, on my way here in the Space Emperor's rocket-flier."

Curt Newton's red head jerked up.

"So Mark Cannig is an accomplice of the Space Emperor!"

His eyes narrowed.

"That eliminates Cannig of my four suspects, at least. But of the other three—"

"Captain Future, do you think there's any hope at all of our getting out of here?" Joan interrupted. "Can we dig steps and climb out of this place?"

"Wouldn't do us any good with those Jovians watching the mouth of pit," Curt told her. His eyes swept the dark dirt walls of the pit. "But there must be some way."

Curt was reduced to his bare hands. Deprived of his belt and pistol, he was robbed of all the instruments he might have used to escape. Even his pocket-televisor was gone.

Joan had sunk to the dirt floor.

"We'll never get out," she said in dull hopelessness. "We'll change into awful creatures and die, down in this pit."

"Like the devil we will!" Captain Future declared. "I was chained to a rock on the Hot Side of Mercury once and left there to die. But I didn't die."

His powerful mind was working at top speed to find a way out of this trap. He went around the dark pit, his keen eyes inspecting the dirt walls.

Suddenly Curt stopped and listened. His ears had detected a faint rasping sound that was barely audible. Quickly he pressed his ear against the dirt wall. And now he heard it much more plainly, a chewing, grinding rasp.

"It's a digger!" he exclaimed in a low voice to the girl. "I don't think it's many yards away from this pit in the soil."

Joan shivered at the mention of the bloodthirsty subterranean burrowers which inhabit the soil beneath the Jovian jungles.

"I hope it doesn't come this way," she said fearfully.

"On the contrary, I want it to come this way!" Captain Future said. "Don't you understand? The tunnels those diggers make connect with each other, and open at many places to the surface. It would be a way out for us!"

"But if the creature came into the pit here and attacked us—" the girl began terrifiedly.

"I can take care of that," Curt told her. "The thing I've got to do now is to attract the beast to come here."

The ingenious fastener of Curt's zipper-suit was made of woven gray wire. He quickly broke a bit of this wire away, and with it he gashed his wrist.

AS blood spurted, Curt smeared it onto the wall of the pit. Then he rapidly bound his wrist with a strip torn from his jacket.

"Those creatures can sense blood for hundreds of yards through the solid soil," he told the girl. "I think that will bring it here."

In a moment he heard the rasping, chewing sound definitely louder and nearer.

"It's coming!" he exclaimed.

Joan shrank back against the opposite wall of the pit.

Captain Future was rapidly unraveling more of the tough gray wire from his woven suit-fastenings. When he had a doubled length of twelve feet, he fashioned a running noose and loop.

By that time the rasping, grinding sound of the advancing digger was very audible, and little flakes of dirt were falling from a spot on the dirt wall. Curt waited beside that point, his wire loop ready in his hand.

"Here it comes—make no sound!" he muttered.

Joan uttered a gasp of horror a moment later. Dirt had fallen from the wall, and through an opening its own jaws had made protruded the snout of a weird and menacing creature.

The digger was like a giant six-foot rat, with a broad, flat face opening in tremendous jaws armed with the big, flat grinding fangs with which it burrowed its way.

Its small red eyes glimpsed Joan Randall and it sprang out into the pit toward her. Curt cast his loop swiftly.

THE loop settled around the leaping brown beast's head, tightened cruelly about its neck as Curt pulled hard. With a muffled squeal, the creature turned on its short legs. But Captain Future leaped aside, tightening the noose.

There was a brief, almost soundless flurry of struggle as the choking creature sought to reach the man. Soon its movements became weaker and it fell on its side, motionless.

"It's done for!" Curt exclaimed. "Come on—we're going out of here through the tunnel it burrowed."

He scrambled into the raw new passageway that the bloodthirsty beast had excavated. It was full of loose dirt, but Captain Future squeezed blindly on through the darkness, with Joan bravely crawling after him.

Presently this raw, stifling passage opened into a larger tunnel, within which they could stand by stooping.

"This is a regular digger run," Curt told the girl. "It may lead to the surface."

They followed it forward, almost suffocated by the heavy, dirt-smelling air. Captain Future's hopes rose as the tunnel slanted slightly upward. The darkness was absolute.

In some minutes they emerged suddenly from the low tunnel into a much larger space. They could stand erect here. But here too the air was heavy, and foul with the odor of old bones and animals.

"Where are we?" Joan asked bewilderedly. "I thought—"

"Quiet!" Captain Future hissed. "See—those eyes!"

In the utter darkness, a dozen pairs of red eyes that glowed with uncanny phosphorescence were watching them.

"We've blundered into a nest of the diggers!" Curt whispered. "And they see us!"

CHAPTER XVII

Chamber of Horrors

JOAN uttered a little cry of horror. At the sound, the phosphorescent red eyes of the watching beasts began moving toward them.

Captain Future swept the girl behind him, against the dirt wall of this underground dirt cave, and awaited the attack of the ravenous beasts.

"Can't we escape back through the tunnel?" Joan whispered frantically in the darkness.

"They'd run us down in a minute, and we couldn't turn to fight in that narrow passage," Curt gritted. "Here we can at least put up a fight."

The scene was enough to affect even the iron nerves of Captain Future. The utter blackness, the stifling atmosphere of ominous odors, and the red eyes that warily advanced.

He clenched his fists, knowing full well that they were useless against the fangs of these gathered beasts. Yet he would go down fighting, he knew fighting as he had fought against hopeless odds from Mercury to Pluto.

Queerly enough, in that moment the paramount emotion of Curt was rage. Rage at the thought of the Space Emperor continuing his nefarious plot unchecked, of Jupiter turned into a hell of horror and struggle to further one man's mad ambitions.

"Look!" cried J o a n suddenly. "What's that?"

Captain Future saw it, at the same instant. It was something flowing down into the digger nest from one of the tunnels, something vaguely shining and liquid.

It looked like a viscous tide of strangely shining j e l l y, gliding smoothly down into the dirt chamber. The sight of it startled Curt with a cold shock.

"It's a crawler!" he exclaimed. hoarsely.

"A crawler?" Joan's voice shook at the mention of the most dreaded of all Jovian beasts.

For the crawlers were almost the most deadly life-form on Jupiter. They were like great viscous masses of protoplasm, moving by flowing over the ground, seizing prey by protruding pseudopods. At first, Earthmen explorers had considered them a very low form of life.

But now it was known that the crawlers possessed a mysterious, high intelligence. Every other creature on Jupiter was in terror of them. And now Curt had visual evidence that they would descend even among the tunnels of the "diggers" in search of prey.

The diggers advancing toward Curt and Joan had not seen the flowing menace entering behind them, for their red eyes were still facing the man and girl. Then Curt saw a pseudopod of the shining viscous creature lick forth and seize a dark digger.

Squeals rent the air, and the diggers dashed in all directions in a wild effort to escape by the tunnels.

And the crawler, its two huge eyes coldly blazing in the midst of its formless body, towered up and sent one shooting pseudopod after another forth to seize the ratlike beasts.

"Out of here before the thing seizes us too!" Captain Future cried to the girl. "Quick, the tunnel it came from—"

He seized Joan's hand and leaped around the rim of the dirt cavern that had now become a chamber of horror.

The crawler, intent on seizing as many of the bolting beasts as possible, did not notice the man and girl until they were entering the tunnel down through which it itself had come.

Then, as Curt pushed the girl up the cramped tunnel before him, he saw the crawler's huge eyes turn on its viscous mass toward him, and a big pseudopod shoot swiftly out.

By main force, Captain Future thrust the girl secret agent up the tunnel, in a tremendous thrust. The pseudopod of shining liquid darted up the tunnel after them.

BUT they were beyond its reach. The viscous arm retreated. They could hear the squeals of the diggers from below as the monster down there seized and ingested them.

"Hurry!" Curt urged the girl. "The thing may follow us! This tunnel must lead to the surface, since it came down this way."

After a few moments more of climbing up the cramped dirt passageway, a circle of brilliant moonlight showed above.

In a moment they were climbing out into the brilliant radiance of the four moons. Joan staggered, and Curt supported her.

He looked swiftly around. They were in the jungle, but he could glimpse the cyclopean m a s s e s of brooding masonry of the Place of the Dead, some hundreds of yards away.

"I've got to go back there," Captain Future told the girl rapidly. "I'll have to find my belt and gun."

"But the Jovians guarding the pit we were imprisoned in—" the girl began fearfully.

"I can take care of them, I think," he said. "Keep behind me, and make no sound."

Silently, stealthily, he advanced through the jungle toward the edge of the great circle of ancient ruins.

Crouching down on the edge of that wrecked city, he peered forth.

The moonlit ruins were now deserted except for six Jovians armed with flare-guns who sat around the ground-drum pit in which they supposed Captain Future and Joan to be still confined.

Curt's eyes searched the ground all around and finally fixed on what he was hunting for. His tungstite belt and pistol! They lay near the pit, where they had been flung by the Jovian who had ripped them from him at the Space Emperor's orders.

Curt motioned for the girl to remain hidden, and inched silently forward in a wriggling crawl. He was only a few yards from the belt and pistol when a Jovian saw him. The green man cried out and jumped up. Captain Future dived desperately toward the weapon.

He scooped it up and pulled trigger in the same swift movement. The pale beam that lanced from it hit the Jovians as they were leveling their own guns, and sent them tumbling into a stunned heap.

"Captain Future, someone's coming!" cried Joan Randall, running wildly out into the clearing toward him.

A dark, humming bulk was diving toward them out of the moonlight. Curt raised his pistol swiftly, then lowered it with a throb of gladness and relief.

"It's the Comet!" he cried.

He ran forward. Out of the little teardrop ship burst Grag and Otho.

The big robot boomed noisily as he patted Curt with heavy metal hands. Otho held Simon Wright's square brain-case.

"Simon, have you perfected the atavism-cure formula yet?" Curt asked the Brain tensely.

"Yes, lad—why do you ask?" the Brain countered quickly.

Curt explained. And a cry of heart-checking rage went up from Otho as he heard.

"He dared turn the thing on you!" hissed the android furiously.

Grag spoke solemnly.

"For daring to do that, I will kill the Space Emperor myself."

"Bring the girl inside," Simon told Curt quickly. "I can give you both an injection at once. Hurry inside!"

IN the laboratory of the Comet, the Brain gave Curt directions. Rapidly, an injection of the pink formula was made into the veins of Captain Future and the girl.

"I don't feel any differently," Joan said doubtfully.

"No, but you are both safe now from the atavism," Simon told them. "The paralysis of your glands had been ended, before it could have any effect upon you."

"What now, lad?" the Brain asked Curt.

"Simon, things are rushing toward a climax," Curt said earnestly. "The Space Emperor plans to lead the Jovian hordes onto the Earthman towns, perhaps this very night. The only thing that will stop the Jovians is the destroying of that black devil whom they worship and follow.

"There's not a chance in the world of our harming the Space Emperor while he can take refuge in immateriality through that vibration step-up. We've got to master that power ourselves before we can come to rips with him."

"You have a plan?" the Brain asked him keenly.

"The only plan possible, and its possibility depends on something I glimpsed in these ruins," Curt answered. "Come with me."

He led the way back out into the moonlight, and hastened toward the great black stone globe that towered between the two ground-drum pits.

Upon its surface, as he had noticed before, were carved outlines of the continents and seas of Jupiter. Set in it were the silver stars that he had guessed marked the location of the long-perished cities of the Ancients. He had formed that guess because one star marked this exact location he stood in now.

Captain Future located the thing about the globe which had aroused his attention when he had glimpsed it from his hiding-place previously. From the star that marked this dead city he stood in, a line had been drawn due northward on the globe in white pencil.

"An Earthman drew that line while plotting directions," Curt told the others rapidly. "And the only one who was likely to have done that was Kenneth Lester, the young archaeologist who disappeared up here weeks ago."

The penciled line ran straight northward toward another silver star, enclosed in a circle, which was set on the southern edge of the big red oval that marked the precise location of the Fire Sea.

"Lester was plotting the direction from this ruined city to some other city or ruin of the Ancients that lies up there on the shore of the Fire Sea," Curt declared. "So that is where Lester must have gone."

"But there couldn't have ever been any city up there by the Fire Sea!" objected Joan. "Why, no one or no thing can live that close to that terrible flaming ocean!"

"The Ancients had a city of some kind there," Captain Future insisted, "but it was different somehow from their other cities, for it is distinguished by a silver circle around the star that marks its location."

"You think then that up there is the storehouse of knowledge from which the Space Emperor got the scientific secrets of the Ancients?" Simon Wright asked thoughtfully.

CURT nodded his red head quickly. "Yes, I do think so. And I think that there I could secure that power of immaterialization for myself, and be able at last to come to grips with that black devil before he can loose an uprising."

"It's a long chance, lad," muttered the Brain. "It's hard, as Joan says, to believe that any city could ever have been located on the shore of that awful sea of flame."

"It's the only real chance we've got of stopping the Space Emperor," Curt warned. "I've got to take it. I'm going up there now, and I'll take Grag with me. We can go in the rocket-flier I left over at the radium mine.

"Otho will fly you and Joan back to Jungletown, Simon," he went on. "It's important that you get that atavism cure working on the victims that

crowd the hospital there."

"But I should go with you instead of Grag!" Otho objected loudly.

Curt silenced him peremptorily.

"Someone has to fly Simon and Joan back. And Grag's strength may be more useful to me up there than anything else. Do as you're told, Otho!"

Grumbling, the android gave in. They entered the *Comet*.

"You can drop Grag and me at the mine, and we'll pick up our flier," Curt ordered.

As they flew eastward over the moonlit ferns again, Curt's mind was worked up to a fever pitch of excitement. He felt that at last there was a chance of getting to grips with the sinister criminal who had thus far slipped through his hands like a shadow.

The little teardrop ship landed in the mine-clearing within minutes. The prisoners and Ezra Gurney were gone. Evidently, a police flier had already taken them back to Jungletown.

"Be careful up there, lad," begged Simon Wright as they parted. "You know that it's death to meddle with that hellish ocean."

"I will take care of master," Grag announced, joyful with pride at being chosen to accompany Captain Future.

The *Comet* shot away, hurtling southward toward Jungletown. Curt and the robot hastened toward the rocket-flier he had left inside the jungle.

In a few moments the little torpedo-like craft rose sharply out of the jungle, and headed northward at its highest possible speed.

Ahead of them the whole night sky was a vivid glare of scarlet, a shaking splendor of wild red rays. Black against the glare stood out the dark, jagged hills that rimmed the southern shore of the Fire Sea.

As they neared the hills, the glare became so intense that their eyes could hardly look into it. Grag turned a little uneasily from the controls toward Captain Future.

"Shall I keep straight on over the hills and above the Fire Sea, master?" he asked.

"Keep on over the hills—we're going to reconnoiter the coast of the sea," Curt told him. He added with a quick grin, "You're not afraid of a little molten lava, Grag?"

"I would not be afraid of a little," Grag answered seriously, "but there is a great deal of it in that ocean, master."

Curt chuckled. "A great deal is right. But it won't hurt us—I hope!"

The flier was now pitching and tossing slightly despite its powerful drive, as it encountered great winds and blasts of superheated air rushing up from the vast, flaming ocean that lay ahead. The whole sky was an unthinkable flare of scarlet from the molten sea.

Curt felt his muscles tightening. They were, he knew, rushing toward one of the most stupendous and perilous natural wonders in the Solar System—one that had claimed the lives of almost all the Earthmen who had ever dared attempt the exploration of its shores.

Whirling blasts of smoke and fumes engulfed the speeding flier, as it raced on over the rocky hills toward the dreaded ocean of fire. Would they be able to survive the fiery sea's perils? Captain Future wondered.

CHAPTER XVIII

The Sleeper in the Cavern

FIRE Sea of Jupiter! Most dangerous and stupendous feature of the mightiest planet, which was spoken of with awe by men from Mercury to Pluto!

It stretched before them now, a vast ocean of crimson, molten lava that extended to the dim horizons and beyond for eight thousand unthinkable miles, and that extended east and west for three times that distance. A flaming sea that was constantly kept liquid by the interior radioactive heat.

The surface of that evilly glowing red-hot ocean was rippled by little, heavy waves and boiling maelstroms. Upon it like genii danced lurid flames,

and whirls of sulfurous smoke. Its radiated heat was overpowering, even through the filter-windows of the rocket-flier.

Captain Future felt awe as he looked, not for the first time, on this incredible fiery gulf into which all Earth could have been plunged.

"Don't go out over it, Grag," he told the robot. "The air-currents above it would capsize the flier. Follow along the shore-line."

"Yes, master," boomed the robot, turning the ship to move eastward. He added naively, "I do not like this place."

"I prefer even the ice-fields of Pluto to this myself," Curt admitted ruefully.

"I see nothing along the shore, master," Grag said.

"Neither do I," Curt admitted. "But there must be something here."

Below them lay the southern shore of the Fire Sea. The flaming ocean's molten waves lapped directly against the great range of black rock hills which acted as a dike to dam them back.

The rock slopes of the hills were heavily encrusted with solidified lava, that showed the tide-marks to which the molten flood reached. But there was nothing else to be seen upon that incredible shore, and indeed, it seemed impossible that ever any living beings could have set foot there.

Captain Future watched with close attention as the flier throbbed eastward along the shore-line. He believed that there must be some ruin or other vestige that would mark the spot which had once been frequented by the Ancients.

Doubt grew in Curt's mind, as the miles unreeled beneath without yielding any sign. After all, he told himself, he had only the evidence of that ancient world-globe in the Place of the Dead to guide him.

An hour passed, in which they had flown steadily east along the flaming coast. Curt made a sudden decision.

"Turn back and fly westward down the coast, Grag," he ordered. "It may be in that direction."

The robot obeyed, and the flier raced back at top speed over the ground they had covered, then moved on westward along the shore.

Again they watched with closest attention. Yet still there was nothing to see but the lava-crusted rock slopes, and the evilly glowing red ocean of molten lava that stretched away on their right.

Blasts of sulfurous air, and howling currents of superheated gases shrieked like fiends around them. The small rocket-flier pitched uneasily, yet Grag held it steadily above the fiery coast.

"Slow down!" Captain Future cried suddenly to the robot, his big figure tensing.

He had glimpsed something ahead—a queer opening in the rock shore at the edge of the lava sea.

THEY glided closer, hovered above the spot. From Curt Newton came an exclamation.

"This may be the place we're looking for, Grag!" he declared.

"But I see nothing, master—nothing but a big round hole in the shore, into which the lava is pouring," boomed the robot puzzledly.

Below them, there was a large, jagged circular opening in the rock slope of the hills, just where the fire ocean lapped against it.

As a result, a stream of the molten lava was pouring ceaselessly down over the lip of that opening, with a dull, reverberating thunder.

"There's a big cavernous space of some kind down there in the rock," Captain Future declared. "And that round opening leading down into it is too round to be natural. It looks as though it had been artificially enlarged at some time in the past."

"Do you think then that the place of the Ancients we are hunting is down in that hole?" Grag asked incredulously.

"It's a chance," Curt said. "We've seen no place else that could be what we're looking for. We'll investigate this."

"But how do we get down in there?" Grag boomed puzzledly. "There does not seem to be any opening except this one through which the lava falls, master."

Curt grinned at the big robot.

"When there's only one door to go through, you can't take the wrong one, Grag. That's our way in."

Grag stared.

"Down through that opening alongside the falling lava? There is barely enough room for the flier to make it without being caught in the fire-fall."

"Enough room is as good as a light-year," Curt shrugged. "Take her on down, Grag."

Curt gave the order coolly, yet he knew the perilous nature of the descent they were about to attempt.

He would have taken the controls himself, but knew that the robot would take that as a lack of confidence on his part. And he had perfect faith in Grag's abilities.

Grag moved the controls slightly, the robot's photoelectric eyes peering downward. The little rocket-flier sank gently toward the dark, jagged opening through which the fire-fall plunged into unguessable depths.

Down sank the little craft, on an even keel, supported by its keel-tubes. The cataract of falling lava was only a yard away on their one side, and its thunder was deafening.

Wild air-currents screaming upward shook the flier as it sank lower. Its stern rasped ominously against the rock side of the opening, threatening to send the ship lurching into the falling lava.

But Grag steadied the craft, kept it sinking directly downward. In a moment they had descended through the opening into a vast, dim subterranean space weirdly illuminated by the red glow of the falling lava.

"Run into the cavern a little and then land, Grag," Captain Future ordered excitedly.

They were hovering near the northern end of the enormous underground space. It extended shadowly southward, a cavern a thousand feet wide and of unguessable length.

The molten red lava of the fire-fall thundered down into a flaming pool, and then ran down the center of the cavern in a sunken channel or canal, a flaming, sluggish river.

Grag landed the flier on the rock floor of the dim cavern, near that fiery river. In a moment, Curt and his companion were emerging.

"This place is incredible," declared Curt, raising his voice above the deafening thunder of the cataract.

"Even the caverns of Uranus are not as uncanny as *this!*" Grag agreed, staring in awe.

Captain Future felt a throb of leaping excitement that kindled higher each moment.

"It's the place of the Ancients we were hunting!" he cried. "See!"

A little farther along the cavern from them, upon either side of the flaming lava river, rose two strange statues of silvery metal.

They represented creatures almost exactly like the Jovians, erect bipeds with round heads, unhuman but strangely noble features, and limbs that ended in flipperlike hands and feet.

The metal figures stood, each with a slender arm upraised, as though to warn Captain Future and the robot back. And upon the pedestal of each statue was a lengthy inscription in queer, wedge-shaped characters.

"The Ancients?" Grag said wonderingly as they paused beneath one of the statues. "But they look just like the Jovians."

"Yes," Captain Future nodded, his gray eyes gleaming. "I believe that the great Ancients *were* nothing but Jovians such as inhabit this world today."

The big robot stared at Curt, his simple mind trying to comprehend the statement.

"But the Jovians today do not build great cities and statues and machines," Grag objected. "They cannot do the things the Ancients are supposed to have done."

"I know," Curt said thoughtfully, more to himself than to the robot. "Yet, I've felt all along that the Jovians are simply the descendants of the mysterious Ancients of whom they tell legends—that the great race of the Ancients had its civilization swept away by some catastrophe.

"If I'm right," Curt added, "the present Jovians have not even a suspicion that the Ancients they revere were their own forefathers. All they

have are vague legends, distorted by ages."

"They look as though they were warning us to stay out of here," said Grag, peering up at the solemn statues.

"We're going on," Captain Future said, striding forward, his big figure animated by driving determination.

They passed the silvery figures, and moved on along the edge of the fiery lava river whose dancing flames eerily illuminated the cavern.

Sulfurous smoke from the lava drifted about them, and the heat from it was fierce on their faces. From behind them came the perpetual booming thunder of the awful fire-cataract.

"See, master!" called Grag, pointing ahead with his metal arm. "Machines!"

Vague, towering metal shapes loomed up out of the dim shadows ahead. They were big mechanisms of so alien and unfamiliar a design that their purpose was unfathomable.

ONE was a complexity of cogged wheels of silver metal, geared to a sliding arm whose end suggested the muzzle of a gun. Another was a huge upright metal bulb that suggested a cyclotron in appearance.

Upon the base of each machine was a lengthy inscription in the queer, wedge-shaped characters of the Ancients.

"If I could only read those!" Captain Future exclaimed tensely. "Here, for some mysterious reason, were gathered all the powers and weapons of that perished race. And I can't translate the key to this riddle, discover those powers!"

"Maybe you can decipher those characters in time, master," Grag suggested.

"Time? There is no time, now!" Curt exclaimed. "Unless we find in here the powers we need to crush the Space Emperor, and return to do that at once, the Jovians will have trampled Jungletown and the other Earthmen towns out of existence!"

Curt was feeling the strain of agonizing apprehension. The knowledge that somewhere southward the Black One was spurring the Jovian hordes on to the attack was like a prodding goad in his mind.

"But we can't decipher these inscriptions at once. Nobody could," he muttered hopelessly.

"I hear someone in here," Grag suddenly said uneasily. "Someone living!"

"Be quiet and listen," Captain Future commanded. "Your ears are keener than mine, Grag."

Curt's hand had dropped to the hilt of his proton-pistol. Standing motionless, listening intently, he cast his glance quickly around.

He could see nothing but the mysterious, silent mechanisms towering about him in the red-lit shadows, the dim spaces of the cavern stretching southward. And he could hear nothing but the thunderous reverberation of the fire-fall.

"I hear it again," Grag asserted in a moment. "Someone moving—"

"I hear too, now!" Curt exclaimed, his keen ears catching the slight, shuffling sound above the thunderous roar. "It's from farther along the cavern."

He drew his pistol swiftly, and Grag imitated him.

"Come on," Curt muttered. "There's someone else in here. If it's the Space Emperor—"

His pulses leaped at the thought, even though he knew that his next encounter with the mysterious plotter might be his last.

They crept forward, big Grag moving soundlessly on his padded feet. They moved around towering, dusty machines, on along the flaming river, deeper into the great cavern.

"There — an Earthman!" Grag boomed, pointing his metal arm.

Curt had seen the man at the same moment. He was not a hundred yards ahead.

A slight-looking figure in a worn brown zipper-suit, the man lay sprawled on his face on the rock floor of the cavern. Near him stood a table which bore an extinguished argon-lamp, and many papers covered with wedge-shaped characters.

"He's either unconscious or sleeping, master," said the robot.

Captain Future saw that the man's limbs were moving restlessly, as though in sleep. It was the sound Grag had heard.

Curt bent over the man, and as he did so he smelled an acrid, unforgettable odor.

"This man's been drugged," he declared. "He's been given a shot of *somnal*, the Mercurian sleep-drug."

He turned the man over on his back. The face of the drugged sleeper was exposed to the red glow of the fire-river.

It was a serious, spectacled, haggard young face that Curt had never seen before. The red-haired adventurer stared down at the man, utterly perplexed.

Then he noticed a monogram on the sleeper's synthesilk jacket. The letters were "KL."

"Kenneth Lester!" Curt cried. "That's who this is—the missing archaeologist!"

CHAPTER XIX

The Epic of Ages

CAPTAIN FUTURE'S pulses throbbed with excitement as he raised the drugged man to a sitting position.

He had felt all along that Kenneth Lester was somehow the key to this whole great planetary plot. And now at last he had found the young archaeologist.

"He's been drugged more than once," boomed the robot. "See the needle-scars on his wrist."

"I can bring him around, I think," Curt muttered.

He fished in his belt for his medicine-kit. It was hardly larger than his finger, but inside it were minute vials of the most powerful drugs known in the Solar System.

Captain Future dipped a sterile needle into one of those vials, and then pressed its wet point into Kenneth Lester's veins.

As the tiny drop of super-powerful anti-narcotic raced through the young archaeologist's bloodstream, he began to stir. In a moment he opened dazed, dark eyes. He looked haggard, worn.

"Why don't you kill me, and get it over with?" he asked hoarsely, looking up unseeingly. "This horrible existence—"

Then as Lester's vision cleared and he saw Captain Future and the towering metal robot bending over him, he uttered a startled cry.

"Who—what—"

"I'm Captain Future," Curt told him rapidly. "You may have heard of me."

"Captain Future?" Lester cried incredulously.

The young archaeologist knew that name, as did everyone in the Solar System. As it sank into his fogged mind, a wild relief showed on his haggard face.

"Thank God you're here!" he sobbed. "It's been a hellish death-in-life for me here, these last weeks. The Space Emperor—"

"Who is the Space Emperor?" Curt asked swiftly, hanging on the answer.

But again he was doomed to disappointment.

"I don't know!" cried young Lester. Then he raged feebly, "Whoever he is, he's a fiend from hell! He's kept me here, for how many weeks I can't guess—forcing me to decipher these ancient Jovian inscriptions for him, and leaving me drugged whenever he went away."

"You were the one who found this place originally, weren't you?" Curt asked.

He had been sure of that, from the first. And he found now that his reasoning had been correct.

"Yes," nodded Lester weakly. "I found it, and I thought I had made the greatest archaeological discovery in the history of the Solar System."

He was sitting up, now, talking with feverish rapidity as he looked up into Captain Future's tanned, set face.

"I came to Jupiter because I had heard of Jovian legends that spoke of a great, ancient race who had once inhabited this planet. I believed that there must be some basis to those legends, and resolved to track it down.

"From Jungletown, I went northward into the fern-jungles and there I tried to learn more from the Jovians, but those primitive creatures became sullenly silent and suspicious when I mentioned the legends of the Ancients. I did learn that they gathered now and then for strange ceremonies at a spot they called the Place of the Dead, so I trailed them there and found it to be a ruined city of the Ancients.

"There was a world-globe map of Jupiter made by the Ancients there. It showed the sites of their cities. But one site was marked differently than the rest, and I guessed it was more important. It was situated on the shore of the Fire Sea, where no city could ordinarily have been.

"So I came north alone in my little rocket-flier and searched along the shore of the flaming sea until I found the opening down into this place. I got down into it with my flier—and found it to be a wonderful storehouse of the powers and knowledge of the Ancients."

KENNETH LESTER'S haggard face lit for a moment with scientific passion as he continued.

"I succeeded in deciphering some inscriptions here, and learned something of the history of those great Ancients. I learned that ages ago they had had a mighty civilization, as high if not higher than that of Earth today. Along certain scientific lines, they had gone farther than we have.

"They had succeeded in solving many a problem that has baffled Earth physicists. They had achieved intra-atomic means of power. They had even been able to perfect a means of making matter effectively immaterial, by causing a step-up of the frequency of atomic vibration which allowed such matter to interpenetrate other matter freely as though it did not exist. They had used this immaterialization process to explore even the bowels of the planet.

"Also their biologists had found a method of causing atavism at will, which allowed them to study the past evolution of their own and every other race. The method depended upon the fact that every living organism has glandular organ which is the real control of its physical and mental charac teristics, and which, if it is paralyzed or atrophied, allows the subject to degenerate rapidly into the past forms from which its race evolved.

"The Ancients had done all these things, but apparently they had not risen above the reach of passions and emotions. For an internecine war broke out finally between their cities. It was carried on with unbelievable ferocity, and it laid their great civilization in ruins.

"Finally when only a few of the Ancients retained the former scientific knowledge, and the rest had become half-civilized tribes wandering amid the ruins of former cities, those few remaining enlightened ones sought to preserve the triumphs of their race. Hoping that some day their people might be willing to forget war and again rise to peaceful civilization, those few Ancients gathered in this secret cavern all the scientific powers and instruments they could collect, so that they might not be utterly lost."

The worn features of young Kenneth Lester showed his deep, bitter emotion as he continued.

"All this, I say, I learned by deciphering some of the inscriptions in this cavern. I realized this was a wonderful storehouse of scientific secrets, which only the proper authorities should know about, lest they fall into the wrong hands.

"So I wrote a report of my find, for Governor Quale. I flew down to Jungletown and mailed it to him, and then flew hastily back here to stand guard over my find. I expected the governor to come here at once.

"But two nights later, as I was sleeping here, I awoke to find myself bound and blindfolded. Someone had learned of my report and had come here to secure the scientific powers of which I had spoken. And that person tortured me into telling all that I had learned so far.

"He learned the secret of immaterialization from me, thus. He used it at once to make himself immaterial, and also he learned the secret of the atavism weapon and took one of the instruments that produce it with him.

"This man whose identity I did not know, the Space Emperor as he called himself, has come here many times since. Each time, he has forced me under threat of instant death to decipher for him more of the secrets of the Ancients. Each time he has left, he has drugged me so that I could not escape while he was gone."

LESTER'S eyes flashed with wild fear as he concluded.

"The Space Emperor boasted to me of what he has been doing with these powers, Captain Future! He has said that he has used the atavism beam on Earthmen, to convince the Jovians that the Earthmen are cursed. He intended to use the Jovians to establish his power over this whole planet!"

Captain Future nodded his red head grimly.

"Yes, that black devil has been doing that. And his plot is reaching its climax, for right now the Jovians are gathering to attack the Earthman towns."

Lester's haggard face went white.

"Can't you stop him some way, Captain Future?"

"Not until I too can achieve the immaterialization that protects him from all attack," Curt replied. "That's why I came here, looking for the means to do that. Can you tell me the secret of that?" he asked tensely.

Curt hung tautly upon the answer. For upon it, he well knew, depended the success or failure of his effort to halt the chaos threatening Jupiter.

"Yes—there are a number of the immaterialization mechanisms here," Kenneth Lester answered quickly.

The big adventurer stared at him wonderingly, though his pulses leaped.

"Then why didn't you use one to escape, and walk through the rock?" he demanded.

"You forget. I've been drugged every moment except when the Space Emperor was here!" Lester reminded. "And when he was here, he stood ready to kill me at my first wrong move. He never allowed me to touch any mechanism. He made me read and translate the inscriptions, and then he operated the things."

Lester staggered to his feet.

"But at last I'm awake, and that

devil not here! Come with me and I'll show you what you want."

Grag held the staggering young archaeologist to keep him from falling.

"The far end of the cavern," Lester said weakly. "This way."

Curt hastened excitedly with Lester and the robot along the dim length of the cavern, through the towering machines by the edge of the flaming lava river.

Captain Future saw that the end of the cavern was just ahead. There was a jagged aperture in its wall, through which flowed the molten lava stream to empty into unfathomable depths beneath.

Kenneth Lester stumbled toward a big metal rack upon which were ranged dusty rows of the instruments of the Ancients. There were many of the atavism-beam devices, like small flat lanterns with translucent lenses.

And there were a number of belts to which were attached hemispherical metal devices with a simple switch.

"Those are the immaterializers," Lester said, reaching forward.

"Master, look out!" Grag yelled suddenly and pushed Captain Future aside with a violent push.

Curt spun around, though off balance, in time to see what happened.

The Space Emperor stood in the front part of the cavern, near their own rocket-flier. Curt knew instantly that the dark plotter had come down through the rock in an immaterial state, for he had not come in any flier of his own.

But the Space Emperor was material for the moment, for he had raised a flare gun and had loosed its beam at Curt's back. Grag had knocked the red-haired man aside just in time.

"The Space Emperor!" Kenneth Lester cried wildly as he saw.

CURT wasted no time in words. His pistol was already in his hand and he was triggering.

But as he moved, his enemy moved his hand also, toward his belt. And Curt's proton-beam again tore through the dark criminal without harming him in the least.

The Space Emperor had again made himself immaterial, just in time. They saw him glide swiftly back toward their rocket-flier and into it, through its walls.

"Get him!" Curt yelled, plunging wildly forward. "He's going to take our flier!"

It was too late. Already the rocket-flier was rising swiftly from the cavern floor and darting toward the entrance of the fire-fall.

The Space Emperor had made himself material once more inside the little craft and was stealing it.

Captain Future shot at it, but though the proton-beam scorched the side of the darting flier, the craft did not stop. It zoomed up past the thundering cataract of lava, and disappeared up through the vertical shaft.

"He got away!" Grag boomed furiously, coming back from his vain attempt to overtake the flier. "Master, how could he know that we were here?"

"He must have heard from Joan or the others when they returned to Jungletown of the quest we'd gone on," Curt exclaimed. "And he came here to trap us."

As he spoke, Captain Future was snatching out his pocket-televisor.

"If I can call Simon and Otho, they'll soon be here in the *Comet* to get us out!"

Again and again he pushed the call-button of the little instrument. But no answer came.

"The devil!" Curt exclaimed. "The rock above us must contain a heavy metal content that screens off our televisor signals. The Space Emperor must have known that, damn him!"

"Then how can we get out?" Grag asked. "We cannot climb up that shaft down which the fire-fall comes —not even Otho could climb out there."

"No, we can't climb out there, but we can get out *through* the rock above us!" Captain Future cried. "We've got those immaterializing mechanisms, and Lester here knows how to use them."

Kenneth Lester was white as death. He swayed as he stood, and shook his head in dull, hopeless despair.

"We can't do it, Captain Future,"

he said heavily. "We'd die if we tried it."

"Why would we?" Curt demanded, puzzled.

Lester shrugged hopelessly.

"We have no suit such as the Space Emperor wears. We'd become immaterial, but we would have no air-supply to breathe in that state. We would suffocate long before we could go out through the rock!"

CHAPTER XX

Power of the Ancients

CAPTAIN FUTURE was undaunted by the archaeologist's objection. The big red-headed adventurer squared his wide shoulders, and into his tanned face there came a determined fighting-look.

"You forget that Grag doesn't need to breathe!" he exclaimed. "He can go up through the rock, and then get us out."

Hope lit in Kenneth Lester's haggard eyes.

"If he could do it—"

Curt hurried back to the rack that held the dusty instruments of the Ancients. He came back with two of the belts to which were attached the hemispherical immaterializers.

He belted one around the big robot, and the other one around his own waist.

"But you won't need one, since you can't go out through the rock," Lester said puzzledly.

"I'll need one if we do get out, when I meet the Space Emperor," Curt said meaningly. "Show me how the things work."

Lester explained.

"The hemispheres are projectors of a powerful electromagnetic radiation whose excitation acts to step up the frequency of atomic vibration of any matter. This action is confined to the wearer of the mechanism by means of this control on the side of the hemisphere, which limits the action to the wearer's body and clothing."

Carefully, with considerable doubt and anxiety, Lester set the control he spoke of on both the instruments.

"The hemispheres also embody a means of projecting speech, even when the wearer is in the immaterial state," he went on. "As far as I can comprehend, it is done by translating the sonic vibrations of the immaterialized one's speech into similar sonic waves in the matter around him, by means of a smaller auxiliary stepdown transformer inside the hemisphere. A similar principle in reverse, takes care of hearing."

"I wondered how the Space Emperor was able to speak and be heard when he was immaterial," Curt muttered.

Kenneth Lester turned.

"It's all ready," he said anxiously to Captain Future.

"What shall I do, master?" Grag asked, looking toward the big redhead with his gleaming eyes quite calmly.

"First you must set your gravitation equalizer at zero, Grag," Curt told him.

The robot obeyed, touching the control of the flat equalizer which he wore upon his breast.

As he set the thing at zero, thus nullifying all gravitational attraction upon himself, the great robot hung floating an inch above the floor of the cavern, drifting slightly this way and that with every little movement.

"Take my proton-pistol, Grag," Curt went on tensely, handing the weapon to the robot. "Now when you touch the switch of this hemisphere at your belt, it will make you immaterial. By firing the pistol downward, the reaction of its force will cause you to float upward.

"You will float up right through the rock above this cavern. You must wait until you have reached the outside surface, and then you must turn off the switch of the hemisphere at once. Is that clear?"

"Yes, master," Grag said doubtfully. "But when I have done that, and am outside, how shall I get you two out of here?"

"You will have to get vines from the jungle and make a strong rope and lower it down that shaft t h r o u g h which the fire cataract falls," Captain Future told him. "Then you can pull us up."

"Very well, master," the robot said docilely. "Shall I start now?"

Curt nodded.

"The sooner the better, Grag."

THEY saw Grag touch the switch of the hemispherical instrument at his belt.

There seemed no immediate change in the robot's appearance. But when Curt thrust forth his hand to touch Grag, it went through the robot as though he did not exist.

"I do not like this much, master," boomed the big metal creature, uneasily. "It makes me feel as though I were not real at all, like those Mind Men we found on Saturn."

Curt made an urgent signal, and the robot pointed the pistol down toward the ground and fired the proton-beam.

At once, under the reactive push of the beam, slight as it was, Grag's huge body rose floatingly from the floor.

Curt and young Lester watched tensely. The scene was weird, incredible. The great, gloomy cavern of looming machines and deep shadows, bisected by the river of flaming lava that flowed down its center from the thundering fire-fall; the immaterialized robot, floating up toward the rocky roof.

The scene became even more weird a moment later. For when Grag's slowly rising body reached the rock ceiling, the robot's head disappeared right into the rock. Then his metal shoulders were hidden, and finally his whole body was gone from sight above.

Curt drew a long breath. There had been a thrilling uncanniness to the sight of the robot entering the solid rock. Even though he understood the scientific principle of the process, that did not make it less weird to his eyes.

"He ought to be on the surface in a few minutes," Curt muttered. "The rock above this cavern can be no more than a few hundred feet in thickness."

Kenneth Lester looked at him fearfully.

"But what if he should lose his sense of direction while he's floating blindly through that solid rock? He might move in the wrong direction and get lost in the rock mass of the planet!"

Captain Future had thought of that. His lips tightened, as he waited.

Minutes went by. Each minute seemed abnormally long to the big adventurer. What was going on southward while he was trapped here? What was the Space Emperor doing?

"Come on, Grag," he whispered under his breath as he waited. "Hurry!"

Yet still, there came nothing to indicate that the robot had succeeded in escaping.

By the time almost an hour had passed, Kenneth Lester's haggard face had lost all hope. The archaeologist sat down as though he had ceased to struggle against the inevitable.

"He didn't make it," he muttered. "We might have known he couldn't."

Curt did not answer. He paced restlessly to and fro, glancing every few moments toward the fire-fall.

Suddenly he shouted in excitement. Something had dropped down the shaft of the fire cataract—a long rope of tough vines tied together, that now dangled with its end swinging a little above the lava pool.

"Grag made it!" Curt cried.

They ran forward, stopping at the edge of the molten lava pool which lay beneath the shaft.

The vine rope hung out of their reach—more than a dozen feet out above the hissing, bubbling lava.

BLINDED by fumes and scorching heat from the thundering cataract of molten rock, Captain Future and Lester stared baffledly at the rope.

"I'll jump for it, and once I get hold of it I can swing over to you," Curt said rapidly, backing away from the edge of the pool.

"If you miss it when you jump, you'll die in that molten rock!" Lester cried appalledly.

Curt grinned at him.

"Miss an easy little jump like that? Why Otho would never forgive me if I did."

Before Lester could protest further, Curt ran forward. All the strength of his superb muscles he put into a

[Turn to page 86]

springing leap that sent him flying out through the air above the glowing, hissing lava.

His fingers caught the vine rope, and held. There was a nasty slipping of the tough vine, as its knots tightened under his weight. But Grag had fastened carefully, and the improvised rope did not give.

Hanging above the lava, Curt began to swing back and forth like a pendulum, the arc of his swing increasing each time.

Finally, he was swinging widely out over the edge of the lava pool, where Lester stood.

The young archaeologist grabbed the vine rope also. They swung back together out over the lava pool. Curt quickly gave a jerk on the vine to signal Grag.

They began to be pulled up. It was a perilous situation, and the unnerving quality of it was increased by the cataract of molten lava that rushed down close beside them, to thunder into the pool below.

Lester's face was ghastly, as he clung.

He cried chokingly to Captain Future, who barely caught the words.

"Can't—hold on—"

The archaeologist's grip upon the vine was slipping, weak as he was from his long, drugged captivity.

Curt grabbed him just in time with his left arm, hanging onto the vine with his right. The weight put a terrific strain on the red-headed adventurer's muscles. No man less perfect physically could have withstood that strain.

Grag was hauling them up rapidly now. The tremendous strength of the robot was standing him in good stead. Upward they rose, revolving slowly at the end of the vine rope, Lester now an unconscious burden inside Curt's arm.

Curt was nearly overcome by the fumes of the falling lava. Wild air-currents from below screamed and howled around him.

Then he glimpsed the mouth of the shaft above.

At the north side of the opening, the lava sea poured in. At the south edge, upon the rock brink, stood Grag's great metal figure.

In a few moments, Curt stood with the robot upon the rock. It was still night, and they stood beneath the combined light of three moons and the red glare of the Fire Sea.

"Good work, Grag!" Captain Future exclaimed, as he lowered the unconscious archaeologist to the rock.

Grag was pleased.

"It took me a long time to get far enough away from the Fire Sea to find vines growing, or I would not have taken so long," he explained.

Curt snatched out his pocket-televisor once more. Again he pressed the call-button.

"Ought to be able to get Otho and Simon now that we're out of the cavern," he muttered.

Presently came the faintest of answering signals from Otho.

"Come in the Comet and get us!" Captain Future ordered. "I'll leave the call-signal of the televisor on as a beam to guide you here."

HE could just hear the faint, distance-dimmed reply from Otho.

"Coming!"

While they waited, Curt hastily examined Lester. The young archaeologist was still unconscious.

"He's in bad shape, but he'll pull through with rest and treatment," Curt declared.

"Master, the Comet comes!" Grag called a little later.

Out of the south like a shooting star drove the little teardrop ship. It dived toward them with a scream of splitting air, and came jarringly to rest on the rock ledge.

Curt shouldered inside, and Grag followed with the senseless archaeologist.

"I've got the immaterializer, Simon!" Curt cried eagerly to the Brain. "Now I can hunt down the Space Emperor and meet him on even terms."

"Too late for that, lad!" rasped Simon Wright. "The Jovians are already on their way to attack Jungletown. They're swarming toward the town from all their villages—thousands of them. By this time, they must be there!"

Captain Future felt the full shock

of the Brain's tidings, his big figure stiffening. And Otho was shouting.

"The atavism cases in the Jungletown hospital have broken loose, too!" the android hissed. "We believe they were purposely released by the Space Emperor, to add to the panic."

"Head back toward the town at full speed," Curt's voice flared. "There may still be time."

The *Comet* jerked upward, and screamed low above the moonlit jungles toward the south.

The night was wild. The silver radiance of Callisto, Europa and Ganymede was paled by the stupendous red glow of the Fire Sea behind them.

Like a meteor, the teardrop ship knifed the air of Jupiter. Curt watched with superhuman tenseness for the lights of Jungletown. If the Space Emperor's hordes of duped Jovians had already reached it—

Far ahead on the rim of the moonlit jungle appeared the clustered lights of the town. They seemed to leap toward Curt, as Otho recklessly swooped to a landing in one of the blazing-lit streets.

"The Jovians aren't here yet!" Captain Future cried as he tore the door of the ship open. "There's still time—"

Then a moment later his face froze in incredulous horror, and he uttered a sharp cry.

"This place has become a hell!"

Jungletown, under the light of the three great moons and the shaking, flaring fire-glow northward, had indeed become an inferno.

Men and monsters were battling in its streets. Monsters—that had once been men!

Hairy ape-brutes, four-footed feral creatures, scaled reptiles that fought and tore.

Captain Future's pistol leaped out and his proton-beam shot to stun a roaring ape-creature that was rushing toward them.

"Come on—we've got to find Gurney!" he exclaimed.

The big adventurer's red head towered above the wild turmoil as he pushed forward through the streets, Grag and Otho close at his side, the android carrying Simon Wright.

The place was a nightmare of terror.

With chaos of panic reigning and monstrous beasts roaming its streets, Jungletown seemed a city of men reeling back toward the brute.

Boom! Boom! Ground-drums out in the jungles were thundering unceasingly now, in a crescendo of fierce excitement.

"The Jovians must be near here!" Curt exclaimed. Then he yelled, "Gurney! Ezra Gurney!"

The marshal was forcing down the street, leading a little group of people who fought off the prowling monsters with their flare-guns.

"CAPTAIN FUTURE, this looks like the end of us!" cried Gurney, his eyes wild in the moonlight. "I can't organize any defense, and the Jovians are near now."

"I'm going out to the Jovians now," Curt exclaimed. "The Space Emperor is out there, and destroying him is the only thing that can stop them now."

Joan Randall, her face deathly white in the moonlight, sprang from behind the marshal to grasp Curt's arm.

"Don't go!" she pleaded. "Eldred Kells went out to try and talk the Jovians into peace, and he didn't come back. And Governor Quale went after him, and he didn't come back either!"

"We caught Lucas Brewer," Gurney told Captain Future hoarsely. "Found him hiding here in town. Not that it makes much difference now, I guess."

"I'm going," Curt told them. "Otho, you and Grag and Simon stay here. This is—"

"Look!" yelled Otho, pointing a finger, his eyes suddenly blazing. "Here they come now!"

A deep roar of thousands of fierce bass voices rent the air at that instant.

Out of the jungle into the clearing around Jungletown, a solid mass of Jovians, on foot and mounted on lopers, was pouring.

Flare-guns gleamed in their mass, ominously.

And at the head of them moved a dark, gliding figure—the Space Emperor.

CHAPTER XXI

The Unmasking

FOR a moment the little group around Captain Future seemed frozen by sight of that fierce, advancing horde.

"It's all up!" Ezra Gurney cried. "There's thousands of those critters."

"I can still stop those Jovians," Curt Newton flashed. "Wait here—all of you!"

"Nothin' can stop them now!" Ezra Gurney exclaimed hoarsely.

But Captain Future's big form was already running out through the moonlight toward the oncoming horde.

The Jovian masses were still pouring solidly out of the jungle. Whipped to fanatic madness by the Space Emperor's playing on their superstitions, convinced that they must destroy the Earthmen, they rolled forward in a solid wave after the dark, gliding figure of their leader.

Captain Future came into full view of the oncoming hordes, his tall figure looming in the moonlight, as he faced the Space Emperor and his followers.

The Space Emperor stopped, in sheer amazement it seemed. And the Jovians behind him stopped also. For a full moment, the horde and its mysterious leader faced Captain Future.

Then Curt Newton cried out in a loud voice to the Jovian masses, in their own language.

"Why do you come here to attack the Earthmen?" he shouted. "They have never harmed you. You have allowed this Earthman to lead you into a great crime."

"He is no Earthman!" cried scores of fierce Jovian voices. "He is the Living Ancient, the last of the great Ancients who has commanded us to sweep away you Earthmen."

"I'll show you," Curt cried, and leaped in a flying spring toward the startled black figure.

As Curt sprang through the air, his hands were on the switches of his gravitation equalizer and of the hemi-spherical mechanism at his belt.

The equalizer he snapped to zero. And as his other hand snicked the switch of the immaterializer, he felt a sickening shock of violent force through every fiber.

There was no other sensation. But he knew that he was immaterial as the Space Emperor now. And then he struck the Space Emperor—*solidly.*

Both Curt and the dark plotter being now immaterial as regarded ordinary matter, they were on a basis of equality. Because their bodies had both received the same atomic vibration step-up, they were real and solid to each other.

But Curt had no air to breathe such as the Space Emperor had inside his suit. He felt a gasping shock of agony in his lungs as he seized the super-criminal.

He and the Space Emperor struggled wildly. And as they struggled, drifting floatingly, they were both floating through the Jovians who had crowded wildly forward. The green natives recoiled in horror.

Curt knew he could last but seconds, without air to breathe. Already his head was roaring. He was trying to reach the switch of the Space Emperor's immaterializer. The other was trying, desperately, to prevent him.

Consciousness seemed draining out of Curt's brain. He vaguely glimpsed Grag and Otho wildly trying to help him, but unable to grasp either himself or his antagonist.

CURT made a savage last effort, putting into it the last of his fading strength. His hand struggled to the switch of the other's mechanism. He snapped it open—

And the Space Emperor became like a phantom in his arms, unreal and tenuous. The dark criminal had been made normal again—and Curt was still in the other, shadowy state.

He glimpsed Grag's great metal fist strike at the Space Emperor. His lungs were on fire, the world dark about him, as he sought to snap open the switch of his own immaterializer. It finally snicked under his fingers—again the sickening shock—

Captain Future found himself staggering on the ground—the solid ground—as he reset his equalizer also.

"The Space Emperor!" he choked. "Did he get away?"

"No, master!" boomed Grag.

Curt stared. The robot's mighty fist had crushed the whole top of the Space Emperor's helmet.

All this swift struggle had taken but seconds. The Jovian horde had watched, frozen with astonishment. Now, with a wild yell of rage, they serged forward.

"Wait!" yelled Captain Future with all his strength. "See!"

And with frantic fingers, he tore the black, flexible suit off the prone figure of the plotter.

An Earthman's body was revealed in the bright moonlight! It was the body of a tall man whose blond head had been crushed in by Grag's awful blow. And his face was the face of—

"Eldred Kells!" yelled Gurney wildly.

It was Kells' dead face that lay there in the moonlight. Kells—the Space Emperor!

Curt Newton faced the Jovians. They had again frozen. In their mien was an incredulous horror.

"You see!" Captain Future shouted to them. "The Living Ancient was a deceiver who duped you. He was not one of the great Ancients, but merely an Earthman like myself."

"It is true," said a Jovian to the stunned horde. "We have been deceived."

"Return then to your villages and forget this mad folly of war against Earthmen," Curt said clearly. "There is room on this great planet for both Earthman and Jovian to live in peace, is there not?"

There was a little, tense silence before the big Jovian who seemed the spokesman answered.

"It is the truth—there is room for both our races," the Jovian answered slowly. "We only prepared to war upon you because we thought the spirits of the Ancients wished it."

Slowly, in a dead silence, the Jovians turned and started to shuffle back into the jungle.

No word was spoken by them. Curt Newton looked after them, pity on his taut face. He knew what a tremendous shock to them had been the discovery that they had been deceived.

Otho and Grag were at his side, and Ezra Gurney and Joan Randall and the others were running forward.

Gurney looked down at the dead face of Eldred Kells as though unable yet to believe his eyes.

"It can't be true!" the marshal muttered.

Joan Randall cried out suddenly.

"Here's Governor Quale!" she announced.

QUALE was stumbling out of the jungle. He came toward them, his face pallid.

"The Jovians captured me when I went out to look for Kells," he said hoarsely. "They released me just now, and I gathered they'd given up the attack—"

His voice trailed off as he saw the dead body of the vice-governor, in its dark suit. He looked up with a wild question in his eyes.

"Yes," Captain Future said heavily. "Kells was the Space Emperor. I've guessed it for some time."

"How could you know?" Quale cried incredulously.

"I knew the Space Emperor was one of four men who could have trapped Joan and me in that Jovopolis hospital," Curt replied. "The four were you, Kells, Brewer and Cannig."

"You were eliminated, Governor Quale, because you were talking to Marshal Gurney on the televisor when I was trapped. You see, I confirmed the fact from Gurney that you had actually talked to him at that time.

"Brewer," Curt added, "seemed the most logical suspect then. He was giving the Jovians guns, as I discovered. But when I found that he was doing it only to get them to dig his radium, I felt he could not be the Space Emperor. He would not stir up a planetary rebellion, when his desire was to get rich from his mine! He'd have everything to lose.

"Cannig," Captain Future concluded, "had been seen with the Space Emperor, by Joan, and so he could not be the plotter. That only left Eldred Kells of the four original suspects."

"I still can't believe it of Kells!" Quale cried. "He was so capable and efficient and ambitious—"

"He was too ambitious; that was the trouble," Captain Future said somberly. "He was chafing here as a mere vice-governor, and when he read the report of his wonderful discovery which Kenneth Lester sent to your office, Kells saw his opportunity to bid for planetary power.

"He saw himself as lord of Jupiter —even as the emperor of other worlds —using the great powers and weapons of the Ancients. He might have done it, too, had he been luckier!"

"Aye," rasped Simon Wright, his glittering lens-eyes staring at the dead man. "That is the curse of you humans—lust for power. It has brought a many of you to their deaths, and it will bring many more."

CHAPTER XXII

The Way of Captain Future

CAPTAIN FUTURE stood in the pale sunlight beside the open door of the *Comet*, with Grag and Otho and Simon Wright. The little ship rested on the ground at the edge of the wilderness outside Jungletown.

The big, red-headed adventurer faced three people—Joan Randall and Sylvanus Quale and Ezra Gurney.

"Must you leave Jupiter now?" Quale was asking earnestly.

Curt grinned.

"It's got too tame around here, now that all the excitement is over."

A brief Jovian week had passed. That week had seen the complete restoration of order in the demoralized colony.

The atavism cases were slowly returning to normal, being treated with the formula Simon Wright had devised. The Jovians were again on friendly terms with the Earthmen, and there seemed no doubt that they would remain so.

A scientific commission was on its way from Earth to consult Kenneth Lester and investigate the secrets of the Ancients stored in that cavern by the Fire Sea. Meanwhile, the place was guarded.

"Everything here's washed up now," Curt was saying. "I called President Carthew today and reported so, though of course this whole affair won't be made public."

Joan Randall spoke impulsively to the big redhead. "Then the people of the System will never know what you've done for them?"

Curt laughed.

"Why should they know? I've no desire to be a hero."

"You are a hero, to every man and woman in the nine worlds," Joan said steadily.

There was a throbbing emotion in the girl's soft face as she looked into the big young adventurer's gray eyes.

"And now you're going back to that lonely home of yours on Earth's moon, to live without another human being near?"

"I'm going back to my home, and my comrades will be with me," Curt defended.

"Captain Future, are you always going to lead this hard, dangerous life?" the girl cried appealingly.

Curt's face grew somber. His voice was low-pitched, his eyes looking far away, as he answered.

"Long ago, I dedicated my life to a task," he said. "Until that task is finished, I must remain—Captain Future."

He held out his hand, and the cheerful smile came back once more into his gray eyes.

"Good-by, Joan," he said. "We'll meet again, somewhere."

He grinned at Gurney. "And I'm sure to meet *you* in that part of the System where trouble is the thickest."

There was a glimmer of tears in the girl's dark eyes as she watched Curt enter his little ship.

The cyclotrons droned, and the *Comet* shot upward into the pale sunlight. Up from Jupiter it roared, out through the dense atmosphere until the mighty planet was a vast white globe behind them, and black, starred space stretched ahead.

Toward the bright gray speck that was Earth, and the smaller white speck that was its moon, the little ship flew.

Curt Newton's eyes were queerly abstracted as he sat at the throttles. He spoke to the Brain, slowly.

"That was a great girl, Simon," he said. Then he added hastily, "Not that it can mean anything to me, you understand."

"Aye, lad, I understand," the Brain answered. "I was human once, too, you know."

"We go back to the moon now, master?" Grag said pleasedly. "I like it on the moon best."

"What's good about it?" Otho hissed gloomily. "There'll be no excitement, no action, nothing else for us to do—"

Curt grinned at the discontented android.

"Sooner or later, there'll be another call from Earth, and then I hope there's action enough for you, you crazy coot."

Yes, sooner or later dire emergency would arise again to threaten the nine worlds, and set that great signal at the North Pole flashing its summons once more.

And when the summons came, Captain Future would answer!

●

COMING NEXT ISSUE

CALLING CAPTAIN FUTURE
Another Complete Book-Length Novel
Featuring
THE WIZARD OF SCIENCE

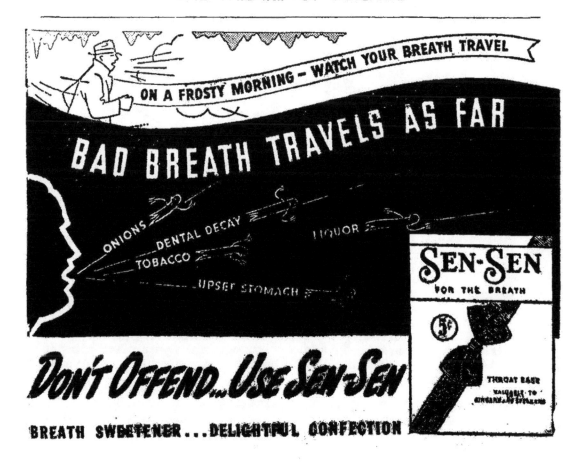

The fluid in the green vial was working!

INVISIBLE

By ERIC FRANK RUSSELL

Author of "Sinister Barrier," "The World's Eighth Wonder," etc.

HASTILY putting down the green vial, "Shorty" Mason flopped upon the settee. His legs twitched, his fingers trembled uncontrollably. The serum from the vial was a veritable hell's brew; he could feel it searing inside, shooting like heated mercury through his tortured veins.

"Highly radio-active," Professor Dainton had said.

It had meant nothing to Mason then, but it meant a lot now.

Shorty lay back, sweat beading his forehead, while Pepito, the professor's Mexican hairless dog, made weird noises out in the yard. According to Dainton's estimate, the liquid from the vial should take effect in half an hour. It had taken only fifteen minutes to perform its work on the dog.

Agony gave way to a dull, listless

ache accompanied by sensations of effervescence in the bloodstream. Mason looked at his naked legs, saw no alteration in their appearance. He stretched his nude form full length and pondered while he waited. Shorty Mason was on his uppers, but with the means to easy money right at hand, Dainton, unwittingly had provided the means. If Dainton had not got himself run over by a car there would have been no need for Mason to take a chance with the scientist's discovery. But Dainton was dead and it was up to Mason to give the stuff in the vial its first chance to work on a human being. What it did to Pepito it could do to him, he felt certain.

Only the previous Wednesday, he and the professor had stood in the backyard and observed Pepito after he had been inoculated with the serum. The dog had scuttled around with its customary joyful genuflexions, but neither of them could follow its movements. For the dog had become invisible.

Stealing another look at his legs, Mason found them becoming diaphanous, indefinite. He blinked, looked again, and smiled grimly as he realized the experiment was going to succeed.

Ten minutes later he stood in front of a full-length mirror, stroking a closely shaved head that could not be seen, feeling smooth legs that were not apparent in the glass. Perfect mimicry! What the chameleon could do in a couple of hours his body could do instantaneously and with complete faithfulness.

His chest reproduced the batik pattern of the wallpaper behind him; his feet and ankles simulated the grained oak skirting board. When he moved, the patterns moved in reverse and held their relative positions. The whole thing was incredible, yet true—the truth evident in the empty mirror. He had made himself transparent—invisible to the normal eye.

He had thought Dainton foolish enough when the latter picked him up at the prison gates and gave him a new start as an assistant. He had been certain that Dainton was unbalanced when he found that the scientist's sole object in life was to satisfy his curiosity about chameleons. Looking at the blank mirror, he knew that Dainton had been quite mad to devote half a lifetime to the development of something that was of no practical use except to crooks.

The old investigator had talked a lot about his eccentric work. Once he had handed Mason a photograph of a blossom-laden bush.

"Some of those are flowers, but others are not," he had said. "They look like blossoms, but they aren't."

"What are they then?" Shorty had asked.

"Examples of perfect mimicry," the professor had replied. "They are clusters of plant-sucking Phormnia, insects of the Fulgoridæ family. Individually, they look like tiny, plume-backed, wax-coated porcupines of the insect world, and they are found in the Bengal Dooars and the jungles of Assam. Their mimicry is so truthful that even birds perching on the same branch can be deceived."

Mason had gaped at the photograph, tried hard to discern which blooms were really blooms and which were insects. It was impossible to tell.

"Countless centuries of evolution had moulded that protective ability," the professor had declared, "yet the chameleon can exercise similar powers in a mere couple of hours, and adapt the effect to circumstances."

"So what?" had been Mason's query.

"It is a longer jump from a million years to a couple of hours than it is from a couple of hours to a split second." A determined gleam in his eyes, Dainton had added, "What I am seeking is the secret of instantaneous camouflage!"

THEN Dainton had plunged into a long, involved speech about chameleons employing some glandular substance that could do to the atoms and molecules of the epidermis what adrenalin could do to the heart. He had talked about chameleons speeding up their vibratory rate until they were reflecting those frequencies of the spectrum compatible with their surroundings. He thought the process could be improved, perfected. Mason had dutifully agreed, without having the faintest idea of what all the talk was about.

But now he knew that Dainton had found success on the eve of his death. How the formula functioned, Mason neither knew nor cared. The effect was what he wanted.

Bending toward the mirror, Mason saw the faint outline of himself. It was difficult to discern. He decided that he could see it because he knew it was there, also because he was standing still and his surface was nearer to the glass than was the surface he was imitating.

TAKING a hand-mirror, he turned around and surveyed his back. It reproduced the batik. All sides of him merged into their respective backgrounds, regardless of the angles from which they were viewed. To all intents and purposes, he was an invisible man.

Satisfied, Mason decided that now was the time to collect the John Legattrick Company's payroll and thus turn another scientific achievement to the practical use of crime.

At the front door, force of habit drove his hand toward his hat and coat. He resisted the impulse, and paused with his fingers on the door-lock. The hall mirror gave him the confidence he required to step into the street stark naked. He set his heavy jaw, opened the door, and boldly stepped out.

The street was drab and sullen beneath the hidden sun, but the air was warm enough to compensate for Mason's lack of clothes. A fat little man hurried along the sidewalk, his feet pattering on the shadowless concrete. He headed straight toward Mason, his eyes studying the dull horizon, his mind occupied to the exclusion of all else. Mason dodged him with a thrill of apprehension, rapidly followed by a feeling of intense relief. The fat man trotted on.

Fourth Avenue was like a game of tag with a million blindfolded players.

Mason had to sneak around standing people, side-step walkers, and jump from the paths of men in a hurry. Several times he narrowly avoided a betraying bump; once he barely escaped being run over by a taxi.

The clock over the First Federal Bank said two minutes to eleven when Mason reached its doors. He had timed himself beautifully. Within two or three minutes a cashier and an armed guard would arrive to claim the Legattrick weekly payroll of forty thousand dollars.

A glance at the still-clouded sky, then Mason jumped for a compartment in the bank's revolving door, entering close behind an unsuspecting customer. Moving to the farther wall, he walked to and fro while he waited. His body was marble against the marble slabs; his constant motion permitted no peculiarity in perspective that might arouse suspicion in the sharp-eyed.

Forty thousand dollars was a nice little sum, he mused. A smart fellow could get around with a wad that size. All he had to do was take it, run like blazes, and hide it in a safe spot from which it could be retrieved later. He had marked out such a place a mere three hundred yards away. Once he'd dumped the money, his pursuers—if any—would have nothing visible to pursue. It was the easiest stunt in the whole history of larceny — and the green vial held enough doses for a dozen more similar exploits. Mason ceased his pondering as the bank's door spun at the stroke of eleven.

A man came through the door, a lumpy man with a big leather bag grasped in his right fist. He was followed by a lean, lanky fellow whose sharp eyes flickered beneath the visor of his peaked cap, and who carried a shoulder holster prominently in view. The first was the John Legattrick Company's cashier; the other his bodyguard.

Both men walked across the floor, up to the glass holes yawning above the counter. The first man dumped his bag on the mahogany and pushed a paper through a gap in the bullet-proof glass. The bodyguard hung around and chewed his fingernails.

Rolls of coinage were shoved across the counter, checked on a slip held by the lumpy man, then placed in his bag. Finally came the paper money, in the form of a flat, square packet. Legattrick's cashier reached for it—and grasped air.

The bundle clutched in his sweating right hand, Mason raced madly for the door. None could see him, but all could see the loot. His imprisoned heart pounded frantically on the bars of his ribs, his ears strained in expectation of shouts and curses; his shoulder muscles cringed in anticipation of impinging, tearing bullets.

No warning yells followed him; no missiles slammed into his spine. The silence was worse than an uproar. He guessed, as he reached the door, that his feet had been faster than the on-

Sprinting for the corner, he almost collided with a pedestrian whose eyes bulged at the magically suspended package. Mason swung an unseen but heavy fist to the fellow's jaw, and the man toppled to the ground. Shorty leaped over him and rounded the corner.

Eighty yards — forty — ten — separated him from the grating. He reached it a few seconds before his pursuers got to the corner. There were several people near, but none had noticed the package; all were staring towards the junction from which came sounds of thudding feet and angry voices.

Mason bent, rammed the payroll between the side of the grating and the dusty window that ran down into the well. The package crimped, slid down, jammed again, then burst

lookers' minds. He was making a successful getaway while they stood dumbfounded by the sight of a packet departing of its own volition.

HE raced through the door like a charging bull, left it whirling behind him. Two hundred yards to the corner, another hundred to the junk-filled grating outside the pawnbroker's shop. If no snoopers were hanging around, he could cache the money there and wander home at his leisure.

The hullabaloo started when he was within fifty yards of the corner. An excited mob poured out of the bank and saw the payroll bobbing fantastically above the payment. Howls of "Stop!", roars of "Get him!" were followed by two sharp reports, and a whine of lead above Mason's head.

through. It flopped into the months' old litter at the bottom of the well.

Beneath the dull but broken sky the hunting pack swirled round the corner a full two hundred strong. They filled the narrow road from wall to wall, their numbers too great to evade.

Grinning to himself, Mason raced up the road. A quick burst to the farther corner and he'd reach the main avenue and lose the baying hounds for good. The money was safe, he was safe, and the world was a wonderful place for guys who knew all the answers. Even Olympic champions didn't get forty thousand dollars for a quarter mile trot. The sun burst through the clouds, beaming in sympathy with his happiness.

Behind, the pack howled. Someone fired a shot, and Mason heard the bullet moan across his shoulder. He increased his pace, still grinning. Let the fools shoot at random if it relieved their feelings.

Another shot, nearer this time. A hoarse command to halt. Mason, taking a hasty, backward look, saw that the mob was gaining. They had passed the grating now, and were less than fifty yards behind him, with a uniformed policeman and the Legattrick bodyguard in the lead.

Even as Mason looked, the policeman fired again. A hot iron seared the muscles of Mason's left arm and blood crept down to his wrist.

With nothing with which to wipe the blood away, he could only rush panting along, licking his arm as he ran. The corner came nearer; the mob came nearer, too. He was within ten yards of the busy main road when two policemen came running in from the other end. Leaping aside to avoid them, Mason gathered his muscles for the final effort which would carry him into obscurity and leave his pursuers foiled.

The policeman behind yelled something unintelligible, fired, and cut a long red flake of brick from the wall at Mason's side. Both of the policemen in front looked startled, snatched their guns, and gestured toward Mason.

"Halt you!" they shouted.

Desperately now, Mason dived for the gap between the opposing officers and the wall. Guns flamed on one side and from behind. Pain, red-hot, speared through him, stabbing his lungs. The force of the blows spun him around, and, as he whirled, he knew that he was performing the pirouette of death.

He tottered off the sidewalk, bloody hands clasped to his abdomen, his shocked mind vaguely wondering how he, the unseen, could have been seen. How had anyone been able to aim at an invisible man? For two seconds he stood with glazing eyes turned toward the sun. Then, abruptly, he collapsed into the embrace of his own shadow. His treacherous shadow, which had been visible to others, even though he himself was invisible!

No. 1—THE METAL ROBOT

GRAG the robot is the largest and strongest of Captain Future's three strange comrades. He is probably the strongest being in the whole Solar System.

He towers over seven feet in height, a massive, manlike figure of gleaming "inert" metal.

This metal, being impervious to most forces and weapons, has protected Grag from destruction many times. Yet old scars show where his body-plates have been broken and re-welded in the past.

IMBUED WITH INTELLIGENCE

Grag was built in the cavern-laboratory on the moon by Roger Newton, Captain Future's father, and Simon Wright, the Brain, according to an intricate design.

The robot was not designed to be merely an automaton, but to have an intelligence and individuality of his own.

His creators endowed him with a brain consisting of metal neurones roughly corresponding to the neurone-pattern of a human brain, though more simple. The thought-impulses

set up inside this metal brain are electrical. Electrical and magnetic "nerves" control the robot's great limbs.

ATOMIC POWER

Grag's source of energy is atomic power. A compact, super-powerful plant is located deep within his metal torso for safety. A small amount of metal fuel inserted into this powerplant inside his body is sufficient to keep his strength for many months.

The metal robot can hear better than any human being, because his microphonic ears are super-sensitive.

They enable him to hear sounds which are above or below the range of human audibility, and Captain Future has sometimes made use of this fact to communicate through Grag with planetary creatures who talk in tones beyond the range of human hearing.

Grag has an immense and unshakable loyalty to Captain Future, which is his chief emotion.

The robot tended Curt Newton through his infancy, and because Curt needed constant watching then, Grag thinks that his master still needs watching over.

THE BRAIN'S HANDS

Toward Simon Wright, Grag feels respect and some awe. For he knows that Simon helped create him.

Also he has long been accustomed to acting as the Brain's hands, performing experiments and researches under the Brain's direction.

But toward Otho, the android, Grag is deeply jealous. For the robot's great desire is to be thought of as human or near-human. Grag has always been angry when anyone has referred to him as a machine, or automaton. He feels that he is just like other humans, except that his body is made of metal instead of flesh.

But Otho, who was also created by Captain Future's father and the Brain, likes to taunt the big robot on that point. Long ago Otho found out that the great, simple-minded robot was most sensitive about his unhuman appearance, and ever since then Otho has gibed about it.

CAMARADERIE

Grag invariably becomes furious at these taunts. Yet the bickering between these two comrades of Captain Future is at bottom one of mischievous camaraderie. Each of them has saved the life of the other, more than once, in a tight spot.

Grag has been able to extricate his comrades from more than one perilous situation, through his great strength or through his special capabilities. One of the most valuable of the robot's abilities is that he requires no breathing apparatus.

This has enabled him to go where neither Captain Future nor Otho could venture.

One time on Venus, when Curt and Otho and Simon Wright were all trapped in deadly peril, and could not be reached in any other way, Grag had walked days under an ocean, over the sea-floor, to reach the island where they were imprisoned. The robot was nearly lost many times in that perilous traverse, in constant danger of sinking into the ooze at the bottom of the sea, but he finally made it and brought help to his trapped comrades.

CAST ADRIFT

Another time, Grag was cast adrift in space when outlaws destroyed the little space-flier in which he was trying to reach his master on Saturn.

The great robot floated in space for many days, helpless and yet still living, needing no food or air, and finally was picked up by Curt Newton. Only the robot could have survived such an experience.

There is a great weld-scar down the back of Grag's metal back, which tells a tale of an adventure that neither he nor his master will ever forget.

Captain Future had penetrated into one of the caverns of Uranus' chasmed abysses, with Grag. The outlaws Curt was after blew up the tunnel entrance to that cave.

Captain Future would have been crushed beneath falling rock had not Grag, with his superhuman strength, held up the masses of falling stone until his master could jump clear. Grag himself was crushed beneath the rock, but Captain Future dug him out later, and the great weld-scar on his back is his memento of the adventure.

NO SENSE OF HUMOR

Grag has no sense of humor, as humans know it. He is puzzled sometimes by Curt's jokes or the sly drollery of Otho. And that makes him uneasy, for the robot's great ambition is to be human in everything.

His happiest moments have been when Captain Future has told him, "Grag, you are more human than most humans I know."

Huge, incredible in strength, his great metal head towering high, his photoelectric eyes gleaming and his mighty metal arms raised, Grag is a terrible figure to evildoers when he goes into battle at the side of Captain Future and Otho.

And woe betide the person whom Grag suspects of trying to harm his master!

The Human Termites

Beginning a great
SCIENTIFICTION
NOVEL

By Dr. David H. Keller

The dark jungles of Africa give up the secret of an invincible dominion when a lone scientist defies immortal intelligence that rules the world!

Hans Souderman

CHAPTER I

After Thirty Years

HANS SOUDERMAN had just returned from a residence of many years in Africa. There he had lived the solitary life of one who is occupied in solving a certain mystery of life and cannot be content until a solution of the problem has been attained. Such men have made our civilization possible. They are not good companions because of their intense introversion, but on the rare occasions when they can be induced to talk about their work they are always able to astonish their audience with their erudition and complete mastery of their life's work.

Such a man was Souderman. For some reason, early in life, he had been stimulated to entomological research. For years he had followed in the footsteps of Forel, Charles Janet, Lubbock, Wasmann and Maeterlinck. He had learned all that these masters of insect life had to teach him. But he was not satisfied with this knowledge. The work of Forel and Maeterlinck intrigued him but left him restless, discontented. He wanted to find one great fact that was unknown to them, solve one puzzle that they had been unable to fathom.

It is typical of the man that he made a calm and dispassionate survey of the entire world of insects before he decided on his life's work. Of the many strange varieties of insect life he studied, one type held an uncanny fascination for him—the termite and its destructive powers.

The terrible powers of these voracious insects amazed him. In the annals of entomology he read of the destruction of the French town, La Rochelle, by termites from San Domingo, which had come in the hold of sailing vessels. Every street was attacked. Before the danger was realized most of the houses fell down. The devastation only stopped when the termites reached the canal of La Verriere.

In 1879 a Spanish warship was literally eaten to pieces by a swarm of termite divers while anchored in the harbor of Ferro. In 1809 these same minute insects destroyed the batteries and munition of the French forts in the Antilles, and made the defense of those islands against the English an impossibility. Souderman found that large portions of Australia and Ceylon were uninhabitable because the termites ate the crops faster than they could be grown.

The more Souderman read about these tiny, blind insects, the more fascinated he was by the many startling peculiarities they possessed. He no longer felt that the bee, the wasp and the ant were the intellectual leaders of the insect world. So he decided to devote the rest of his life to a study of the termite.

Severing all relations with his European associates, securing an income from one of the large research endowment funds, he went to South Africa to study the termites, not by observing them, but by actually living with them.

Such workers have been few. The price that has to be paid is too great. Everything has to be abandoned. A lifetime has to be spent to attain one little fact. And yet the men who do this feel that the attainment of one addition to the store of human knowledge is sufficient reward for all their sacrifice. And it is. Suppose one man spent a lifetime with the cancer cell, not merely studying it, but actually living with it. He would think of nothing else during his waking hours and dream only of it during his sleep.

Month by month and year by year he would become more intimate with this enemy of the middle-aged. To him the cancer cell would become a separate race of living creatures, a parasite enemy of mankind. He would learn its history, its folklore, its traditions.

TIME would pass and it might be that old age would come on and still the secret of prevention would remain a mystery. As a last resort he would deliberately inoculate himself with the cancer cell, make of his own body a laboratory so that he could make a last, final effort to gain an insight into the soul of the individual cell, the group intelligence of the cancer mass.

On his death bed, perhaps, he might whis-

• BEGINNING A GREAT SCIENTIFICTION NOVEL •

per the great truth which would make the human race free from this parasite that now kills one out of every four who reach the age of forty. Surely this man would die happy in the thought that he had contributed one fact that would make the life of his race happier. That is the great sacrifice. Every generation produces at least one man of this kind. Such a man was Souderman.

He went to Africa when he was forty-five. He came back when he was seventy-five. During those years his loved ones in America had died. Most of the scientists he had grown up with were solving the puzzles of another world. Saddened by the realization of the changes in his social life, still horrified at the final revelations of his African studies, he decided to go to New York and there place the results of these years of sacrifice in kindly hands before his death made it too late.

For when the final truth had dawned upon him it had made him afraid. Deathly afraid.

The student of termites came to New York. He then visited Chicago and Philadelphia. His record, his knowledge, made him a welcomed guest in the homes of fellow scientists. Souderman talked little, listened intently and observed much. Finally he found one man who had the peculiar mental qualities and the scientific vision necessary for an appreciation of what Souderman had to tell him.

This man had youth, enthusiasm and an excellent education. In addition he had a respect for the aged. The old man at times wished that the course of his life had made it possible for him to have a son like that. Subconsciously he adopted him.

Having finally found his man Souderman spent a few months in becoming acquainted with him. He wanted to leave this man all the knowledge accumulated in those long years of African residence, but he did not want to make any mistakes. He had a strange secret to tell.

It is interesting to note that there were many men in America who were more brilliant than Adam Fry. There were scientists who had forgotten more than this young man knew. But Adam Fry had one trait that Souderman considered necessary for the complete understanding of his secret—imagination. That was a trait that many scientists lacked, in fact most students of the world felt that imagination had no part in their lifework. Yet Souderman had developed his imagination and by means of it had come to at least a partial understanding of one of the world's greatest secrets.

He felt that unless his heir possessed the same peculiar mental trait he would not listen to what might seem the ravings of an old man. He wanted a man with the combination of Galileo and the far-seeing vision of Jules Verne, a scientist who understood insect life as Fabre and Maeterlinck did and yet had the imagination of Wells and Poe. In Adam Fry he believed that he had one of these peculiarly combined personalities.

The reactions of Adam Fry to the older man were all pleasant. In a singular way he had always been accustomed to respect

Adam Fry

age. The mere sight of this wornout, shriveled, old man, who had spent a lifetime in isolation, awoke an intense pity and even love in the young scientist. He felt that this man knew something, and to the youngster all knowledge was sacred. He desired nothing more than to learn what this white-haired man had to teach and regretted that his comparative poverty made it impossible for him to spend a few days or a week with him.

So it was a gratifying shock to learn that the old man had money, and was anxious to adopt him as a student for the rest of his life. All of Fry's financial worries could cease and he would do nothing but listen day after day to Souderman and write a complete statement of the conversation. This statement was to be put on pure linen paper, with indelible ink that would last for ages and two copies made, one for the Congressional Library in Washington and one for the Public Library in the City of New York.

The two men decided to rent a small apartment overlooking Riverside Drive, do their own housework and cooking and devote their entire time to the completion of this manuscript. Souderman did not feel that he was in the best of health. He did not fear death, but he did dread the thought of dying before his life's work was securely placed on paper and burned into the mind of his pupil.

Hans Souderman was so impatient to begin his story that he could hardly wait until they were installed in their apartment. Adam Fry, trained as he was through years of scientific work to take notes, made a beautiful task of assembling and arranging in logical sequence the old man's conversation, which at times was rather rambling and disconnected. The completed manuscript can be examined by anyone who cares to take the trouble to do so, though it tells only a part of the complete and final story resulting from the work of years of patient toil completed by Souderman in Africa.

CHAPTER II

Souderman's Story

THE story as told the young man by Souderman during these daily conversations, arranged in some order and avoiding repetitions, was as follows:

In order for you to understand fully the end of my work, Adam, (he began) you will have to listen while I tell you something about the beginning of it. I went to Africa many years ago to study the termites. Many people think that they are ants and their common name is the White Ant, but they are very different from the ant. It is not hymenopterous, and therefore has no close relation to the ant, and the bee. It is usually classified in the order of *orthoptera*, of the division *Corrodentia*.

They are very old. One hundred and fifty species have been found in fossil amber. Go back a million years and there were the termites. Go back to the endless night of the Primary and there is the termite associated with the *Protoblattidae*. Some men have placed their beginning one hundred million years before man appeared on this globe. Surely a very respectable age.

During all this time they have lived and through these countless ages they have adapted themselves to their surroundings and necessities. Otherwise they could not have survived. Man, supposed to be a most intelligent creature, has just begun to learn a few of the things that the white ant has been doing for millions of years. But they are able to live efficiently in many ways of which we are ignorant and yet, though the knowledge might be beneficial to us, so far we have been unable to learn the secrets of their lives and apply this knowledge to our own.

Doomed to an existence in darkness, they have adjusted themselves to the life of the blind. Without defensive armor, weak, pitiful little things, they have perfected an architecture so secure, and built their houses of material so strong, that they could not be broken into by any of their natural enemies, until man came with tools of steel and dynamite.

They build their homes of intestinal secretion mixed with small particles of sand or vegetable debris. This forms a wall that is hard and a perfect protection against their natural enemies. Their houses are perfectly ventilated and at the same time kept warm by some heating system, probably generated by decaying vegetable mould. While they need moisture, they are enabled to live in tropical countries where the rain falls very seldom. Do they make water? Or conserve it? Who knows? At least they have all they need.

COMPARED with their size, the height of their buildings is enormous. Suppose man was to build according to the same scale? Then his houses would have to be 1,800 feet high, something that so far has never been attempted by the race we are so proud of belonging to.

In architecture they show the most astonishing variation, especially when you consider that all of the actual building is from the inside, out. Their houses have spires, domes, columns, facades. They imitate every known geometrical shape known to mankind.

They not only build houses but they build tunnels. Destroyed by the light, unable to defend themselves in any way, they go enormous distances for food and always through tunnels of their own construction. At times enormous colonies are connected by tunnels apparently for no other reason than a desire to form a social contact with each other, perhaps some union, political and economic.

They have solved the problem of food. Everything they touch can be eaten. They eat their dead, the useless members of their colony. Nothing is wasted, nothing is useless. In time of surplus they place little piles of food in corners. Certain workers have nothing to do but to supply food to other groups of their political organization.

They continue their group life by hatching and caring for the eggs and young of the Queen. She is an enormous creature ten or fifteen times larger than her subjects. She simply lies in the royal cell and for a life of five years she lays one egg a second, thirty million a year or one hundred and fifty million in her lifetime. When she grows old she is eaten and replaced by a younger Queen.

The eggs are fed different foods and consequently develop into different kinds of termites. Some are workers, others inside policemen and still others soldiers. A few are specially fed to become future queens, others to be the husbands of queens. I want you to remember that these are all raised from the same kind of eggs and they are produced according to the need of the colony. If soldiers are needed, then they are produced until the need is supplied.

Do you see anything wonderful about that? Compare it with man, the so-called intelligent creature. What can he do? A man and a woman can produce a child. They cannot even determine that child's sex. It will be some kind of a child but can they make a musician, an artist, a mathematician out of it? Can they determine its shape before it is born? The termite does all that, and more too.

It has successfully solved all the problems of life. The community it lives in is a dark, sad, and gloomy one, but it is highly efficient. The individual is in every instance sacrificed for the group. But they have survived through the ages.

For ten million years the Ant has been at war with the termite—but the termite still survives. It lives on, not as an individual but as a colony. Who directs it?

On a single acre in Africa there may be twenty colonies. Each house seems to be separate and yet there seems to be a uniform rhythm of life. They do things in the same way and at the same time. Some naturalists have thought that this can be called instinct. That all the deeds of this wonderful little thing are without intelligence.

I studied this matter. Was there an intelligence? If so, was it an individual or a group matter? Perhaps there was an electrical phenomena, something resembling the contact of our neurones and dendrites. I spent years searching for an answer. For a while I thought that the Queen headed the group. But I learned that she was subject to the same immovable laws that governed all the rest. She was simply a highly specialized, glorified worker and, when her usefulness was over, she was killed and eaten just like all the rest of the colony.

There seemed to be some occult power, some super-termite intellect directing the affairs of each house. I hunted for it and for years I could not find it. I tried to apply every known physical law to the problem. All that I attained was failure. Twenty years passed. During that time I had done nothing but live and think and study termites. I tried to become one of them.

I felt that if I could only put myself in the place, say of the Queen, that I could understand the mental reactions of the unit, the house, the colony better. I got nowhere but to the depths of despair. I felt pitifully dumb, ignorant, helpless. I was on the outside, separated from the Great Truth, not so much by the colony wall, but by sheer lack of intellect. These little termites, helpless, blind, small, were living a mental life so complicated that I, a scientist, could not begin to understand it.

Then I suddenly wondered about the noise. For there is a noise that comes from the colonies. Some think that it is music. Others call it cracklings, tic-tacs, whistles, cries of alarm. If the ear is placed on the wall of a termite colony these sounds are plainly heard. I had known of them for years. Now it came to me, like a stroke of lightning, that perhaps those sounds could be interpreted!

Thanks to the new improvements in the science of the amplification of sound I was able to assemble a rather satisfactory apparatus to help me. First there was a bell-shaped stethoscope, a little similar to the instrument used by physicians to examine the heart. It had a rim of soft rubber which had little holes in it. When this was pressed to the wall of a colony house, it remained there by suction. Inside was a diaphragm.

I had the sound augmented by radio tubes, and finally transmitted to me by a loud speaker. Now all I had to do was to sit in my observation tent and listen to the sounds that were being formed in the termitary. Naturally, the first instrument was not satisfactory. The little fellows promptly ate it. They made short work of my first acoustophone, but I fooled them the second time. I made a study of the cement they used in building. I was able to make a fairly good imitation and covered all the apparatus with that. I guess they thought it was a part of their colony house; at least they did not try to eat it.

Now followed long days of study. I realized that my life was not long enough to do all the research, especially when it came to the interpretation of a new language, so I enlisted the help of a linguist, Johanson. He was a wonderful linguist, but he just hated bugs of all kinds. I made hundreds of phonograph records for him and let him study them in comfort in his house at Cape Town.

It was odd. I did not even tell him what the recordings were; just told him that it was a new language and that I would like to see if we could isolate it and understand. The conclusions he reached after two years were astonishing and were very useful to me in reaching my final conclusions.

Working independently of him, I was able to isolate certain sounds. But as I had no idea what actions were accompanying those sounds I at once saw the need of actually *seeing* what those little fellows were doing. That made me undertake a special study of the physics of light rays. I left Africa and went to France, and a Frenchman and I made a little machine that would enable me to look right through the wall of the colony house. It had some of the principles of the X-ray, but was far easier handled and a great deal more satisfactory.

Its penetrating power was only three feet but that was better than nothing. Now I could look into different parts of the colony house. I could *see* the life lived there under normal conditions. It was my hope to obtain some harmony of purpose between action and sound.

We learned the language of the termite. At least we thought that we did. You remember that I said that the philologist in Capetown simply knew it was a language but did not know that it was a language of ants. The poor fellow went wild over it. He said that he believed it was the oldest language in the world and the parent tongue of all human speech. He isolated root words, established derivations, and finally wrote a glossary composed of over five hundred words.

That was what I wanted. I made a few hundred more records for him, promised that I would finance his book when he was ready to publish it, and then went back to my own work, determined to learn and use this new language as soon as possible.

I experimented for at least two years. For example, I took a very sharp auger and bore a hole one inch wide through the wall of the house to which I had my acoustophone attached. Now I was able to look into that house and hear what was going on and note the reaction of the termites to this opening of a hole. As usual, a number of soldiers came out and formed a solid ring around the sides of the hole. Then workers came, each either dropping a globule of liquid cement or a small piece of sand. Within an hour the opening was closed.

Were these orders given? Did some supreme mentality realize the danger and close the opening by giving orders?

I procured an ice machine and literally froze a small portion of the wall. I had a thermometer in the wall, but it showed no result. The termites simply rushed large masses of fermenting mould to that spot, and in spite of my efforts they kept the temperature to a point where they could live.

I WOULD bore you with a detailed study of all these experiments. At last I came to some very definite conclusions. Each termite had some nervous system. They were able to understand certain sounds, and originate certain sounds. These sounds were used in a way to resemble speech; at least they served as a means of communication. But there was no sociability, and the conversation seemed to consist mainly of orders. Some power issued orders and the millions of occupants of one termitary said "Yes, Sir," and at once obeyed.

Then I was faced with a new problem. Whence came these orders? What constituted the initiating force? Here was a plunge into the realm of the unknown, a leap into the darkness of the Great Void. For listen to me, and pay attention, Adam Fry, to this next statement. These colonies are thousands of years old. Perhaps one house is a million years old. How can we tell? They are indestructible.

Listen to me. Man since the day of Magellan has sailed and walked and flown around the world. They have gone up in the air and down into the deep seas. The North Pole has been looked at and the South Pole will soon be a commonplace. Where has man not been? Everywhere? No! There is one place that the foot of man has never trod, and that is the real inside of a termitary. What is there? How deep do they extend into the ground?

What we see may be only an outer shell. These are the questions I asked myself. I knew that they were old. Was the intelligence governing them old? The life of the human being is but a trifle compared to the race history of the termite. I felt that in all these million and hundreds of millions of years, they had attained to mental processes that we could only imagine.

So far I had seen only the carrying out of orders. The termites seemed to be but servants. Where was the greater mind? Could I communicate with it?

By this time I knew the five hundred words. I had isolated sentences, in fact I was beginning to talk their language. For example, they had certain sounds to indicate that a hole was broken in the wall and that it must be repaired. I reproduced that series of sound on a phonograph and then transmitted it by vibration through the wall.

I watched the result through my visual apparatus. At once the soldiers came to guard the opening. Instantly the workers came with their liquid cement. Of course there was no hole to repair and there was a resulting confusion. I waited a day and repeated the experiment. Once again there was no hole to repair and there was no reaction. Attaching my acoustophone, I carefully bored a hole in this same colony house. At once there was an order given but it was not the same as I gave. Some new sounds had been introduced. The soldiers and workers obeyed at once and closed the hole.

Here was a novelty. Someone had learned that their orders were being duplicated, and consequently their orders from the inside were changed, and the workers instructed to pay no attention to the old form.

I went to another termitary and gave the original order. There was no response. Then I gave the *new* order and for two days it was obeyed but on the third day it provoked no reaction. I went one mile away and the result was the same. A hundred miles away, and there was no difference.

CHAPTER III

The Great Discovery

SO I worked a game of chess with this thing that ruled the colony house (Souderman continued). I would live with the receivers of the acoustophone attached to my ears, and by a specially ingenious invention I learned to talk to the termitary with such a changed voice that it was an exact duplication of the tone used by the insects. And gradually it dawned upon me that there were two languages being used. One for the issuing of orders and the other—dare I say it?—for the communication of the Supreme Intelligences of the various colony houses.

When that idea dawned upon me I went rushing down to Capetown. I was growing old, and there was no time to spend in isolated working. To my surprise Johanson in Capetown had arrived at the same conclusion I had—that there were two languages. We talked over the matter for a day and were convinced of that fact. One language is very simple and is used only for the giving of orders. The other is vastly more complicated, only imperfectly understood by the soldiers and workers and apparently used as a means of communication between the Intelligences of different colony houses.

Johanson hated insects. He just naturally could not stand the thought of an ant crawling over him, but he came with me to my termite colonies. I will give him the credit for staying there two weeks. Then he left me. The work we accomplished during those two weeks placed me on the threshold of a great discovery.

I ceased to worry about the lesser language. In fact, I found that the vibratory scale of the two languages was so different that I could tune in the greater language and tune out the lesser one. On the day I started to do this I was nearly sixty-eight years old. And the thought came to me, irresistible, tremendous, awe-inspiring, that the words I was hearing were being produced by an intellect that was perhaps a million, perhaps ten million years old. And I was trying to understand it!

WHEN I was seventy I heard them talk and understood them. Do you see what that meant to me? For two years there had been no experimental work; I had attempted nothing new; I had simply sat there in a chair or rested on my cot with the receivers in my ears. I learned the language. And then the Great Idea came to me.

This termitary with the millions of termites, all carefully differentiated in shape and ability to perform the various forms of work required for the successful functioning of the Colony, was not composed of millions of individuals but was simply one large animal! The Colony House was the skeleton, changed according to the growth of the animal and its needs.

Think this over well. *One large animal.* Does it mean anything? Think of an animal a million years old, ten million years old. Imagine the wisdom that it would have accumulated! And these things we called termites, they were just so many cells in the body of this animal. With the conception of this fact, I realized that I was faced with the wisest, most remarkable life that had ever appeared, or would ever appear on this globe.

All the forms of life that had been coincident with it had disappeared, unable to withstand the changing conditions of earthly existence. The Palaeozoic types were all gone. The pterodactyl, mammoth, cave bear, saber-toothed tiger had all failed to adjust themselves. But this animal I was thinking of had slowly conquered continents and was threatening Europe and Northern America. And I was studying it! Alone, unarmed, incompetent, I had the temerity to place my intellect above that of a million years.

Other lives were gone but they lived on. They had met such obstacles as changes in moisture, temperature, sources of food. In every instance their intelligence had been sufficient to provide security against a threatening danger. In all the studies made by over fifty careful observers only one termitary was found lifeless. Thus there was no death rate. They lived on and on. I believed that their ambition was eventually to rule the world.

That gave me food for thought. I knew that the area they lived on was slowly expanding. Now and then new cities, fresh agricultural areas were over-run. Was there a method back of this? Could they plot, prepare and premeditate an attack? Each one was helpless in its stationary position. It could not move, but it could form new members.

Across the field it would send a cement tunnel and through this blind tunnel the workers would go perhaps for a hundred feet and there a new Colony House would be erected. I saw that happen. For two years I saw such a house grow, and during all those two years it was ruled by the Intelligence from the first house; and then—you must believe me, for this is one of the greatest of proofs—the tunnels were broken, the two houses became separate, and in the second house was a second Intelligence. And it was not a new form, but had the wisdom and apparent endless age of the first. Was it a part?

I determined that what I had seen was simply a budding, a cleavage, a peculiar form of birth of a new individual. And thus, by slowly establishing new individuals, all with the same mentality, they hoped to conquer the world.

I remained silent. As I said, for over two years I did nothing but listen. And finally I could stand it no longer. Their plans were so heartless, so coldly diabolical, maddening

in their cleverness and deadly in their ability to wait for a thousand, a million years, if only at the end of that time they were able to rule the world and drive out all other forms of life. It was all so horrible that I just had to do something.

You will remember that I had never tried to talk to them. But now I determined to do so. I formulated a phrase in their language and I vibrated that phrase through the walls of a hundred Colony Houses in the immediate neighborhood of my laboratory.

"This is a large world," I said. "There is room for all. Why try to destroy all other life?"

And then I went back to my favorite termitary, replaced the acoustophone and started to listen. And what I heard was this. I wrote it on a piece of paper, and put it in my wallet. Here is the paper and here is the message:

For a long while we have been studying you. Because of this we have tolerated you. Now you must leave. We can tolerate no interference with our plans.

For years I had been unmolested by the termites. Here was the explanation. To complete their knowledge they had to study man. In order to do this they had to have a man near them. They could not catch a man and make him a source of observation. For all these years I had obliged them by remaining in one place. I thought that I was studying them, whereas the truth was they had been studying me!

For once in my life I was absolutely at a loss as to my future conduct. Restless, I went to bed. The next morning, after a bad night of dreams, I woke to find my laboratory a wreck. Everything was gone, eaten, cut to little pieces. My records, apparatus, food supplies, were gone. They had told me to leave, and this was the final warning. I had the clothes on my back, some memos in my wallet, and that was all.

OF course, the very valuable phonograph records were safe in Capetown. At least I thought so. I hurried there, but I was too late. Poor Johanson had been attacked the same night, only he had been killed, literally eaten alive by millions of warrior termites. His records, in fact his entire house, had been destroyed. I was horrified, and at the same time I felt that they might now decide to get me after all. Here was time for deceit.

I arranged to leave Capetown on a certain steamer. I told dozens of people that I was going to do so. I even went out to a colony of Termitaries and shouted the news and then at the last minute I left in an airplane. That ship sank the day after it sailed from Capetown and all on board were lost. Divers examined the hull and found that it had been literally eaten to pieces by termites.

* * * *

Souderman smiled wistfully at young Fry.

"Looks as though they tried to get me, doesn't it?" he asked. "I do not think they can in New York City. It is too cold. But

105

they are working on the problem of living in cold climates. They have to solve that and then they will creep over the world. So there is my story and there is the danger. Johanson could corroborate it but he is dead. Our records are destroyed. Only my intellect survives and I am now an old man. Well, Adam Fry, stop writing. Do you believe me?"

The young man smiled.

"Certainly I believe you. Why not? At one time I studied medicine. The anatomy of the human body is proof that you are right. For days I have been listening to you describe those colony houses and all the time I have been thinking, making use of my imagination, trying to compare your termite organization with the human body. You have made the comparison worthwhile. You told me when we first met that what you wanted was a man with imagination, a young man that could think outside the beaten track. Well, I will reward your search and I will make a statement. The only difference between the Termitary and the Man is one of age and intelligence."

Souderman laughed, almost hysterically, as he patted his student on the back.

"My dear boy, my real son. You see it. You see it! You saw the analogy all by yourself. Only by arriving at this conclusion separately could you show me that you were worthy to share my secret. Now I can die happy for I know that you will carry my work on. With the foundation I have laid you will be able to build a superstructure that will perhaps save the human race from a future terrible destruction. I believe with you that there is a universal pattern of life of which the combined life of a single termite colony is the oldest and most remarkable form.

"It must have been the oldest form and all the other life on the earth since its development must have been foolish efforts to imitate that type of life. With what success or failure you can judge. We think man has been the great achievement of the ages. Well, man is due for a surprise!

"I talked about a single pattern of life. We are a form of termite colony, only we are infinitely lower than the Giant Termite of the tropics. We live sixty, seventy years and then we are dead. I wonder if the real Termite knows what group death is. We prate of our nervous system, our red and our white corpuscles, our muscle, bone and digestive cells, but are they under the control of our wills? Not at all, and yet in the case of the Giant Termite every function is absolutely governed by the Central Intelligence.

"Everything we do is childlike, puerile, infantile compared to their profound efficiency. If we knew what they knew we would be able to prolong life indefinitely, become efficient in any line of endeavor. We call ourselves human beings; in reality we are simply a collection of a number of interrelated but at the same time independent cells living within a colony wall called the skin, and so far we know absolutely nothing concerning the real governing of these cells by means of the higher intelligence, mind, or what-can-you-call-it of the central nervous system.

"The Central Intelligence of the Giant Termite issues direct orders to all the individual cells which form his body. Consider them as cells, or as individual living creatures, little termites, whatever you please, but no matter how you call them they are absolutely under the control of the Central Monarch, the IT of that colony.

"Can we do that? If our liver cells are sick, can we make thousands of new ones? If there are too many white corpuscles, the policemen of our blood, can we order that one third of them be destroyed and eaten for the public good? Can we form new human beings? You say 'yes' but will they automatically be possessed with the accumulated power and wisdom of the past hundred million years? How about the idiot, the epileptic, the defective we procreate? There is none of that in the Giant Termite.

"MAN knows a lot, but when he comes in conflict with these stationary animals who have serenely wandered down from the past eons he has to surrender. He cannot live with them, or, in fact, near them. They strike in the dark, but when they finish there is no place for the man-form of termite. Some day they will come. Perhaps for some centuries a few of the human beings will survive shivering around the Poles. I see it all, and you do too, because you have imagination. But who else will see it? Can the race be warned?"

"They cannot!" replied Adam Fry. "They will almost kill themselves laughing at us if we try to warn them. Tornadoes they understand, death from war and tidal waves, destruction from famine and pestilence they have at least read of, but that whole nations should perish through the silent working of a creature that they would only see as a small, helpless, defenseless, blind white ant, they will not understand. They are too grandiose, too sure of their position in the world in which they live."

"But the race must be saved," insisted Souderman. "We are men. It is incomprehensible that our brothers should be so stupid, but we must save them in spite of their asinine lack of imagination. I say that we must save them. In reality you must because I will not be here much longer. You have the secret. In the little time I have to live I will teach you all I know and then as you grow older you must teach some one else. Perhaps when the real test comes, when there is the final struggle, the one man who is our descendant might save mankind."

"I feel," said Adam Fry, slowly, as though he was not sure of his statement, "that the first thing we should do is to preserve your knowledge of the language of the Giant Termite on records. Then there is another idea which can be developed in the course of the next few years. I feel that your work was cut short, and that it is incomplete without an effort made to actually find, and see one of these things, whatever you might call it, which is the head, the actual intellectual force behind the animal you call the Giant Termite. I feel that something might be learned if one were actually captured. If its knowledge is so superior to ours perhaps some compromise might be reached. How about it?"

"Your first idea is a good one," replied the old scientist. "Work once done need not be repeated. Many years of my life were spent in the endeavor to learn this peculiar language. If some one repeated that work it would be simply time wasted. It will be an easy matter for me to make phonograph records and I could also teach it to you. In regard to your second suggestion, it opens interesting possibilities. Of course, you realize that I left Africa the way I did because I felt that some one should know the secret and I was convinced that the Giant Termites were going to do all they could to stop me.

"They killed Johanson. Of course some would call that a coincidence but I do not. I have tried to imagine what such a thing looked like but I have failed. If one could be located and captured—"

"Well, there is nothing like trying," said Adam Fry bluntly. "Nothing can be accomplished without the primary effort. Suppose we get the language put into an imperishable form and then some years from now I may go to Africa myself. I want you to make a map of that region for me. I want to go there and locate that special Giant Termite you talked to, the one that threatened you. Perhaps I could catch him."

CHAPTER IV

The First Invasion

ALL that spring the two men worked and on into the summer. Phonographic records were made, maps were drawn, detailed blueprints were made showing the various scientific instruments used by Souderman in his years of African study. As soon as Adam Fry was able to sustain his share of the conversation the two men talked in the termite language of the workers, which Souderman called the "Command" language. Then they advanced to the speech of the Giant Intellect, used only in intercommunication between the Egos of the different colonies.

Gradually the two manuscripts neared completion, and finally they were finished. The one was sent by express to the Congressional Library at Washington, while the other was in a drawer, waiting to be delivered personally to the New York City Library.

It was an interesting sight to see the two men on that morning. The one, old, stooped-shouldered and white-haired and yet with the gleam of youth in his eye; the younger man, keenly alert, physically capable of any exertion, brilliantly equipped in every way to play the part in life that fell to his lot. They wore bright neckties this morning and were freshly shaved. Souderman even insisted on carrying a cane. He said that a man was as old as he feels. They ate a hearty breakfast of soft-boiled eggs, bacon, toast and coffee. Then they prepared to start out.

But when they opened the drawer the book was gone.

It was a manuscript book, the pages and soft leather cover held together by steel rings.

Only these steel rings were in the drawer. The two men looked at each other. At last Souderman said, with a deep sigh:

"The summer has been hot."

Then he pulled the drawer wide open and pointed to a long tube the size of a straw and about the same color. The tube stretched from one corner of the drawer over to the middle, where the book had been.

"Termites," he whispered.

Adam Fry looked at him as though a thousand questions darted from his eyes. But all his tongue could say was:

"A coincidence?"

The old man smilingly shook his head.

"We might fool ourselves by thinking so, my lad, but with the Giant Termites nothing happens by accident, by coincidence. No! This is simply the first attack of the enemy. It might not have happened in the winter, but they have taken advantage of the long and very hot summer. How did they locate us?

"You cannot think? Where is your imagination? I am sure that they did not look me up in the telephone directory. Look, here is the thread of life, the channel through which the attack was made. Suppose we try to follow it downward. They probably came up through the leg of the table. I recall now that it has not been moved since we came here.

"Suppose we tilt it over on its side. There! See that hole in the bottom of that leg? Now where did it connect with the floor? Just as I thought. There is the hole. Now, somewhere in the ground under this building is the main body of the Giant Termite that was assigned to this work. Can you imagine the cunning, the intellect, the enormous mentality of such a being? Immobile, not capable of changing his home, he yet devised methods to be carried to New York by ship, locate himself in the city, find us here. Then he established stations for observation in our rooms.

"No doubt every word we said, all of our plans, perhaps, for all I know, even our thoughts were understood, appreciated, and stored in the storehouse of memory. We think that we were shrewd in placing one copy in the Congressional Library. Perhaps even now a Giant Termite is waiting there to destroy it when it comes. Well, boy, our partnership is over. From now on, our only safety lies in separation and rapidly moving from place to place. Fortunately we duplicated the phonograph records. We will each take half of them. I am going to secure a skilled linguist and go to some cold country like Labrador and teach him the termite language. You do what you think best, but be careful of yourself, because one night will ruin your hopes."

"Do you still think that they want to kill us? They had a thousand chances."

"I do not know. They never tried to hurt me so long as they thought I was not going to fight them. Just as soon as they considered me an enemy they came close to destroying my life."

ADAM FRY sighed.

"Are you going to try and find this individual Termite that is living somewhere under this building?" he asked.

"No," replied Souderman, vigorously shaking his head, "the best thing for us to do is to pack our things and get out. Suppose we spend three hours tracing this slender hollow tube of cement to the basement. By the time we return we might find the entire surface of every phonograph record smeared with a glasslike cement, and utterly ruined. We had better leave. I said out loud that I was going to Labrador and you said out loud that you would stay in the city. We had both better change our plans and think them instead of saying them. Perhaps they are able to read our thoughts. Perhaps not. But you have ample funds, and all I know you do. You go ahead. The safety of the human race lies in your hands."

Without the loss of any more time the two men packed the most valuable of their possessions and left the small apartment that had been their home for so many interesting months of companionship. It was not till they were several miles away from the apartment house that they ventured to speak. Souderman took out a paper and pencil and wrote an address on the paper.

"I will be here if you want me," he whispered, and handed the paper over to Adam Fry. The young man looked at it a long time memorizing it, then burned it and placed the ashes in his coffee.

"Fine," he commented. "There could be no better place. I will let you know from time to time how things are going. Goodby, my dear friend, and take care of yourself."

And so they parted.

The young man took his heavy bundle of records and went to a cold storage plant. He left the phonographic records of the Giant Termite language there and walked out on the street. To all appearances he looked just like any one of ten thousand men he passed every few minutes. There was this difference. He knew what danger menaced them and he cared; they neither knew nor cared. He was on his way to save them. He went to a cheap hotel and registered for twenty-four hours.

Once in his room he simply sat and thought. He had the beginnings of an idea and he wanted to find some one who would have sufficient mentality to take that thought and push it over into actuality. Even as Souderman had hunted for a man with imagination, so was Fry searching for a super-mind, an intellect that would be able to think in channels, hitherto unknown to mankind.

Fry reviewed the men he knew, the great men in the world who were really doing work of vast importance. There were scientists, economists, business men, politicians, world visionaries, lawyers, physicians, psychologists and leaders of religious thought. Where among such men could he find a man who would willingly listen to a perfect stranger? None of them would listen to him, but perhaps he could force one to hear him for at least a few hours, until interest made it impossible for the listener to break the thread of the narrative.

With this new viewpoint he again went over the list of the men he knew or had heard of and finally selected a bank president.

Here was a peculiar choice. Bailey Bankerville was the descendant of the famous Bankerville who had largely financed the American Revolution. No one knew just how long the family had been financiers. Bailey, or B.B. 4th as he was known to his intimate friends, had become the head of his family on the early death of his father. He had handled the affairs of an enormous corporation with the greatest ease by finding capable men to do the work for him. Consequently, he had found sufficient time to take things easy, to play.

HIS play would be considered by other men as work. For example, he spent a large sum and a year of his life making a careful study of the monoliths of Easter Island. His book on the subject, printed in a limited edition, is one of the most prized works sought by anthropologists.

This work, which he laughingly called play, was but one of a number of similar adventures in which he sought to wrest from Mother Earth her secrets. He had been so busy doing this and at the same time augmenting the family fortune that he had no time to play in fields feminine. So far he knew woman simply as the female of the Genus Homo. He was fairly well familiar with her attributes as an entity, but never willingly sought the company of any woman except his mother and sisters.

This was the man that Adam Fry picked out to finish the thinking of his great thought. Fry knew the man had imagination, boundless perservance and an education that equipped him to at least follow the bare outline of any scientific discussion.

Bailey Bankerville was artistic and therefore temperamental. To a great extent he was a man of moods, quick to react to little, peculiar stimulations. When Fry sent in his card, requesting an interview, the banker was annoyed.

"Tell him I am out!" he roared at his secretary. "Tell him I refuse to see him. Tell him anything you like, but show him the door."

Adam Fry came back the next day—and the next. And never again, at least not to the banker's office.

The following Saturday night the banker had a very uncomfortable dream in which there seemed to be an inability to move. Waking, he found that this was an actuality, for he was securely tied to the bed and also gagged to prevent his calling for help. In the dim light he saw a man at the foot of the bed and now that this man saw he was awake he started to talk.

"I am Adam Fry. I wanted to see you; in fact I had to see you. I called at the office three times and you would not have anything to do with me so I was forced to visit you at your home. I am not a robber or a murderer; my motive is neither commerical nor religious. I feel that if you will listen to me talk for an hour you will listen to me to the end. I hope that I can take the gag off and unbind you. Will you agree not to call for help?"

The banker had a saving sense of humor. For a week he had been making fun of this man without ever seeing him. Now the man had him.

"Sure I will listen to you," he said as the gag was untied, "Let me free and we will go to the library and spend the rest of the night. I think you are a bothersome interloper but anyone who is clever enough to pull this stunt is worthy of consideration. I suppose you are some new kind of bond salesman, one of those go-getter devils. Let me turn on the light and locate my bathrobe and slippers and for goodness' sake put that gun away. It might go off and break something like a looking glass. Hard luck, you know, to have a looking glass break."

In a few minutes they were in the library comfortably seated in overstuffed leather chairs. Then Adam Fry started to talk to the banker. He first told all about the Giant Termites as studied by Souderman. He was still telling about them when the butler entered the room to open the shades and let in the sunlight. Bankerville jumped up with a start.

"Let's shave and dress. We can talk while we are shaving. Then we will have breakfast. I will send word to the bank that I will not be there today. I never had so much mental sport since Tige was a pup. I do not know where you have been staying but I know where you are going to stay from now on. You are going to be my guest. I do not know how much you have to tell me but you are going to tell it all before you quit. Send for those records. I am going to send the best linguists I can hire to examine them and learn that language. You either are insane or you are up against the largest problem that ever hit mankind since the flood. You high-jacked me into this and by the Sacred Cow of Benares I am going to stay in as one of the leading actors till the play is finished."

"That is what I wanted you to do," answered Adam Fry.

He was greatly pleased. In fact he felt that now he could begin fighting in earnest. At the same time he realized that, even though the rich man was thrilled with the story of the Giant Termites, there was still a large question, and a very important one, to be answered.

WOULD the man's brain leap over the gap that had stopped the mental processes of Adam Fry? There was a secret there somewhere. Fry felt it, could dimly sense the outline of a great truth hidden behind it all. But it needed something better than a Fry brain to help solve it.

The two men shaved and prepared for breakfast.

At that time a rather startling surprise awaited Adam Fry. Bankerville had a sister, and that young lady, Susanne Bankerville, was very much in attendance on the two men. In any household, news spreads like wildfire and the banker's sister, greatly pleased at the idea of anyone actually hogtying her brother and forcing him to listen to a wild-goose yarn, had violated all feminine rules and was at the breakfast table, charmingly clad and apparently anxious to make toast for the two men.

Bankerville's sister had accompanied him on all of his queer expeditions and the fact that she had obtained an excellent scientific education made her a very valuable aid to Bankerville in his anthropological researches. She was looking rather attractive this morning

Adam Fry was at a loss to know how to consider her after the introduction. Could he talk freely or must he be guarded in all he said? Bankerville lost no time placing him at his ease, as he followed up the introduction with a long tirade concerning the real worth of his sister and at the same time what a tremendous nuisance she always was when they visited the far-off places of the earth.

"This young lady," he began, "refuses to let me get out of town without her. She ran away from school to go to the Easter Islands with me. Though I try mighty hard, I can never shake her from my trail. This is the first time in five years that she has had breakfast with me. Why? Because she smells a rat. She thinks that I am into something and she refuses to be left out.

"She looks real cute now, but you ought to see her in her war togs. You can say anything you want to in her presence; she is absolutely to be trusted. And I will say

[Turn page]

"I TALKED WITH GOD"

(Yes, I Did—Actually and Literally)

and, as a result of that little talk with God some ten years ago, a strange new Power came into my life. After 43 years of horrible, sickening, dismal failure, this strange Power brought to me a sense of overwhelming victory, and I have been overcoming every undesirable condition of my life ever since. What a change it was. Now—I have credit at more than one bank, I own a beautiful home, drive a lovely car, own a newspaper and a large office building, and my wife and family are amply provided for after I leave for shores unknown. In addition to these material benefits, I have a sweet peace in my life. I am happy as happy can be. No circumstance ever upsets me, for I have learned how to draw upon the invisible God-Law, under any and all circumstances.

You, too, may find and use the same staggering Power of the God-Law that I use. It can bring to you, too, whatever things are right and proper for you to have. Do you believe this? It won't cost much to find out—just a penny post-card or a letter addressed to Dr. Frank B. Robinson, Dept. 711-12, Moscow, Idaho, will bring you the story of the most fascinating success of the century. And the same Power I use is here for your use, too. I'll be glad to tell you about it. All information about this experience will be sent you free, of course. The address again—Dr. Frank B. Robinson, Dept. 711-12, Moscow, Idaho. Advt. Copyright 1939 Frank B. Robinson.

this; her brain is better than mine for she has feminine intuition."

That was the end of his speech. Susanne Bankerville smiled.

"And now, Mr. Fry," she said, "tell me all about whatever there is to tell about."

"Giant Termites, my dear sister," corrected the brother.

"Do you know anything about Termites, Miss Bankerville?" asked Fry.

"I certainly do not, but don't mind me. You start right in where you left off. The information I have is so confusing. Brother says he asked you to have breakfast with him and others say that your conversation started during the night."

"Well, let our guest eat and then we will all go to the library. I have sent for those records and when they come I will play them on the orthophonic. I know sis will like to hear them. She is wild about all those foreign jabbers."

The rest of the meal was very quiet and almost formal. The young lady soon showed that she was the perfect hostess and Adam Fry was at once placed in a position where he had to acknowledge that he was having a very pleasant time.

CHAPTER V

Fry Delivers a Lecture

SOON after they were again seated in the library. But at this, and for that matter at all future sessions, Susanne Bankerville was an interested member of the audience.

"There is no doubt," continued Adam Fry, "that the millions of little blind termites enclosed in a colony house simply compose so many parts of one animal, which Souderman called for convenience the Giant Termite. I feel that for a correct understanding of our problem we must consider the colony as an outer shell or skeleton. The various workers, warriors, even the Queen and her husband are all dispensable and replaceable. But, irrespective of the death-rate of the individual termite, the Giant Termite lives on as he is always absolutely able to replace any of his dead individuals."

"Just one minute," interrupted Susanne Bankerville. "Do I understand that each individual termite has a separate intelligence?"

"They must have. I compare them to the cells of a human being and yet the microscope shows that they are really formed of many cells. They have the ability to understand speech because they obey orders. They have a definite speech with words, and yet they have no initiative. All they can do is obey. Communal life social discipline is carried to such a point that every one of them has to be finally sacrificed to the good of the community. They work for the good of the Central Intelligence but have no part in any happiness or benefits. The entire social order is predicated on self-sacrifice of the individual in order that the mass, the entire animal, might live."

"Another question. Do you think that the cells within our bodies have a similar individuality, a peculiar type of mentality? Do they know anything? Can the blood cell, the little bone cell, the muscle fiber, think, reason, do anything but obey a nervous impulse?"

Adam Fry looked at the girl curiously as he replied.

"Honestly, I do not know. Certainly there is not the beautiful control of our cells that the Central Intelligence of the Giant Termite exercises over his individual termite cells. We cannot force our cells to perform certain acts. Of course, we can, in a limited way, as in walking, but the efforts we make to manage the affairs of our body are pitifully infantile."

"Yet every part of the work done by the Giant Termite is duplicated in our bodies?"

"Practically. But poorly. It is as though we were just learning; as though, after a million years we were just out of our infancy, barely beginning to understand life. Nothing like that with the Giant Termite."

"How much do they know, anyway?" growled Bankerville.

"How can I tell? Souderman worked with them for years and he was completely nonplussed at the end. He even accused them jokingly of finding our apartment in New York by making use of a telephone directory. Perhaps they have all the wisdom of the entire preceding ages. Perhaps they know a hundred times more than we do. They certainly have perfected a bodily structure that is infinitely more remarkable than ours. They have, by Jove! What an idea! They have put legs on the corpuscles, taught them to walk instead of swim and then taken away their blood liquid.

"Their cells literally run around in dry arteries, juiceless capillaries, and yet are able to perform all the necessary work. The human female has an ovary, bilateral. If all the conditions are right she may be able to reproduce herself, but in doing so she is subject to a thousand adverse conditions. The Giant Termite reproduces at will any of its cells and when it is ready divides its Central Intelligence, whatever that may be, and forms a new individual."

"And I suppose your idea is that all life is like the Termite, only not so highly organized?"

"Something like that. It seems that perhaps the dog, the fish, bird, and human being are all simpler forms of the termite colony."

For a while all three were silent. An oppressive silence seemed to hover like a mist over them. Then, for all his accustomed poise, Bailey Bankerville started in to tremble. It seemed that he was tortured by the effort to think. The sweat started to break out on his forehead.

"The devil!" he exclaimed angrily. "I am trying to think of something and it eludes me. Something about us and the Giant Termite and I cannot get it out. Can you help me, Adam Fry?"

"I cannot. I have had the same feeling for a week. That is why I came to you. There is something there that I ought to see, but for the life of me I am unable to. I feel it. It just comes so far up to the threshold of consciousness and then it sinks back without crossing. I have been unable to sleep because of it. I thought you, with your vaster experience in the mysteries of the world, could fathom it."

AND then Susanne Bankerville jumped up and began to dance around the room like a whirling dervish. And as she whirled she sang.

"I have it! I have it!"

Both men looked at the girl, puzzled.

"The idea is too big for me," the girl began. "But it is what you men were hunting for. I just know it is. You said, Mr. Fry, that all life had a certain pattern and that the oldest and most perfect pattern was the Giant Termite. You said he was formed of millions of little white ants and then you said that each little termite was formed of little cells. In making your comparison with man you said he was on a par with the Giant Termite. But you gave man too much credit. He is simply on the level physiologically and psychically with the LITTLE termite.

"He has no initiative, no spontaneous ability to control his actions. I cannot explain it, but I believe that all the people in the United States are simply little termites, the cities are large colony houses. The cities are connected with roads, rails, even air routes, but over all the millions of inhabitants is a Central Intelligence that governs and directs.

"There is a Central Intelligence for each nation — Mexico — France — Turkey — Germany—Russia. And the people of each nation are just like those poor little blind termites that sacrifice everything for the good of the nation."

The two men looked at each other in silence.

"Not a very pleasant thought, Adam Fry," the rich man said finally, "to feel that one and all of us human beings are just running around doing what we are told to do by a Central Intelligence that has not even the brains of a Giant Termite."

"Not pleasing, but it sounds as though it could be true. I feel that this is the thought I have been looking for. The world has to be saved from those white ants. Meantime, the human races, poorly governed, badly directed, expend their strength fighting among each other while all the time the termite terror becomes more real."

The brother turned almost fiercely on his sister:

"What do you mean, Susanne, by a Central Intelligence governing the United States, and another one governing Mexico? Do you mean the political power, the combined thought and determined purpose of the people, the will of the mass to rule, a combined psychic impulse jointly held by the entire nation?"

"Nothing of the kind!" was the determined reply. "If life has one pattern and the Giant Termite is the pattern, then everything you say is nonsense. Mr. Fry says that Souderman proved positively that the little termites were hopeless and helpless and all they had to do and all they could do was to obey the orders of the supreme intellect, I think he

called it the Central Intelligence. They do just what he or it says. The queen lays so many eggs and when he says 'Enough' they kill and eat her. The eggs are developed into so many workers, so many outside warriors, so many internal policemen, so many nymphs according to his orders. If food has to be secured, the colony defended, a new termitary formed, then he orders and they obey. If they are too many he commands that a certain percent be eaten.

"Not in a single instance, as far as I can learn from your talk, is there the least suggestion that at any time they are capable of independent thinking or action. In the scale of life, in this uniform pattern of existence we men and women correspond to the little, helpless, blind, insignificant termites, and if this is true then we have nothing whatever to do with our government. We may think that we have—but that is just a delusion. No doubt our President is selected rather like the Queen termite is. When the Central Intelligence is through with him he is thrown out of the White House."

"Well. Let's go on with the argument. This is growing interesting. We are all little termites and have nothing to do with our lives or actions. All is controlled by a Higher Central Intelligence. Is it God?"

"No."

"Less than God?"

"Of course. Far less than even the Central Intelligence of one little colony in South Africa."

"Where is it?"

"I will answer that," said Fry suddenly interrupting. "One of the things that Souderman failed to do was actually to see the ruler of a termitary. Mark you, he talked to one. He was convinced that there was one. He was sure that they were able to talk to each other and that there was perfect accord and a communicated harmony between them. But he never saw one. He says that no man has ever seen the inside of a colony house. That is, he means entirely. He did not know how deep they extended into the earth. But down there somewhere in the termitary is this Central Controlling force.

"I have the blueprints of all of his instruments. The study he made of the two languages, one of the command tongue and the other used for the intercommunication of the rulers, is preserved for us on phonographic records. Souderman actually talked to the THING, and IT talked back. Now if all life has the same pattern and we could actually see this THING that rules a colony house, then we might be able at least to imagine that something like that ruled the separate Human Termite nations."

BANKERVILLE started to walk the floor. Suddenly he exclaimed:

"Perhaps we are all wrong. Surely if the three of us are just little helpless termites of humanity we are doing a lot of criticism of our Central Intelligence. We are doing a lot of independent thinking. Perhaps sister is mistaken."

"That is a logical statement," answered Fry. "But you must remember that the animal of which we are a part is still in a very experimental state. I do not think that conversation, dreams, and criticisms such as we have been indulging in would be possible between three little white ants. They have had all such independent initiative crushed out of them by millions of years of communistic life.

"Their motto is, 'One for All.' The all for one disappeared from their lives many centuries ago. I feel that our seeming independence is simply a proof that the animal that we are a part of is in a very early state of its intellectual development, and we all know that man was nearly the last animal to appear on the earth.

"Nevertheless, since we have the thought that we are supreme we can at least play the game bravely. If we could look into the future we might recognize even now the hopelessness of the struggle. But as it is, why not fight? Three of us, all loyal to each other and consecrated to the betterment of our fellows. Then there is Souderman, brave old man, fleeing to a cold country so his knowledge can be preserved. He can be counted as number four."

"That sounds good to me," said Bankerville. "Any suggestions as to our line of attack?"

"I think that we ought to try and solve the question of just what the Central Intelligence of the Giant Termite really is. I have the exact location of the Giant Termite that ordered Souderman to leave Africa. That is the one to go after. We will duplicate Souderman's machinery for listening and conveying sound and then, after we have learned the higher language, we will talk to this THING. Miss Bankerville, you have been of the greatest help to us, but you must not go to Africa. You have no idea of the danger. If a man like Souderman is thoroughly alarmed over the situation, it is certainly no place for a girl."

The girl walked over to Adam Fry and took hold of his shoulder.

"What do you think I am, Mr. Fry?" she said. "Here I have been fretting my life away in the city for over a year, and now, at the first chance I have had for real sport, you say it is too dangerous. You and brother need me. Did you know that I can speak seven foreign languages? Do you realize that I have a flair for languages, a real appreciation of sound? I have to go along with you men!"

Bailey Bankerville threw up his hands in well-simulated hopelessness.

"You see how it is, Fry. This girl has bossed me ever since she was a baby. I guess the only way to get rid of her is to take her with us. I am going to send for your clothes and you will be our guest until we start. I think I will send a long message to the Librarian of the Congressional Library warning him to protect that manuscript. It would be a good idea for him to make a few hundred photostatic copies and distribute them throughout the world.

"I am going to send for some manufacturers of scientific apparatus and start them to work on those acoustophones that Souderman used in listening to the conversation of the termites. I think that it will be a good idea to hire a few expert philologists and one or two entomologists. We need a first-class staff of scientific workers, at least to start with. I feel that the closer we keep our secret the better for us, because I do not think it will help any to broadcast our intentions. Hell's bells! If those white ants can read a telephone directory, they may be able to read the newspapers!"

CHAPTER VI

Going to Work

WITH a man of Bankerville's training to think was to act. He converted several rooms of his house into a workshop and installed over a dozen scientists, all of whom were famous in their particular line. Not until the third evening was there any relaxation and then, for some unaccountable feminine whim, Miss Bankerville dragged the unsuspecting Adam Fry to the roof garden of the Bankerville mansion.

It was a beautiful evening, a lovely location and a supremely attractive woman. Adam would really not have been to blame if he tried in any way to duplicate the conduct of his namesake of the Garden. However, such a procedure was far from his thought. For the time being he could think, talk and dream of nothing but the termite.

The woman realized this. At the same time she was a woman.

"Those termites seem almost devoid of emotion, Mr. Fry."

"They certainly are. Of course, they may have thoughts that are unknown to us. But mainly their life is a cold, cruel, materialistic one."

"Then there is no love as we know it?"

"I doubt it. The entomologist, K. Escherich, was fortunate enough to open a royal apartment and observe it for a few minutes before the alarm was given. He drew a picture of that apartment and its inhabitants which I have been seeing in my sleep; it haunts me like a nightmare. Souderman had a copy of it and we used to study it. He felt that it was very true to life. He saw the Queen, a large, inert, white creature, a feminine God, created for one purpose only, the laying of an egg every second. In a large ring around the outer sides of the room a solid ring of enormous warriors are constantly on guard. A ceaseless line of workers deposit drops of food into the mouth of their motionless sovereign. Other workers seize each egg as it drops, wash it and carry it away to the nurseries. Around the Queen small policemen guard her from any possible attack. For five years she lays an egg a second. Then, her usefulness over she is deprived of food, dies of starvation and is, like all other dead termites, eaten."

Susanne shuddered.

"I am glad that I am not a Termite Queen. Has she a husband?"

"Yes, a poor little, insignificant thing. He is only a small fraction of her size and spends most of his time hiding underneath her to avoid being eaten by the workers. It is thought that he fertilizes her eggs after she voids them."

Susanne shuddered again. This gesture drew her closer to Adam Fry.

"I am glad," she said, "that you are not a termite male."

And Adam Fry replied that he was glad that they were just human beings, able to look up to the stars, and smell the flowers and know what the love of life really was.

After a month of hard work the scientific expedition was ready to start to Africa. It was the last of July. The boat was all ready. The talk that night was not about termites, but of the social changes that would take place in the world if the controlling Force of the nation could be discovered, and influenced for the good of the common people.

Then something altogether unexpected happened. About ten P. M. several terrific explosions were heard and the entire house was rocked on its foundations.

"Earthquake?" asked Fry.

"Earthquake nothing. That was some kind of dynamite or T.N.T. Hell's bells. Hear those shouts. Sounds like a mob. That is a queer thing. First time I knew anyone had it in for me. We will investigate this later on. The thing to do now is to get out and do it quick. Let's slip out through the garden and back to the car and beat it to the boat. I smell smoke—perhaps they are trying to set fire to the house. Here, Fry, take a gun, and you, Susanne, take this pair of automatics. Thank goodness you know how to use them. Now let's beat it."

And in the darkness that just preceded the flare that told of the burning of the house they rushed to the automobile and down to the ship.

Once on board the ship Bankerville telephoned the various members of the expedition, urging them to join him at once. All night he stayed at the phone, giving a thousand orders, and not once did he make any remark about the attack on the house. Before daylight all were on board and orders were given to start down the bay. It was not until the ship was several hundred miles out from New York that he seemed to notice the other members of the party.

They, unable to help him in his complete absorption of the various problems arising from the sudden leaving, had spent part of the night listening to the news that was coming over the Radio Sun of New York. Newspapers were still in existence, but many millions of urbanites received all the news of the day over radio newspapers and a part of the equipment of the ship consisted of a radio and television news service.

The three, Bailey Bankerville, his sister Susanne and Adam Fry, gathered in Bankerville's cabin before breakfast.

"What happened last night, Sis?" he asked.

"Enough. An unorganized mob attacked our house. Some member of that mob had dynamite. They blew up part of the house, set fire to all of it, plundered what they could. Three of our servants were killed, including James, the butler. The police were at once notified, but by some mistake went to the wrong part of the city. By the time they were on the job the damage was done.

The fire department came out, but the mob cut the hose lines. There was a terrific riot.

"It was the belief of the reporters that the three of us were buried under the ruins of the house. Apparently our quick getaway fooled them. The police are at a loss to understand the reason back of the attack. Several of the rioters were arrested but could give no explanation for their conduct. They simply said that for some reason they had to do it. They saw a crowd running and they ran along.

"The Police Commissioner submits a peculiar report. He states that for some reason there were hundreds of traffic violations at that time of the night, at least ten times more than normal. He says his men were so busy trying to get things fixed on the streets that he could not handle the riot as well as he might have on other evenings, and of course that in itself is peculiar. It all looks like a mess to me, Bailey."

"WHAT do you think about it, Adam Fry?" asked the banker.

"Well, the suddenness with which this happened, the dazed condition of the prisoners, their inability to understand what it is all about, the coincident traffic difficulty, the fact that the police went to the wrong part of the city, and the cutting of the fire hose all seem to me to point to one thing."

"And what is it that you men think?" demanded Susanne.

The two men looked at each other.

"I guess we think the same, don't we?" finally asked the banker.

"Right!" said Fry. "The Central Intelligence of this United States, the Ego or whatever you call it that we talked about when we compared the life of a nation to the life of a Giant Termite—well, that Central Power, wherever and whatever it is, grew tired of our independence and original thinking and criticism of his stupidity and inefficiency and He ordered a mob to go and destroy us."

"That is just what I think," said Bankerville, emphatically. "Of course, I would not have thought that some months ago, but it really is a beautiful demonstration of our hypothesis. No doubt many of those people from the President down thought they were acting on their own initiative whereas in reality they were just obeying orders like the workers or soldiers in a Termitary. For some reason we were able to think a trifle faster than the Central Power. Of course, if he had known we were on the boat all night he could easily have gone ahead with the killing. He is capable of a good many things, but he is not omnipotent by any means.

"The three of us are perhaps insulated in some way against his power. We irritate him, but he cannot get rid of us. Perhaps he feels about us like a human being feels about a beginning cancer. Now the question arises as to what his next move is going to be. Will he think that we are dead, under the burning building? Or will he be able to locate us on the ship? If he can, perhaps he can command the crew to mutiny and kill us here. He can easily find out where we

113

are heading for, as the ship's clearance was for Capetown. What do you think we had better do, Susanne?"

"I believe we had better get lost."

"What do you mean?"

"Can you depend on the crew to be loyal?"

"I believe so. Most of them have been with me before."

"Then send a wireless out to the effect that the ship, under orders, left New York last night, but that the three leaders of the expedition are missing and it is believed that they were killed in the riot. A few hours later send an S.O.S. that the ship is sinking. Then send another that the situation is hopeless. Then put the crew to work painting a new name on the ship and changing her generally.

"Slip into some little South American port and bribe the port authorities to give you false clearance papers and just go out on the seven seas as a tramp steamer. No use going to Capetown, for there are all kinds of reasons what they will be waiting for us there, not only the Giant Termites but the representatives of the Central Human Termite Power. No doubt the English and American Powers are in sympathy."

"Well, they would control Australia."

"Certainly, but we would not go to any port, and even if we did we would not be recognized in our new disguise. Maeterlinck says that at Cape York, Australia, large groups of termitaries can be seen from shipboard. We have had an exciting twenty-four hours, but we must not lose sight of the fact that the main reason for this expedition is to find just what the real ruler of the Giant Termite really is like. We decided that we had to know that in order to come to any understanding of the same force in the national termite. Let's go on and do what we started to do."

"Your entire plan sounds like common sense, Susanne," said her brother. "Do you know, Fry, that this little woman is right just about all the time?"

"I wonder why that is?" asked Fry.

"That is because I am a woman," replied Susanne. "You know we are right because we use intuition instead of reason in arriving at our decisions."

During the next two weeks Susanne's programme was carried out to the letter. Gold bribed a Central American Port official. Dirty linens, unshaved faces completely changed the appearances of the officers and crew. All entered into the spirit of the game and it was hard to tell Bankerville from the most villainous seaman. Susanne, as the cabin boy, made a thoroughly hardboiled lad. Several times they were stopped by war ships, but in every case their general looks and false papers were sufficient to fool the inspecting officers.

THUS they finally came to Australia. It took another week of careful sailing to locate Cape York. Several miles out they were forced to anchor, but the termite colonies could easily be seen through glasses. There were hundreds of them rising many feet in the air in every possible shape. Bankerville called a meeting of Susanne, Adam Fry and the captain. As they gathered in his cabin he almost shouted.

"Well, we are here now. The voyage is over."

Then he started to write on a piece of paper, signaling to the three that they should watch him. This is what he wrote:

"I believe that our destination is known to the various powers that are determined to destroy us. The only way we can escape from them is to think faster than they do. I am sure that they can hear the vibration of the voice over great distances and that is how they came near killing us in New York City. I want them to think that we are here and going to stay.

"In reality we are going to wait until dark and then slip out to sea. To the east of us are the New Hebrides. There are thirty islands in this group, but only twenty of them are inhabited, as the termites are so bad on some of the smaller ones that the inhabitants have despaired of growing anything. One of these uninhabited islands is called Whitsunday and that is where we are going. Do you understand?"

The three silently nodded.

Bankerville struck a match and burned all he had written. Three hours later the tramp steamer raised anchor and slowly steamed eastward. Four days later it found a pleasant and safe harbor on the east side of Whitsunday Island. It was over seven weeks since they had left New York. During the voyage their destination had been changed three times. Now they hoped that in this safe harbor of an isolated, uninhabited country, they could start in their study of the Giant Termite and the occult power that ruled it.

That night Bankerville for the first time called a staff meeting of all the scientists. These gentlemen had not been at all idle on the trip, but had spent long hours of study, some at the extensive library on the Termite, others learning the language from the phonograph records, while the poison expert dabbled in his laboratory, concocting new and deadly liquids and gases to use if necessary. As usual Bankerville ruled this meeting.

"Gentlemen," he began, "I suppose you all are aware of the real purpose of this expedition. We are here to make a complete and thorough study of the Giant Termite. Some of us have peculiar ideas of just where this study will lead us, but irrespective of those views I would urge all of you to be true to your scientific education. If your observations fail to show that Souderman was right in some of his ideas I want you to say so.

"For example, you may arrive at the conclusion that what Souderman thought was a language is simply a coincidental conglomeration of natural sounds proceeding from the termitary and not in anyway connected with mental processes of any kind or form of life. You must remember that Souderman led an isolated, anti-social life for many years. He thought of nothing, saw nothing, heard nothing except it was in some way connected with the termite. Under these circumstances it is entirely possible that he may have had hallucinations.

"He made double records, but the Giant Termite talking back to him may have been nothing but the other side of his dual personality. In other words he may have had the true schizophrenia of the paranoid praecox. In all of your scientific study of the termite remember these things. If one of you makes a discovery, do not accept it as the truth, but see if three or four of your fellows are able to arrive at the same conclusion independently of each other.

"**I** WANT you also always to bear in mind that we feel there is a possibility that we are here dealing with a personality that is very old and very intelligent. It may be that the things we call the brains of the Giant Termite are far more intelligent than we are. They had no trouble in killing Johanson in Africa to keep him from spreading the facts about their dual language. They traced Souderman to New York and ate his manuscripts. Be on your guard. Because they are so small, always out of sight, do not underestimate their power. Because you never saw a thing happen do not think that it cannot happen. They are cunning. They have been known to eat a picture, frame and all, and at the same time cement the glass to the wall to keep it from falling and waking the people in the room.

"With such insects the only safe way is to remain constantly alert. There is no telling what they will do next.

"I feel that we should finish this work as soon as possible, but we do not want to finish it before we are through. By that I mean that we do not want to be forced to leave. The least relaxation of caution, the slightest break on our part may be the means of driving us from our work on this island. I want each of you to make as much progress in his specialty as possible, but at the same time I want all your work to bear on one problem. Has the Giant Termite a Central Force or Intelligence? Can this Central Force be understood, apprehended by the senses of man by sight, hearing, touch, or is it something in a new dimension, that might be thought of but would not be tangible like objects in the three sensual dimensions.

"Finally I want you to recall that we are dodging the influence of some peculiar occult power that has threatened us since that fateful night in New York. So far I think that we have been able to keep one move ahead of that power, but at any time these influences may find us. I am going to ask you to be very careful of your own feelings. If you become angry, mad at one of your fellow men, report the matter at once to either Mr. Fry or myself. It may be that your desire to harm your fellowman is a desire that is put into you by this occult power. There may be even mutiny. Please think of this. Remember that our success has a large influence on the future hopes of mankind."

The next day they started to work.

How does Adam Fry combine the resources of modern-day science with human strategy to combat the sinister intelligence of the giant termite? What are the plans of Hans Souderman, the aged scientist who was the first man to establish communication with the termite civilization? How will mankind react to the first blow of an insect rebellion?

The Answers to These and Other Questions Are in the next Installment of

THE HUMAN TERMITES

Appearing in the Next Issue

A DEPARTMENT OF ASTRO-GEOGRAPHY

JUPITER

JUPITER, mighty monarch-world of the Solar System, was first colonized by Earthmen in the year 2005. But men had visited it some years previously, and had brought back reports of the giant planet's wonders.

As every school child knows, the first space flight was that of Gorham Johnson to the moon, in 1971. Johnson was a veteran of the Second World War who spent years trying to perfect a rocket that would make use of the newly discovered atomic power. Soon after his first great flight to the moon, he made a second voyage in which he reached Venus and Mercury, and a third in which he touched Mars and Jupiter.

Johnson was accompanied on this great third voyage of 1988 by Mark Carew, inventor of the gravitation equalizer. When they sailed on that voyage, their crew did not know that they meant to go beyond the orbit of Mars. Had they known, the men would never have signed up for the trip.

After leaving Mars, Johnson and Carew headed on outward through the asteroidal belt. Carew, in his book (*Spaceward to Glory*, 1994), says that the men became mutinous when they realized that the voyage was to continue to Jupiter. They believed, like most other Earthmen at that time, that the outer planets were all too cold and poisonous of atmosphere for human existence, and that they would surely perish there.

Landed at Callisto

To quiet them, Johnson told them he would not land on Jupiter, but on one of its larger moons. Their rocket, the *Pioneer II*, made a landing on Callisto. There they were attacked by the crystals of that moon, which Carew calls "a creeping diamond horror." And it was there on Callisto that Gorham Johnson was stricken by a swift fatal sickness, his frame enfeebled by the incredible hardships of his three stupendous voyages.

Carew in his book (Page 434) tells how Gorham Johnson, dying, asked that they carry him out of the rocket and let him look up at Jupiter, whose vast, cloudy white bulk filled the sky over them.

"I will never live to reach it, but you must land there," Johnson murmured to his loyal lieutenant. "It will be safe. The day will come when Earthmen will have cities on that great world—yes, and on the worlds beyond, even out to Pluto."

In the Void

A little later, Johnson died. His last speech, Carew tells us, was his famous dying request that they release his body in space, to roam the void in death as in life.

Johnson's prophecy that Jupiter would be habitable was fulfilled when Carew landed there. Beneath the upper poisonous levels of the atmosphere they found a clear, breathable atmosphere, and a world warmed by inner radioactive heat. They were amazed by the vast continents and endless seas. They marveled at the limitless fern-jungles, dotted with ruins of a vanished civilization, and the colossal and terrible Fire Sea. And they met the Jovians and made a friendly contact with them.

Carew went back to Earth from Jupiter, to lead his famous expedition to Saturn and the farther planets the following year. For some time, in the excitement of the exploration of those outer worlds, Earthmen heard little of Jupiter.

Site for Earth Colony

But explorers had visited Jupiter in 1990, 1994 and 1997. They had fixed a site for a possible Earth colony in the continent which Carew named South Equatoria, for it was here that deposits of valuable uranium, radium, iridium, platinum and other ores had been located.

A concession for a huge area was obtained from the Jovians by a fair treaty. In 2005 the First Jovian Expedition sailed from Earth, under command of Robert Caswell whose name is immortalized by the Caswell Strait between North and South Equatoria.

The expedition stopped at Mars for replenishing of supplies, and then sailed for Jupiter. Three ships were meteor-struck during passage through the asteroidal zone, but there were no other casualties during the long trip.

Landing was made on the southwest coast of South Equatoria, on June 12, 2005 (Earth calendar). A monument of simple design, bearing that historic date and no other legend, now rises from the shore near Jovopolis to celebrate the event.

(Concluded on page 129)

FIRE SEA

FIERY RIVER

CAVERN OF THE ANCIENTS

PLACE OF THE DEAD

LAVA BEDS

RADIUM and URANIUM MINES

RUINED CITY OF ANCIENTS

JUNGLES

JUNGLETOWN

JUNGLES

NORTHTOWN (EARTHMAN TOWN)

JUNGLES

OCCIDENTAL OCEAN

JOVOPOLIS

SOUTHTOWN (EARTHMAN TOWN)

SOUTH EQUATORIA (SOUTHERN PART)

GREAT SOUTH OCEAN

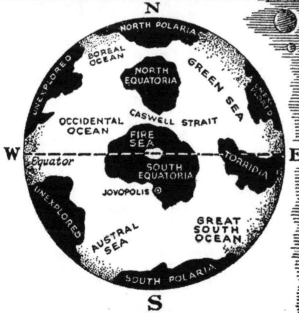

N

NORTH POLARIA

BOREAL OCEAN

NORTH EQUATORIA

GREEN SEA

UNEXPLORED

UNEXPLORED

OCCIDENTAL OCEAN

CASWELL STRAIT

W   Equator

FIRE SEA

TORRIDIA

E

SOUTH EQUATORIA

JOVOPOLIS

UNEXPLORED

AUSTRAL SEA

GREAT SOUTH OCEAN

SOUTH POLARIA

S

WESTERN HEMISPHERE OF JUPITER

JUPITER

DISTANCE FROM SUN 483,000,000 MILES

DIAMETER · 87,225 MILES

VOLUME · · · 1312 TIMES THAT OF EARTH

LENGTH OF YEAR · · 11 YEARS, 10 MONTHS, 17 DAYS. (EARTH)

LENGTH OF DAY · · 9 HOURS 55 MINUTES. (EARTH)

NUMBER OF MOONS · · 11

Around Infinity

By OLIVER E. SAARI

Author of "Stellar Exodus," "The Time Bender," etc.

THROUGH the three quartz windows showed darkness, far deeper than the black of interstellar space. It made one feel totally alone, forever removed from the familiar things of Earth.

The ship's single room was small and the three men made it crowded. The insistent hum of the engine gave some feeling of reality, but one had to keep his eyes away from those windows. For utter emptiness of inter-universal space was a thing no man could stand for long.

Dr. Leslie Chapman was hunched over the controls, guiding the ship on its strange flight. Over his stooped shoulder peered tall, dark-haired Ivar Augustus, watching his every move. Dr. Chapman was like a child, eagerly demonstrating the wonders of his new toy.

And Ivar was watching, with something more than interest. Ever since the ship had left familiar space and plunged into this mysterious inter-dimensional continuum, Ivar had kept his eyes on those controls.

Behind his saturnine countenance Ivar was thinking dark thoughts which the white-haired doctor and his assistant could not guess. He masked his feelings well.

He knew why the white-haired man had invited him on this trial flight—to gloat over him, to bask in the success of his supreme invention. It would make Dr. Leslie Chapman the greatest scientist in the world.

Ivar knew he could never surpass this machine. The knowledge of his failing prowess in science had been thrust upon him too often. There was something that made the thought of his failing almost unbearable. It was a boast made long ago, when he and Chapman had been vying for top honors

"Indeed this is a strange planet," said Ivar slowly

in the same college. He knew he could not fulfill it.

Besides, Dr. Chapman's invention would net him well over a half million dollars in the numerous scientific awards it was sure to bring. Ivar knew of some very good uses for that much money.

He fondled the little smooth-handled object in his pocket. A little invention of his own that might have brought him much. Perhaps it would yet help bring him more. Anything could happen in another universe!

Ivar Augustus' Murder Plan Could Beat the Law—But Not the Laws of Physics!

Suddenly Dr. Chapman cried out.

"We've done it!" he said. "Supraluna pulls—"

A subtle force wrenched the ship, twisting the very atoms. It was like a long fall coming to a sudden stop—against nothing. And it had brought them to a new universe.

Ivar had seen the last of Dr. Chapman's manipulations. Now he closed his eyes for a moment, then turned his attention to the view in the ports. A green light appeared in one of the windows. In silent wonder the three explorers eyed its source.

It was a colossal disc of pale luminescence in a background of starless space. A huge, bloated world of purest jade. It must have measured all of ten degrees from edge to edge. Its light was soft and soothing, but curiously mottled, an interplay of dark and glowing areas.

"A planet," Dr. Chapman whispered. "A great, sunless planet—"

But Dave Manning, the doctor's young assistant, pointed to the control board.

"The indicator shows that it has no mass, no gravity. Look! The needle's pointing in the other direction!"

They all turned and saw a disc of light exactly like the other, but smaller. Its edges were sharp and distinct, and it was obviously a solid body not far away.

"That *is* a planet," said Dr. Chapman. "A little smaller than the Earth, to judge from our indicators."

"Let us approach this world," said Ivar. "That is, if your machine can propel itself through ordinary space."

Dr. Chapman smiled, moved a lever. A slight acceleration tugged at them. The ship was moving through the alien void, toward the planet.

"Rockets," he explained. "I had an inkling we might materialize here in the middle of space so I installed them."

THEIR objective soon grew into a world of appreciable proportions. It was like a huge ball that was splotched with radium paint. This strange, sunless world furnished its own light. Dr. Chapman remained at the controls and the dark-haired man still watched. Ivar wanted to learn every operation of this ship. He might have to fly it, soon . . .

Finally a grinding of metal on rock told them the ship had landed. Dr. Chapman's machine had brought them to a planet more remote from Earth than the farthest galaxies!

The ship rested on a level plain that curved away on all sides to a nearby horizon. In the heavens there were no stars, no sun. The great disc of green light they had first seen was still visible, but a strange thing had happened to it. The ship had gone in a direction away from it, but its apparent size hadn't grown smaller with distance. Instead, it now seemed many times its former size, covering nearly all the sky with its pale light.

Ivar was the first to notice the phenomenon. "Look," he said, gesturing. "What kind of a universe is this your machine has brought us to?"

Dr. Chapman and his assistant were gazing upward, puzzlement showing on their faces.

Like a mammoth lid the light hung over the world, spreading to within a few degrees of the horizon. There it faded away, leaving a narrow band of dark space to meet the eye.

"I think I'm beginning to understand," said Dr. Chapman. "I've told you the theory on which I based my ship: the idea that there are many three-dimensional universes, having movements and orbits of their own in a four-dimensional space—just like a planetary system on a larger scale. They are simply 'planets' or spheres of curved space. Our own Universe is a huge three-dimensional space-world. It has its satellites, smaller universes, circling it, just as the planets have their moons.

"What we have just done is to travel to one of these satellites—this one. I call it Supraluna. But that light in the sky is explained by the fact that this is a small universe. Its curve is sharp, its circumference small. Infinity, here, is near at hand. That patch of light in the sky is this same planet on which we stand, and which we see *around the universe.*

"When we neared the planet, we decreased the number of possible lines of vision that did not intersect with this world. Therefore the image grew in

(Continued on page 122)

THE MARCH OF SCIENCE

SCIENCE AT THE WORLD'S FAIR

•

Flight Through Space

YOU can visit alien planets!
Other worlds can actually be visited at the Theater of Time and Space. This is an astronomical exhibit which simulates a journey into space, accomplished by ingenious photography. The audience leaves New York City in a rocket ship. The full sun of noon goes into an eclipse, the stars come out, a new moon grows full and its craters and valleys come into view.

Presently you pass Venus through a shower of meteors, speed past Mars with its polar ice caps, pass the spiral nebulae and Saturn with his three rings and nine moons. Then, to the accompaniment of roaring rocket exhausts, you race back to Earth!

Microscopic Magic

GIANT cellular organisms stalk the Fair!
One of the exhibits at the Westinghouse Building is a micro-vivarium in which magnified microscopic demonstrations are projected on wall screens. Walking across the wall as big as life —considerably bigger, in fact, since they are magnified more than 2,000 diameters—can be seen tremendously enlarged images of ciliates, *Didinium nostum,* hydras, and other varieties of microscopic aquatic life. Invisible life made huge through the miracle of science!

The Artificial Heart

THE human heart can survive independently of the body!
This fact is graphically illustrated by a model of the famous Lindbergh-Carrel artificial heart, at the Hall of Medicine. The model, constructed of glass and metal, pumps a colored fluid to demonstrate the mysterious action of the heart. As an added feature, a thyroid gland from a dog is shown in the perfusion apparatus—in action!

Man-Made Lightning

SCIENCE can create artificial lightning!
High voltage electricity is demonstrated in an exhibit of General Electric. Here you may watch ten million volts hurl a bolt of man-made lightning across a 30-foot gap, with the thunderous report of a rifle-shot. The vivid streaks of super-flame race across the gap at an incredible speed —yet science has them under perfect control!

Perfection Plus

THE instruments of science are extremely sensitive!
A delicate thermocouple in the General Motors Building can measure the heat generated in the air by your hand! Another meter indicates, in millionths of an inch, the extent to which you can bend a steel rail by slightly pressing against it with your finger.

And under a magnifying lens you may see strandlike, human hairs through which holes have been drilled, through the medium of the most delicate instruments known to science!

(Concluded on page 128)

AROUND INFINITY
(Continued from page 119)

apparent size. Probably this is the only world in the entire cosmos, for there is room for no other!"

Ivar, who had been listening to these theories with apparent lack of enthusiasm, interrupted the doctor. "These are all very well in the way of abstract explanations," he said. "But just what are we going to do now? Had you anything planned?"

The gray-haired scientist smiled.

"Dave, unpack the space-suits," he said to his assistant, who had just finished testing a sample of the atmosphere.

Dave Manning obediently pulled open a trapdoor at one side of the floor and took out three large bundles.

"Oxygen suits," he explained for Ivar's benefit. "The air here is helium at minus 160° Centigrade. Not very breathable!"

The suits, when unrolled, turned out to be one-piece affairs, made of some thick fabric and topped by rigid helmets. Goggles of reenforced glass permitted vision. Ingress was made through a slit in the side, which was closed by a heavy zipper-like device.

In a few minutes the men were attired, ready to emerge. Manning went out first, through a cramped airlock. Soon after, his bulging figure appeared in one of the ports.

Ivar bowed to Dr. Chapman.

"After you, Doctor," he said.

When the doctor had climbed through, Ivar picked up the object he had lifted from his pocket. It was a small, hollow tube with a metal handle and an enclosed mechanism at one end. He was glad he had brought it along—that athletic looking assistance might prove troublesome. Ivar grasped it in a space-gloved hand.

The terrain was hard beneath their feet, and full of little prismatic glitters, as though it were composed of pulverized diamond. But here and there were softer places where the crystals were absent and the ground was porous.

All around them were the luminous areas, where the mineral glowed with a vivid green radiance. At close range these could be seen to consist of tiny threads of light that spread and branched, pulsing with an alien living energy.

"Life," whispered Dr. Chapman.

The others heard him through the small ether-wave units in their helmets.

"What do you mean?" asked Ivar.

"Life," repeated the scientist. "The simplicity of this universe forbids more complex forms. Life here is simply a radiation, feeding on pure matter."

"Indeed this is a strange planet," said Ivar slowly. "Unbelievably removed, inhospitable. What a place to die!"

He felt the tide of resolution rising within him. Now was his chance. It would be so simple and safe. No one on Earth knew of this trip. He, Ivar, could go back alone, and eventually announce the dimension-rotor as his own discovery.

(Continued on page 124)

Nervous, Weak, Ankles Swollen?

(Continued from page 123)

Dave Manning had caught his cryptic mention of death.

"What do you mean—die?" he asked, rising.

Ivar was edging toward the ship. He returned, the tube in his hand.

"This is something of an act of self-preservation on my part," he said coolly. "Fate has given me no other alternative."

Dr. Chapman looked up at him, his bewildered face shining through his goggles.

"Why—" he began, but Ivar broke in with a laugh.

"My meaning is simple enough," he said. "This dimension-rotor of yours is a wonderful machine. One which might add credit to my genius as well as yours."

He waved the tube in his hand.

"Besides," Ivar went on, "I have long felt that I could follow my scientific pursuits better if Dr. Leslie Chapman were not around to anticipate my discoveries. Do you see? This Supraluna of yours is a wonderful place to disappear into without leaving a trace."

"You wouldn't—" choked the white-haired man.

Ivar's icy laugh came through the earphones.

"I'd advise you both not to try to follow me to the ship. This little device in my hand projects a beam of high-frequency radiations, enough to kill any living creature. A little invention of my own, almost as wonderful as yours, Dr. Chapman."

SLOWLY Ivar stepped backward toward the ship, watching the others. Dr. Chapman was pale. He seemed overcome by this sudden turn of affairs. It was only the assistant, Manning he had to fear. He could see they were afraid of the tube in his hand, and well they might be. For he had not lied. In that tube lurked death.

But death of a worse sort awaited them on this bleak world. Ivar could almost read the thoughts of his victims. He could see Manning gathering his muscles for a leap, and brought his weapon to bear with a jerk.

And when Manning suddenly lurched aside, Ivar grimly pulled the trigger. A thin beam of ionization leapt from the weapon's muzzle.

It sliced through the space Manning had occupied a split second before. A continuous beam—so much more efficient than a bullet, Ivar reflected with cool pride. He started to flick the ray across the moving man. And that was the last thing he knew, before the greatest darkness of all blotted out his consciousness.

To Manning, keyed as his senses were to the highest pitch of efficiency, it seemed like a slow-motion picture.

Ivar Augustus was standing there with his space-suited figure outlined against the rim of black space. From

(Continued on page 126)

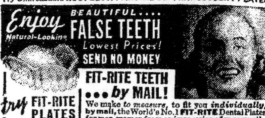

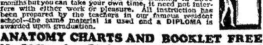

(Concluded from page 125)

this blackness, from an infinite distance, a bright beam of light lanced down. Only for a moment did it touch Ivar's broad back. Then it flickered aside and was gone.

The weapon went dark. The tall figure swayed, melted down, and toppled loosely to the ground. Manning rushed ahead and bent over the still form. One look at the place where the ray had struck was enough.

"Dead," he said softly.

Later, as the single world of Supraluna diminished beneath their spheroid, the white-haired man said to his assistant, "I am still wondering if we did right to leave the body of Dr. Augustus back there on the alien world."

"It might have been hard to account for," Manning pointed out.

"You know, of course, how he died?" Dr. Chapman asked.

"Of course. Ivar's weapon projected parallel rays. He forgot, when he fired it, that the rays would follow the curvature of this space, all the way around infinity, and back to the point from which they issued.

"When it missed me, the ray curved completely around this universe! Only Ivar happened to be in the way of the returning beam. Ivar Augustus died by his own hand!"

NEXT ISSUE

•

CALLING CAPTAIN FUTURE

Another Complete Book-Length Novel

Featuring

THE WIZARD OF SCIENCE

and the Men of Tomorrow

PLUS OTHER STORIES

BEST FUN, FICTION AND FOTOS

THE FUTURE OF CAPTAIN FUTURE

By
EDMOND HAMILTON

Author of "Captain Future and the Space Emperor"

I FEEL that CAPTAIN FUTURE AND THE SPACE EMPEROR is the most thrilling story I have ever told. Captain Future has three assistants . . . but all during the story a fourth, invisible companion shared in their adventures. That companion—myself. For the story seemed so real to me that I felt as if I actually were participating in the dangers and exploits of these men of tomorrow.

As to forthcoming adventures of Captain Future—that depends a great deal on the readers of this magazine. For I want to know—shall the scope of Captain Future's quests be limited to our Universe? Or shall his experiences plunge him into the fourth dimension—into the past, remote eons of time—or into the far-distant vistas of eternity a million years from today?

I don't know. I'd like to write about them all.

As for the companions of Captain Future: Do you like the pleasant rivalry between Otho the android and Grag the robot? Which of Captain Future's three assistants do you think is the most human?

Another thing. Would you like to see Captain Future take on additional aides, possibly a fourth or a fifth associate? Or would you rather the quartet remain as is?

As I've said . . . all this is up to the readers. I'll take Captain Future anywhere in the Universe you want me to. And I promise that wherever he may go the result will be exciting. When the four greatest scientific wizards of all time get together, something is bound to pop.

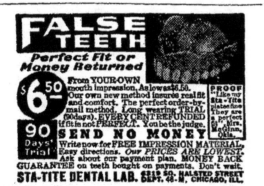

THE MARCH OF SCIENCE
(Concluded from page 120)

City in Miniature

THE world's greatest metropolis has been reduced to miniature size!

The principal feature of the Consolidated Edison exhibit is a thrilling diorama so large that virtually the whole of New York City is brought to life in miniature. More than 4,000 buildings, studded with 130,000 windows are included in the model.

The twist of a dial, and ultra-violet light floods the entire scene, throwing into brilliant illumination more than a quarter mile of colored lines representing the vast metropolis's underground electric, gas and steam networks.

Wonders at the Fair

VODER, a synthetic human voice, who answers your questions. . . . "Reado," the new radio device which plucks your morning newspaper out of the airwaves and unrolls it for you beside your breakfast table. . . . A model of the 200-inch Mt. Wilson telescope. . . . A large model of the eye, through which you may actually direct your own vision and observe reality as it appears to the near-sighted. . . . An illuminated graph which shows the retreat of death in the last 150 years. . . . Transparencies, which illustrate the functionings of the ductless glands. . . . The germs that cause pneumonia—enlarged 40,000 times. . . . The Time Capsule—which will be opened six thousand years from now! . . . The marvels of television. . . . The Hall of the Future, where you can see the farms of tomorrow, equipped with solar power units. . . . The 1/100th of a second stop watches used in timing meteorite flights. . . . Three-dimensional movies. . . . The "Court of the Atom," in which there is an animated copper atom . . . and miraculous devices used in micro-technique work, which determine the amount of oxygen in minute samples of water.

BEST FUN, FICTION AND FOTOS *IN*

THE WORLDS OF TOMORROW

(Concluded from page 116)

The first step in establishment of the Earth colony was erection of smelters which rapidly poured out a stream of metalloy from the rich Jovian ores nearby. Metalloy sheets were rapidly built into the structures of a city, and that city, called Jovopolis by Robert Caswell, grew quickly from a straggling village, to a considerable community.

Progress in Trade

Contact with the Jovians was maintained on a friendly basis. Authorities were careful not to offend the planetary natives by granting any mining or other concessions near the mysterious ruins which the Jovians held sacred. Within five Earth years, ships were traveling from Jupiter back to Earth and Mars, heavily laden with grain, new hybridized Jovian fruits, super-valuable radium, uranium and other rare metals, and a variety of miscellaneous Jovian products.

Robert Caswell, the first governor of Jupiter, was an ambitious explorer and mapped large portions, not only of South Equatoria, but of the neighboring continents of North Equatoria and Torridia. Of course, he was able to chart only the main continental outlines, and the great part of Jupiter's actual surface remains unexplored to this day. Caswell was killed in a crash-landing in the jungle outside Jovopolis, in 2012.

A Miniature Jupiter

The colony prospered, however. Expeditions were sent to Europa, Io and Ganymede, the other three of the four great moons, to explore. Europa was found to be a miniature Jupiter, jungle-covered and quite habitable, though lacking valuable minerals as far as could be ascertained. Io, on the other hand, was as harsh and forbidding as Callisto, though uninhabited by the crystal-creatures that tenant Callisto's wastes. Ganymede, the fourth moon, is still a mystery. Three expeditions sent there have failed to return, and further attempts at exploration there are temporarily prohibited.

In 2015, the Jupiter-Earth ship-lines were terrorized by radium bandits who held up the craft carrying back the precious metals to Earth. Development of the colony was set back for a time. But as the Planet Police got the radium bandits under control, colonial development prospered again, and was destined to meet no further danger until there suddenly developed the dark, unbelievable menace of the atavism horror—a menace that seemed fated to sweep Earthmen from Jupiter forever.

THE WORLDS OF TOMORROW
—will appear in every issue

EVERY ISSUE OF COLLEGE HUMOR 15c EVERYWHERE

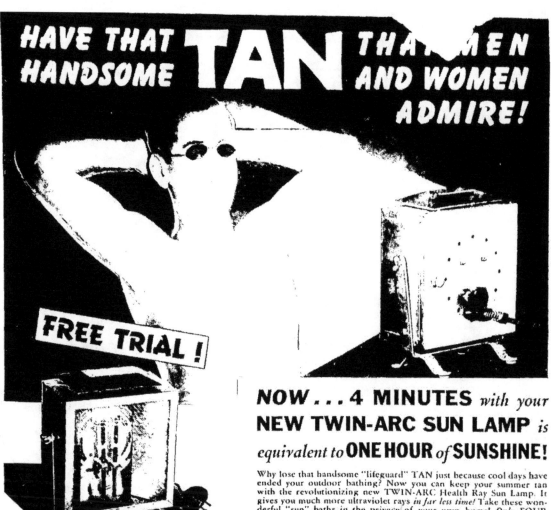